Praise for Jim (

Inside My

'Provocative, honest and gripping … a must
Telegraph

'Witty and hard-hitting dialogue and
a compellingly written storyline'
Irish Post

'To say this is a page-turner is an understatement …
This is a journey of discovery, high-octane excitement
and eventually pure, living terror'
Flipside Magazine

'One of the most thought-provoking and compelling books
I have read … There should be a copy of this book in
every secondary school library'
Book Zone 4 Boys

'Wonderfully honest and tremendously tense'
TheBookbag.co.uk

In the Bag

'A thoroughly good read and teenagers,
especially boys, will love it'
TES Magazine

Drive By

'Carrington keeps us guessing, right up to the very last page …
an absorbing narrative'
Books for Keeps

'A very, very pacy and unputdownable contemporary novel'
Love Reading 4 Kids

Also by Jim Carrington

BOY
23

BOY 23

JIM CARRINGTON

BLOOMSBURY
LONDON OXFORD NEW DELHI NEW YORK SYDNEY

Bloomsbury Publishing, London, Oxford, New York, New Delhi and Sydney

First published in Great Britain in November 2015 by Bloomsbury Publishing Plc
50 Bedford Square, London WC1B 3DP

www.bloomsbury.com

Bloomsbury is a registered trademark of Bloomsbury Publishing Plc

A CIP catalogue record for this book is available from the British Library

ISBN 978 1 4088 2277 7

Typeset by Integra Software Services Pvt. Ltd.
Printed and bound in Great Britain by CPI Group (UK) Ltd, Croydon CR0 4YY

3 5 7 9 10 8 6 4 2

To Sonja

Jesper

Suddenly the whole world shifts underneath me and I'm wide awake.

And I'm falling.

Only for a second.

Because then –

SLAM.

I land on my side.

And in my head I can hear this never-ending noise, like:

RRRRRRRRRRRRRRRRRRRRRRRRRRRRRRRRRRRRRRRR RRRRRRRRRRRRRRRRRRRRRRRRRRRRRRRR …

My heart's racing and my head's pulsing.

I don't know what's happening.

I try to stay calm and take deep breaths. Except my breathing doesn't feel right, cos there's something against my face. Cloth? Like a mask or a hood. It scratches at my skin every time I move. It tugs at my neck, as though it's been fastened there.

I try to lift my hands to my face, to figure out what's going on, but I realise they're behind my back and they won't move. My skin feels tight at the wrists. They're bound together, aren't they? My feet too. I writhe around, trying to free my hands and feet, but it's no use.

And all around me I hear that noise:

RRRRRRRRRRRRRRRRRRRRRRRRRRRRRRRRRRRRRRRR RRRRRRRRRRRRRRRRRRRRRRRRRRRRRRRR …

Angry and roaring, ugly and vicious. Like a monster or something.

Only it can't be a monster, can it?

Cos for one thing, there's no such thing as monsters – they're made up. There's people and animals in the world and that's all.

And for another, if it was a monster, how come the sound is all around me, like it's the only thing in the world and I'm inside it? I'd have to be in the monster's belly for the noise to be surrounding me like this, like it had eaten me. And that'd mean I was dead.

I can't be dead though, can I? Cos I'm thinking this. And I can feel and hear and smell. If I was dead, I wouldn't be able to feel how my arms and my legs are tied, would I? I wouldn't be able to feel this thing over my face.

Except I don't have time to think about that right now, cos all around me that noise keeps on going – inside my head and my guts and my skin like it's a part of me. So I decide to do something logical. I stay as still as possible, listening so I can work out what the noise is.

RRRRRRRRRRRRRRRRRRRRRRRRRRRRRRRRRRRRRRRR RRRRRRRRRRRRRRRRRRRRRRRRRRRRRRRR …

It goes on and on and on like it's never ever gonna stop. And the longer it goes on, the more I realise it doesn't sound like anything natural, not like a person or an animal. It sounds like a machine. It sounds powerful. It changes pitch, goes up to almost a squeal and then back down to a low-bellied roar.

It fills my guts with fear, makes them jump around inside me like they're tying themselves in knots.

I'm thrown into the air again and I land with a *SMACK* against something hard and I stop thinking about the noise for a second, cos I'm thinking about the pain in my side instead.

And then I start thinking about where I am.

Cos I'm not in My Place.

Nothing like this has ever happened before.

What normally happens – what happens every single day – is The Screen plays the Waking Sound – '*Cock-a-doodle-doo*' – and I wake up and open my eyes and I see that I'm in My Place and the lights are coming on. And when I get up my provisions are waiting – juice, cereal, toast. And Feathers, my squawk, is fluttering round his cage, squawking. Same every day of my life.

Except today.

RRRRRRRRRRRRRRRRRRRRRRRRRRRRRRRRRRRRRRRR RRRRRRRRRRRRRRRRRRRRRRRRRRRRRR …

I don't feel right. I've got a fuzzy feeling in my head. The water in my provisions last night tasted bitter. Maybe that explains this – weird things always happen after they give me the bitter water.

The ground shakes – another almighty jerk, bouncing me up through the air. I slam against something hard with my shoulder – *BANG* – and crash back to the solid ground. I feel

3

something crack in my shoulder, and the pain makes me want to scream.

Then, suddenly, ALL the movement stops.

No more shakes or jerks or shunts.

Even the '*RRRRRRRRRRRRRRRRRRRRRRRRRRRRRRRRR RRRRRRRRRRRRRRRRRRRRRRRRRRRRRRRRRRR*' doesn't sound so angry any more. It sounds slower. Lower-pitched. Rumbling.

And then the noise splutters and finally stops completely. Gone.

All there is, is darkness.

I gulp. Because maybe this is it. Maybe now I'm dead.

I wait for something to happen, to prove this isn't the end.

And eventually it does.

CLUNK.

Then another noise, closer this time – sliding metal – and a blast of cold air.

Something closes around my ankles and I think it's a hand. Two hands. Someone's touching me. I feel sick. I think I'm going to vomit. I flinch away from the touch, try to wriggle away, but I can't. I scream but the noise stays inside me, refuses to come out of my mouth.

With a sudden jerk I'm moving again, dragged along by the ankles. Then I feel the hands move to my shoulders. I shrink from the touch, but the hands grab me, pull me till I'm sitting up. Completely disorientated, feeling sick.

'Stand up, Jesper.'

4

The sound startles me, sets my heart racing anew. Cos it was The Voice, wasn't it?

The hands pull me till I'm standing, unsteady, my legs bowing underneath me. I fall to the ground. Pain shoots through my body. And I'm panicking again, gasping for air, tasting the cloth covering my face.

The hands pick me up, haul me to my feet.

And then nothing. Except I know something's close to me. Someone. The Voice. I feel his breath on me, sense his movement. Then I hear a metallic noise – *SHING* – which sounds like a knife.

I've seen them on The Screen; I know what they're for. Cutting, stabbing, tearing flesh.

Surely he isn't gonna do that to me? He looks after me, doesn't he?

I say a prayer in my head, only I can't think of anything except this crap:

Dear Lord,

I'm sorry for whatever I've done wrong. I promise to be better in the future. Please save me, Lord. Please.

Amen.

I brace myself, waiting for the stab of the blade in my flesh. But instead I feel a tug at my wrists – *ping* – and my hands are free. Seconds later, the same at my feet. And for a second I'm thinking my prayer must have worked.

'Jesper, are you OK?'

My body stiffens with fear.

'Jesper,' The Voice says again, 'are you all right?'

It definitely is The Voice. It sounds like he's actually there in front of me. I shiver. I don't understand what's happening.

I open my mouth to answer that I'm OK, but all that comes out is a cough. No words.

'Get out of here. You're free. Don't look back.'

Cold air blows over me and I shiver again. I sniff back tears and snot.

'This is for your own good, Jesper. You're at risk in Huber. It's the only way to save you. I'm sorry.'

My heart thumps. Why's he doing this to me? The Voice usually looks after me.

'Get as far away as you can. Use everything I've taught you. You'll find your scroll in your pack, which will keep you moving in the right direction – north-west. I'll come looking for you when I can.'

My brain fills with a million questions, only when I open my mouth nothing comes out except a little whining sound.

I hear another metallic noise – something being put away (the knife?). Footsteps. A clunk as something opens and another clunk as it closes.

The '*RRRRRRRRRRRRRRRRRRRRRRRRRRRRRRRRRRR RRRRRRRRRRRRRRRRRRRRRRRRRRRRRRRR*' starts up again, loud and fierce, but this time the ground doesn't shake and it doesn't feel like I'm inside the noise. It sounds far away. There's a crunching sound and then the roaring moves further away, as though it's leaving me. It fades until it's gone.

6

And now I've heard it from the outside, I know what it was. I've heard cars on The Screen a million times before.

But it's gone, hasn't it? And I'm here and alone, with nothing except silence and darkness and the cold wind.

My shoulder's in agony. It feels like something's broken. The pain is so intense that I barely even notice the pounding in my head. But my body tells me I need to move. I get to my feet unsteadily, and as I straighten up I hear the cracking noise, feel my bones crunching back into place, mending themselves, feel my skin heal. In a few seconds I'm upright and on my feet and the only pain left is a sore feeling.

Everything's still dark though. I put my hands up, feel the material that's around my face and head, and I pull at it. And as it comes off, I squizz at it and see that it isn't a hood or a mask at all: it's a cloth bag. Only I don't think about that for long, cos as soon as my head's free I feel my guts churning as though they're surging up through my body, and I have to bend over.

Weeeyyyuurrkkk.

Weeeyyyuurrkkk.

Weeeyyyuurrkkk.

My vomit goes all over the ground and all over my shoes and everywhere.

I crouch down, bent double, heaving, retching, trying not to chuck up again. I close my eyes and concentrate on breathing in and then out while my head and my stomach spin and the world won't hold still.

But the cold air helps and after a while the spinning stops and the feeling passes.

I open my eyes and wipe the cold sweat from my forehead and the sick from my mouth.

And only then do I see what's in front of me.

I can barely believe what I see.

This definitely isn't My Place. There's no Screen. No bed. No walls. No carpet. No ceiling. No light bulb. No toilet. No shower. No provisions. No Feathers in his little squawk cage.

Nothing.

Just darkness. Night-time, like the picture on The Screen when lights go out and it's time to sleep. It's the sky, isn't it? It's all covered in dark blue/black and there's millions of stars so white and so bright that it hurts my eyes to look at them. The moon's brighter than anything I've ever seen.

And it's different to the pictures I've seen on The Screen, cos there's no end to it, no edges. It just keeps on going, round and round and round, surrounding me, making me feel dizzy.

Cos it's real, isn't it? It's actually there.

I'm outside.

I take long, slow, deep breaths.

Only staying calm isn't easy, cos I don't understand what's happening. I don't know where this place is or why I'm here.

8

And then I think, *What if this is a test?* They could be prying on me, seeing how I react.

Only when I squizz around, I can't see anyone prying. Not that you ever can. You just know they're there. Always.

All I see is endless dark sky and trees and grass and hills and a river.

And all I want to do is go home back to My Place, to be inside, surrounded by walls. Except The Voice just told me not to do that, didn't he?

I look down and I see something dark on the ground, a metre or so from where I stand. A bag. I grab it so I can squizz inside. The bag's tied at the top with a bit of stringy rope and a toggle thing. And the first thing that I see when I open it is a bit of paper, folded into a triangle. I take it from the bag and unfold it:

PLEASE BURN THIS NOTE AFTER READING
  Jesper,
  The place you know as My Place isn't safe for you any longer. The Huber Corporation want you dead. They will come looking for you, so be careful. I will be doing all I can to help you.
  Whatever you do, don't return to My Place. Stay away from all humans. Stick to the woods as much as you can.
  Head north-west, across the border with the Low Countries – the scroll I've provided you with has a map which will guide you. I will meet you as soon as

**I've attended to business here. The Spirit of Resist-
ance will help us.**

**Use everything I've taught you and you will stay
safe and well.**

The Voice.

I read it through once and then go right back to the start and
read it again. It doesn't make sense though. I could read it a
million times and still not understand.

And even though the letter said I should burn it, I fold it
back into a triangle and put it in the pocket of the coat I'm
wearing – cos maybe I'll read it again later and it'll make
sense then. I look around me again before opening the bag up
to see what's inside.

There's all sorts of stuff: a torch and a bottle of water and a
book with plain empty pages and a pen and a thick blanket
and some thin string kind of stuff. There's a scroll in there –
shiny and smooth and exactly like The Scroll. I drag my finger
across it and the screen comes to life, showing a map with an
arrow pointing north-west and a pin marking where I am
now.

There's food too – bread, cheese and fruit. There's a firelighting kit, like I've seen on The Screen before, and a
telescope with buttons on the side of it to extend it and to
zoom in. And there's a knife, which I take out to look at. It's
one of those knives with loads of blades which all fold into
the handle. I open them out – a sharp knife, tiny scissors, a

blade with an edge that is kind of bumpy and rough, a screw-driver and loads more that I don't know what they're for. I fold it all back and put it in my pocket, in case I need it.

And then I use the scroll to find north-west and I start yomping, cos that's what The Voice said to do, isn't it?

Carina

I stopped being able to sleep at night at the same time they brought me to this place.

When the lights go out I close my eyes just like everyone else, but my thoughts race and my heart pounds and I lie awake for hours. It's then that the unwanted memories drift into my mind. They're the kind of thoughts I spend all my days trying to avoid by being busy. Thoughts of my family and how I ended up here. And whenever I get so tired that I fall asleep, the thoughts turn into dreams. Before long I wake up, sweating and panicking, grinding my teeth, thinking it's happening again.

So on nights like tonight, when the memories are coming thick and fast, the best thing to do is to get out of bed and walk the empty corridors. I swing my legs from beneath the scratchy sheets and my bare feet touch the wooden floor. I pad over to my wardrobe and root around underneath my grey uniform until I feel my hairgrips. I grab a couple, hide them in my nightdress pocket and creep through the dormitory, past rows and rows of beds with deep breathing and whimpering and snoring noises coming from them, towards the door. As I pass Sabine's bed, I hear a noise that makes me freeze.

It takes me a second to realise that it was nothing more than Sabine coughing in her sleep. She tosses and turns in her bed, but her eyes stay closed and I carry on walking.

In the corridor I step carefully, avoiding loose floorboards. Moonlight streams in through the windows, lighting my way. Twenty doors line the walls of the corridor where my dorm is. I know this because I count them every time I walk this corridor. Behind each one there are girls, all sleeping soundly, some in dormitories like mine and some in smaller rooms with just a few beds. There are also a couple of single rooms, which are always kept locked, and a medical dorm/quarantine.

On the other side of the building there's another corridor, identical to this one, except that behind the doors there are boys rather than girls.

I reach the end of the moonlit corridor and creep down the wooden stairs. Everything is still.

At the bottom of the stairs I take a moment to check I am definitely alone. Because what I'm doing is forbidden. If I was found out of bed I'd be in trouble. I'd be put in one of the detention rooms, locked away, allowed out only to work. I've been doing this long enough to know how not to be found out though.

I scamper across the big entrance hall, the stone floor cold beneath my bare feet. I head over to the large double doors that lead to the food hall, where the daily slop gets dished out.

As I get to the door I reach into my pocket and take out a hairgrip, checking behind me once more before sliding the grip into the lock. I work it around inside, listening and feeling for clicks and clunks, adjusting as I go. After a minute it unlocks with a final clunk and I push the door. I'm inside.

I hurry across the food hall, where the smell of greasy cooked meat hangs thickly in the air. At the far end is the door to the kitchen, which I pick and let myself in. I head straight for the cupboards, ignoring those with food meant for us girls and boys and making for the supplies reserved for the priests. Inside I find what I'm looking for – bread, ham, cheese and biscuits – and I help myself to a little of each.

Jesper

I yomp through the night, following the arrow on the scroll, and I try to convince myself this is the most natural thing in the world. Only it isn't natural. It doesn't feel right. Cos for a start, it's night-time and that means I ought to be asleep. And for another, the wind is cold and biting. Even the ground feels strange. The grass is wet and springy under my feet and that's all right. But all the rocks and stones? Well, I can feel them poking into the bottoms of my shoes as I walk over them.

It feels weird being able to go wherever I decide, that there aren't any edges or walls or locked doors. I can decide to walk to my left or my right or backwards, and nothing's in the way and nothing stops me.

But I don't go wherever I want, do I? I go north-west, like The Voice told me, checking the scroll every few minutes. Cos if I keep walking in the direction The Voice said, surely everything will be all right. Everything will start to make sense soon.

The darkness hides everything. Someone (or something) could be hidden from view, prying on me, waiting for me. (Cos they're always prying, aren't they?) With every nervous step I take, my eyes squizz this way and that for movement. My ears tune into the silence, waiting for the tiniest sound.

And there are loads.

'*A-HOOOOT.*'

I stop in my tracks, terrified, holding my breath.

I squizz into the darkness all around, trying to figure out what made the noise.

Except all I see is darkness.

Shadowy outlines of trees.

The sky and the stars and the moon.

All cloaked in darkness.

And then the noise again. '*A-HOOOOT.*'

I stay frozen to the spot, still squizzing, still listening.

But I think I've worked out what it is. It's gotta be an owl, hasn't it – a scary-looking squawk with enormous haunting eyes? And then I remember the bag on my back and I carefully take it off, open it and silently take out the torch. I press the button on it. Nothing happens. So I stare at the torch and I work out why; there's a handle on it cos it's one of the wind-up ones. I turn the handle – round and round, trying to do it quietly – until I've counted to a hundred in my head, and this time when I press the button a beam of bright white light shoots out. I aim it into the darkness, lighting up the bushes and trees, showing their real colours – brown and green and all the colours in between. But I don't see any haunted eyes prying out from the bushes. No owl.

I'm not taking any chances though. I get the knife from my pocket. And then I carry on walking, torch in one hand and the knife (biggest, sharpest blade out) in the other. Only now I'm not so much yomping along as edging forward, nervous, cos I'm wondering what else is out there.

Up ahead is a bend in the path, and as I reach it my torch

beam catches something hidden away in the bushes and trees. A building, made of stone, just like My Place.

I creep forward, thinking all the time about what I know from The Screen about buildings. They're where people live and work, aren't they? And The Voice told me not to go near people. My heart is beating so fast it feels like it's gonna thump its way outta my chest.

I calm myself with deep breaths.

I have to go to the building, don't I?

Cos buildings also have *things* inside them that could help me work out what's going on, what the Low Countries are. There could be a screen. I could speak to The Voice through it. Maybe this is what I'm meant to do – this building's been put here for me to find.

Or.

Cos there is an 'or'.

Or maybe it's a trap.

I take one wary step at a time, squizzing nervously around.

As I get closer, I see the building's all beaten up. Worse than beaten up – it looks wrecked, falling down. Bits of wall are missing. Plants have started to grow up and over and through it, like they're trying to hide it away. And as I walk closer, I see a tatty sign standing on a post in the ground. It's yellow and black and there are words on it which are starting to fade to nothing. Only they're words that don't make any sense, cos they're not really words at all, just letters that make no sense:

WARNUNG. NICHT BETRETEN.
KONTAMINIERTER BEREICH

There's a symbol on it too – like three C shapes joined together, on top of an *o*: ☣ And I have no idea what it is, what it means.

Where the windows should be, there's nothing but air. This place looks like it's been hit by a bomb. And that makes me think that maybe there aren't any people in this building – cos who'd want to live in a place like this?

I shine the torch through the gap where the glass should be, but the gloom swallows up all the light and I still can't see anything. So I continue creeping round the outside, dragging my hand along cold rough stone walls as I go, till I come to a doorway with no door.

Beyond the doorway is more deep darkness – empty, black, ready to swallow everything. My torch beam cuts enough of a hole in the dark so I can see where I'm going. I walk through the doorway, feeling the ground beneath me, hearing it crunch as I step, feeling my heart pound in my chest.

When I'm inside, I see there isn't much here – broken walls, scrubby grass, bushes, trees growing up from the ground and out of the walls. It looks like there must've been squawks in here, cos the floor is covered in their dung. I squizz up to see if I can spot them roosting, thinking about Feathers, about how he'll still be in My Place, snoozing on his perch in his cage, wondering where I've gone. But all I see above is sky and stars and the outlines of tree branches, and I realise that there isn't a roof or a ceiling or anything. It's been smashed to pieces. And when I shine the torch down on the ground, I see that most of the roof's fallen down and broken into hundreds of pieces on the floor. Some of the pieces are black and charred like they've been burned.

I move slowly and carefully through the building. The bad news is there isn't much of anything – no screen, no bed, no food, no chair. But there are walls, and that makes me feel better, cos walls are safe.

I sit down on the dirty ground, wrap the blanket around myself and make a decision. I'm gonna stay here till it gets light, until it's daytime. Maybe things'll make more sense when I can see properly.

Or maybe I'll wake up back in My Place and find none of this has really happened.

Carina

Inga stumbles into the dormitory looking bedraggled – hair tangled and matted and clothes even dirtier than is usual for this place.

She's been out for a week.

The dormitory pauses to look round and stare at her.

'Are you all right?' I ask as she approaches my bed.

She looks up at me and says nothing.

'Did they beat you?'

'What do you think?'

'New Dawn?'

She nods again. 'And Father Frei too, when I was brought back.'

Neither of us speaks for a second or two. I can sense the rest of the dorm is going back about its business.

'Where did you get to?'

Inga sighs. 'About ten kilometres from the town where my uncle and aunt used to live. I know people there. They would have taken me in …'

'So what happened?'

She shrugs. 'I hadn't eaten for three days. I was starving, and I saw some bread in a house, just inside a window. So I broke the glass and took the bread. And then they caught me.'

'That's bad luck.'

Inga shakes her head. 'It was stupidity,' she says. 'Another few hours and I'd have had all the food I needed.'

And she shuffles on towards her bed.

Jesper

The digits of the clock on my wall change to 19:00 just as I squizz up at it. I hear a clunk as the door hatch opens. I drag my finger across The Scroll in an X to switch it off. I head straight for the hatch cos I'm starving and I can already smell my provisions.

I take a squizz under the metal bowl that covers my plate, keeping my food warm. And I'm amazed, cos it's roast chicken, potatoes and gravy – absolutely my favourite meal. The smell is fantastic. I take it to my table, sit down and start scoffing right away.

Feathers flutters around his cage as I eat, chattering to himself. Then he perches on the side of the cage and pecks at it with his beak. And that makes me feel bad, cos he's shut in. My knife and fork clatter on to my plate as I get up and open the wire door. Feathers doesn't waste any time – he flies outta the cage, wings beating at a million miles an hour, and he's off flying laps of My Place.

I sit back at the table, tuck into my dinner again, wondering, thinking, until Feathers lands on the table and stands right in front of me, gawping straight at me, making the funny clicking noises he sometimes makes with his beak and his throat.

'What's up, Feathers?'

Except he doesn't answer, does he? He just waddles around my table and then takes off and flies around the room again.

All of a sudden there's a voice (The Voice) and it makes me jump. 'Are you enjoying your food?'

I squizz over to The Screen, which has just started to show one of my favourite clips – the one where this man makes a camp and catches a bushtail and makes a fire to cook it on.

'Yeah.'

'Good, Jesper. Savour every last mouthful of it, won't you?'

So I eat, like The Voice says, but in my head I'm thinking, What's this all about? Cos this isn't what normally happens. There weren't any tests today and I didn't earn any credit, so I shouldn't have rewards. I didn't get asked to choose a clip or what food I wanted, but still I got my favourites. That isn't right, is it?

So, eventually, I decide to say something. 'What's happening?'

There's quiet, except for the sound of me scoffing more chicken meat, slurping up gravy to stop it running down my chin, and Feathers' wings beating the air as he flies to the top of The Screen.

'How come I got my favourites today? The food and the clips.'

And still there isn't an answer, not for ages. It's like The Voice is thinking of what to say, and that isn't like The Voice at all, cos it always knows everything straight away, quicker than looking something up on The Scroll.

'This is to mark a special occasion, Jesper.'

'What do you mean?'

'For all your achievements, Jesper. To mark a change in your life. You're becoming a man.'

And I don't know what The Voice means, but seeing as I've got my favourite food and my clip, I decide not to ask any more questions, but to enjoy them instead. So that's what I do – finish my provisions and watch the clip, and when that's done I have a *shower, change into my nightclothes, clean my teeth and all that sort of stuff.*

When I come back through, I grab the water from my provisions and I drink it all back in one go. It's down my throat and in my guts before I realise what I've just done, what was in the water. Cos it tasted bitter, didn't it? And I know exactly what that means. But it's already too late. There's nothing I can do about it apart from make myself sick. And if I tried that, they'd realise what I was doing.

And this time the bitter water must be stronger than normal, cos as I pick up the tray to take it back to the hatch, I get this dizzy feeling, like the world's swaying. I stop for a second to let it pass. Only all that happens is another rush of dizziness fills my head, and before I know it the tray slips from my hands and crashes on to the floor.

The room lurches. Everything swirls, nothing staying still. I close my eyes to try to stop it moving, but that doesn't work, does it? The whole world spins. And my thoughts spin with it and I'm thinking about the tray and that it needs to be picked up, and how my hands feel strange, like my fingers are too big and too sensitive. And the walls – I'm suddenly thinking about how they're white and I'm wondering if they were always white or did they used to be grey, and I'm wondering who changed them if they did. And Feathers – cos if I sleep now, who's gonna put him back in his cage?

And then I realise I can't feel my legs any more and I start wondering whether they're even there. And then I'm falling on

22

to my bed, lying there, unable to move, not even to open my eyes.

I hear a voice echoing through my brain: 'Sleep well, Jesper. Tomorrow's the day.'

And the rest is darkness.

I don't hear any *cock-a-doodle-doo* of the Waking Sound, but I wake up anyway and I open my eyes and squizz around. My eyes don't see what they're hoping to though. There's no tray with provisions waiting for me, and no hatch in the door for it to come through neither.

Cos I'm not back in My Place, am I?

I'm scrunched up underneath a scratchy blanket in a dirty, broken building full of squawk dung and cold air.

Above me, through the broken roof, I see the tops of trees and light beginning to creep into the sky, cancelling out the stars.

I rub my eyes.

I tried to stay awake through the night, watching the darkness in case something happened. But I must have fallen asleep. All I remember is my eyes feeling heavy and closing them for a second.

But now it's morning and the sky's full of light. And maybe that'll make it easier to see where I'm going, to figure out what's happening.

There are noises above me. Whistling. Cracking. Something's alive in the trees above the building, prying down on me. And I don't like it. It can see me but I can't see it.

23

I squizz around where I'm sitting, find the knife – biggest, sharpest blade still out – and I hold the handle tightly. I gawp around at the tree above. Something moves suddenly amongst the leaves. I tighten my grip on the knife.

Then I hear a flapping noise and I look up. An enormous funny-looking black squawk flies from the tree, up into the sky, big wings beating so hard I can feel the air move.

It's just a stupid squawk. I'm safe.

And I'm an idiot too. Frightened by a little squawk. It was twice the size of Feathers, but it's still only a bundle of feathers and a beak and some eyes. It couldn't do me any harm.

I shift myself on my bed of squawk dung and dust and blanket. The fuzziness in my head has gone, but I feel hungry and thirsty. I take the food and water from the bag. There's just a little dribbly bit of water left, which I finish in one gulp. The bread and cheese and fruit's squashed, but I'm too hungry to care, so I scoff it all.

Except when it's all gone I don't feel any better. Still hungry. Still thirsty. Still confused.

This is the first day ever when it's been morning and there are no provisions left for me. They're always there without fail. I gotta find a way to get more food.

And while all those thoughts are bouncing around my head, I realise something else, cos I haven't been to the toilet in ages and right now I need to go.

Only where do you go to the toilet when your toilet isn't there?

24

Cos I already know there isn't a toilet in this building – I checked last night.

I shiver as I get out of bed, creep outside into the forest and find a place amongst all the bushes to squat and do my business. And while I'm at it, I do some thinking about the things I know:

- The Voice said to head north-west, to the Low Countries. (And I have to do what The Voice says, because that's who gives me what I need, who keeps me safe.)
- I have a map on the scroll to guide me.
- The Screen and The Voice have been teaching me things lately that I can use – like working out from the sun what time of day it is, and how to make fires to keep warm and cook. (Maybe what's happening is they're testing me to check I've learned it.)
- Someone from My Place is probably following me, but I don't know who they are or what they look like, cos I never saw anyone before in my whole life.

I squizz around for something to wipe my backside on and I see something, hidden amongst the trees and bushes. There are crosses stuck in the ground – each made of two bits of wood tied together. A shiver runs down my spine. Because I've seen things like that on The Screen. On graves.

I pull my trousers up in a hurry and run back to the building, then scramble around getting all my things together and into the bag as fast as I can. I don't want to be near dead people. I have to keep moving. So I yomp out into the forest again, knife in hand, following the arrow on the scroll.

Blake

The sun's beginning to come up behind the main building, as I approach. I'm met by armed guards before I get to the door.

'What's happened?' I ask. 'The power in my quarters is out.'

'Power's down in the whole facility, Mr Blake, sir,' the guard answers.

'Really? Why?'

'I don't know. Technicians are trying to restore it right now. You need me to let you in?'

I nod.

The guard puts a key into the bottom of what's meant to be an automatic door and then slowly pushes it open.

Inside the windowless building it's pitch black. I take a flashlight from my jacket pocket and aim the beam into the gloom, following the corridors round until I reach the control room, where I find Hersch and Henwood. A small portable lamp illuminates the centre of the control room.

'What on earth's going on?' I ask.

Henwood sighs. 'All we know is the power failed in the early hours of the morning.'

'Shouldn't the generator have cut in?'

'It should have,' Hersch says. 'We're trying to find out what went wrong.'

'Are the inmates OK?'

Henwood nods. 'As far as we know. But no power means no video feeds, so we can't see what they're doing. Hopefully they're all still sleeping – it's dark in their rooms so they'll assume it's still night.'

I nod. 'Good.'

At that moment the lights start to blink back on. One by one the bank of screens in the control room flash back to life. I watch the screens as the inmates start to wake, looking confusedly around them, no doubt wondering why there was no Waking Sound.

'Oh no,' Hersch says.

'What?'

'Boy 23 isn't in his room. Look!'

I stare at the screen. The room's empty all right. 'Switch cameras,' I say. 'Try the other angles. Maybe he's just hidden from the camera.'

Hersch flicks through one camera after another, each revealing another view of the room, vacant except for the boy's pet bird.

'He's gone. We should alert Mr Huber right away,' I say.

Hersch nods. 'Let me try his tracking chip first,' he says. 'It should tell us exactly where he is.' He taps at a keyboard, staring at the screen in front of him. He shakes his head. 'This can't be happening ...'

'What is it?' I ask.

'Boy 23's chip has been deactivated.'

Jesper

I walk all day. I watch the sun go right across the sky and start to go down again. And in all that time, nothing happens – no provisions, no humans, no buildings. Nothing except from time to time a hopper jumps out of the bush and scutters across the path in front of me, making me jump.

Once or twice I even try to speak out loud to The Voice, like I would in My Place.

'Where am I?' I ask him.

'Where can I get food?'

I ask other questions too.

And I don't need to even say that The Voice doesn't answer, do I?

There are times when I want to cry and other times when all I want to do is fall down to the ground and rest.

But I don't. I keep following the arrow to the north-west cos that's what The Voice told me to do. And The Voice has never been wrong about anything, has he?

Carina

I open my eyes when I hear the bell toll. My head feels heavy with sleep. I didn't get to sleep until it was almost light. I kept remembering things I didn't want to. I wandered the corridors. When I came back to bed, I heard Sabine crying in her sleep, turning from side to side.

Much as I'd like to, I can't stay in bed though. It's time for church. Around me, the dorm's a hive of activity as everyone gets ready. Reluctantly I join the rush and get dressed.

As I'm hurrying towards the dorm door, I notice Sabine. She's still lying in bed. Her face is pale and sweaty and her eyes are closed. I stop and bend down close to her, feel her weak breath on my face.

'Are you OK, Sabine?'

She doesn't answer, but she opens her eyes and looks at me. For a second I'm reminded of my mum.

'It's time for church. You need to get up.'

Sabine shakes her head ever so slightly and her eyes close again. I can't help but wonder what's wrong. Marsh Flu? But it can't be; we've all had the inoculation. It's just, the way she looks and sounds, it's like what Marsh Flu did to Mum. And millions of others.

'Stay there, Sabine. I'll fetch help.'

I rush into the corridor, looking for one of the priests, but none are around, so I run along the corridor and then down the stairs until I spot Father Liebling at the foot of the boys' staircase.

'Father, come quick,' I shout, running towards him. My voice echoes around the vast entrance hall and I'm dimly aware that everyone else stops what they're doing to stare at me.

Liebling looks up, startled.

'Sabine's sick. I think she has Marsh Flu.'

He stares at me for a second while the words sink in and then he turns to one of the boys and instructs him to go and get a medic.

'Take me to her,' Father Liebling says.

I lead the way back to the dorm as he hobbles along behind.

Her eyes are still closed when we get to her.

Liebling gets uneasily to his knees beside Sabine's bed. He reaches a hand out to her brow. 'She has a fever,' he says.

He takes his hand from her head and feels her pulse underneath her chin. Sabine lies still, eyes closed. I'm not even sure she knows we're here.

30

'Can you hear me, Sabine?' Father Liebling says.

Sabine says nothing. Her eyes remain closed. She doesn't stir even when he asks her again more loudly and shakes her shoulder. I fear, for a second, that she's dead. But I notice her chest still slowly rising and falling.

There's movement over near the door. I look up to see Father Lekmann – the medic – arrive, a bag in his hand. He wears a mask over his nose and mouth. He hurries over to Sabine's bedside, moving Father Liebling and me out of the way. He opens the clasp of his leather bag and takes out a thermometer and a stethoscope. Without a word, he checks Sabine and he frowns.

'What's the matter with her?' I ask.

Father Lekmann ignores me.

'Is it Marsh Flu?'

He carefully pulls Sabine's nightdress to one side so he can place the stethoscope on her chest and then he listens, still ignoring my question. I turn to Father Liebling, who's watching like I am. 'Do you think it's Marsh Flu, Father?'

He shakes his head. 'She's had the Marsh Flu inoculation. It must just be a fever.'

The bell stops tolling.

'You'd better hurry to church, Carina,' Father Liebling says. 'You'll be late. You'll get into trouble.'

I look once more at Sabine, at the medic leaning over her. I don't want to leave her, but Father Liebling's right.

I hurry to the corridor and towards the church.

Jesper

At first it's just a sound in the background and I don't pay it any attention. But as I walk on, it gets louder. The sound of movement. Trickling and rushing. And I realise it has to be water, doesn't it?

And by now I'm so thirsty I don't even think about it, I just yomp in the direction of the sound, away from the path and through the darkness of the trees, crunching twigs underneath my feet, till I'm at an opening in the trees where there's grass and plants and flowers and the sound of trickling water is louder.

A riverbank, and cold running water.

I stand and gawp for a second cos I've never seen anything like it in my whole life. I mean, of course there are taps and water and a shower in My Place. And I've seen a river on The Screen before, but that doesn't even get close to this. This river looks alive – water constantly moving and rippling, making shapes as it travels around rocks and fallen tree trunks. But all that'll have to wait, cos there's only one thing on my mind and it isn't thinking how pretty the river is. I crouch down at the river's edge, scoop up a handful of cold water and gulp it down. And the truth is that it tastes kind of dirty compared to the water in My Place. It's all I've got though, isn't it? And it doesn't have the bitter taste. So I slurp handful after handful, till it's dribbling down my chin and I don't feel thirsty any more and then I take my bottle and I fill that up too.

For a while I stand and gawp at the way the water moves along, how it never stops still even for a moment. The sunlight reflects on it, making it sparkle. I watch flying bugs flit about just above the surface. And I'm still gawping at them as a tiny squawk comes swooping along and catches one of them in its beak.

Only I don't have time to just stand and gawp, do I? I need to keep moving. I look at the scroll and see that if I turn left and walk along the riverbank, I'll be heading north-west. So I yomp along, trampling the grass as I go, listening to the trickling water.

My stomach rumbles and gurgles as I walk, and I can't help but think about how I'm gonna find some provisions. The Screen showed me clips all about how to find food in the forest – fish and hoppers and berries and mushrooms and all sorts. But seeing it on The Screen and doing it for real are two different things, aren't they?

And then I squizz to my right, down at the river, and I see something that makes me stop dead. Something in the water. It looks sort of like a squawk, except it's enormous – long and white and thin and hunched over, with legs like great long sticks. Around its beady yellow eyes it has a black feathery stripe, like a mask. The eyes pry into the water, deadly and still. And on the front of its face there's this beak – long and sharp and like a spear.

And I'm frozen to the spot, not knowing what to do. That beak and those eyes and the size of the thing make me nervous. All I can do is hope it doesn't see me. I watch it stalk through the water, away from me. One step, two steps. Beady eyes squizzing the water. It stops, absolutely still, beak just above the water. Seconds pass and nothing happens except I think about whether I should just run away but maybe it would chase me. And then, suddenly, it stabs its beak into the water and a second later brings it out again and there's something in its beak, thrashing about, trying to escape. A fish. Silver and smooth and shiny.

And that's when the squawk's head turns and it squizzes straight at me. The fish still thrashes around in its beak. I stand frozen as it gawps at me. What's it thinking? What's it gonna do?

The squawk turns its head away again, scoffs down the fish whole and then opens its enormous wings and takes off.

And I stay frozen to the spot, heart thumping.

Blake

I follow the grey, windowless corridors to Huber's office. His door's already open, as though he's been waiting for me. He sits behind his desk, speaking on the phone, but as I stand in the doorway he looks up and gestures for me to come inside. As I enter, he finishes his conversation and puts the phone down. I sit in the chair opposite his.

'Mr Blake, I assume you know what's happened.'

'Yes. Boy 23. I was in the control room when we discovered he was missing.'

'I don't need to tell you how serious this is, do I?'

I shake my head. 'No. Boy 23 has never been outside before. He's in all kinds of danger.'

Huber raises an eyebrow, causing the scar that runs the length of his right cheek to stretch. 'That's not what I meant. He provides a direct link to the origins of Marsh Flu – a disease we were tasked with finding a vaccine for.'

I nod. 'Which we developed a vaccine for.'

'Yes,' Huber says. 'But as far as anyone out there knows, the disease came from a meteorite. A freak occurrence. A one-off. We can't risk the truth being discovered. It would cost us everything we've built up and, even worse, what we are preparing for.'

I nod. 'Of course.'

'After the findings of Girl 7's autopsy, we must make sure nobody's aware of where these diseases originated. We're supposed to be covering tracks, not creating new ones. Today was to be the day that Boy 23 was decommissioned – the beginning of the end of the Sumchen project.'

I nod.

'As it stands, there's a very real likelihood of a new outbreak, Blake, a new pandemic. Boy 23's presence in the outside world could easily lead back to us. If they trace Marsh Flu back here, we're finished. All of us. Boy 23 needs to be found and destroyed as a matter of urgency.'

'Understood.'

For a second we sit in silence.

'Do we know if Boy 23 is a carrier? Has his sample been tested?'

Huber shakes his head. 'His sample is missing.'

'So you don't know whether he's a danger to the public?'

Huber doesn't answer.

'I don't understand how this could have happened,' I say.

Huber sits forward in his chair. 'Nobody understands "how" at the moment, Mr Blake. I'm trying to establish the facts of his disappearance.' There's something in his tone that makes me uneasy. He leans forward. 'I'm suspicious that he escaped on the eve of his decommissioning. Especially given the missing sample.'

I don't feel comfortable. I shift in my seat.

'Have you noticed anything suspicious recently?'

'Nothing,' I say. 'Until the power came back on and we saw he'd escaped, I had no idea anything was wrong.'

Huber sighs. He says nothing for what seems like an age, but he stares at me as though he's trying to read me. I can do nothing but look back at his hard, lined face and his cold blue eyes. Eventually he breaks the stare, glancing down at a notepad on his desk. 'The basic facts, as far as we've been able to establish, are that at twenty past eleven yesterday evening Boy 23 was in his room asleep.'

I nod. 'I finished my shift at ten and he was snoring. He went out like a light not long after his provisions.'

'However, at twenty-one minutes past eleven, the power failed across the entire facility, knocking out all the cameras. The back-up generator had been tampered with – fuel had been drained from it in order to disable it. Boy 23 escaped from the facility without a trace, having dug the tracking chip from his neck and left it in his room. Nobody knows how.'

Huber says nothing for a while, but he gives me a searching expression, trying to read me. Eventually he clears his throat and speaks again. 'Did you notice anything strange about his behaviour recently?'

I think for a second. 'I don't know. He asks a lot of questions. I thought he was just trying to understand the world outside the facility.'

'Did he ask questions about who he was? Where he was? What was going to happen to him?'

'Nothing that gave any indication he was aware his life was coming to an end, no.'

Huber nods. 'There was nothing suspicious at all?'

'There were times when he tricked us. He'd got wise to the fact that we laced his water with a tranquilliser when we needed to work on him. There were occasions when he didn't swallow the water and therefore wasn't anaesthetised. On one occasion he opened his eyes when we were running a test. He saw the team of doctors. We terminated the test immediately and gave him a shot of anaesthetic. It's possible he might remember that.'

Huber nods again. 'Do you think there's any way he could have become aware of the fact that he was to be decommissioned soon? Could he have overheard something?'

I shake my head. 'Impossible,' I say. 'Even if someone had said something, Boy 23 would have had no way of understanding. He has no context outside of his room in the facility and his own experience.'

Huber says nothing.

Carina

I get into church just as Mass is coming to an end and everyone's leaving their pews to go to breakfast. I join the crowd, try to get swallowed up by it, hoping nobody noticed I wasn't there for the service. It isn't long before I feel a hand on my shoulder though. I stop and turn to see Father Frei staring angrily at me. He pulls me out of the crowd.

'Is attending Mass now voluntary, Carina?'

I shake my head.

'Then why did you miss most of the service? Did you over-sleep?'

'No.'

'Did you have somewhere more important to be?'

I shake my head again.

'Then explain yourself.'

'A girl in my dormitory was ill. I went to get help for her.'

Father Frei raises an eyebrow.

'Father Liebling called Father Lekmann out for her. I think she has Marsh Flu.'

For a couple of uncomfortable seconds, Father Frei stares at me, before clearing his throat. 'Well, whatever the reason for your lateness, Carina, you must understand that religious observance is a mandatory requirement of your board at St Jerome's.'

I sigh. The chance of getting thrown out of St Jerome's would be a fine thing indeed.

'Which work team are you on today, Carina?'

'Kitchens.'

Father Frei shakes his head. 'I think today you should join the team working in the clearances, Carina. The wagon leaves from outside the home five minutes after breakfast has finished.'

I nod. He thinks clearing houses is a back-breaking punishment, but I know there are perks to the job.

Jesper

I stand on the bank, totally still. It takes a while for the ripples I've made to calm, but when they do, the water's completely clear. I see a fish in the river, an arm's length from the bank, and right away I think of filling my belly. Except, as I'm prying and thinking about how to catch it, the fish flicks its body and darts off, quick as anything. I've lost him.

I squizz all around the river again, searching for another fish. Only I don't see anything but water. Not until I catch a glimpse of something zooming through the river like a rocket – there one second and the next it's gone. And then I spot them – a big group of fish, all kind of swimming together but staying pretty much in the same place. They're little ones, not even the size of my hand.

Are they too little to eat?

Not when I'm as hungry as this.

All I have to do is catch one. Or two or three.

Except maybe that isn't gonna be so easy. On The Screen I've seen them do it, but they have this long stick thing, with some string on it with a hook on the end, and they put food on the hook, and the fish bites it and gets stuck.

But I don't have any of that stuff, except the string. I could go into the trees and find a stick, but I'm hungry right now and the fish are here now. So I gotta use what I have with me – my hands, a knife, a bag and not much else.

As I stand and pry at the fish, I think about the best way to do it. Yomp right in there and grab one with my hands? Try and stab one with my knife?

Or maybe I could do what I saw in one of the fishing clips on The Screen – they had a net and they scooped the fish into it. The bag could be my net. I empty the contents on to the ground, and when the bag's empty I take off my shoes and socks and roll my trousers up until they're above my ankles.

As soon as I step into the water, I realise it's freezing cold and way deeper than I thought, coming up above my knees.

But I'm in here now. And I have to do this. I roll my shirtsleeves up and stand still, letting the water settle again, squizzing for the fish. They're still there, moving their tails but staying exactly where they are. They must be pretty stupid, if they don't realise what I'm gonna do. But who cares? I get ready with the bag. And in my head I count:

One

Two

Three ...

I break the surface of the water, plunging the bag down and swishing it in the direction of the fish, only it isn't as easy as the big squawk made it seem, cos as soon as the bag's in the river it doesn't move so fast and I have to kind of drag it through the water.

I lift the bag back out of the river. The water drains slowly out of it and all over me, until I hold it away from my body. When all the water's gone, I squizz inside. There's no fish in there, just a few little stones. I sigh, tip the bag up to let the stones plop back into the water. And then I try again. Plunge my bag in the river where the fish are, try to swish it through the water and then watch them all escape.

I've gotta come up with a better plan, haven't I? I've gotta outsmart the fish.

I ready myself for another go. This time I sink the bag under the water and hold it there. I let the water settle before looking for the fish. And you know what? They must be even more stupid than anything, cos there they are again, swimming real close to me.

I step just a little closer, so slow they don't even seem to notice me. And then, when I'm within swooping distance, I steady myself, count to three in my head:

One

Two

Three ...

I swoop, faster this time, bringing the bag up from underneath them, pulling it up to the surface so they can't get away. And when it comes out of the river and all the water starts draining out, I can tell that it's worked, cos there's fish in there, flapping about as the water drains away.

I yomp back through the river and climb on to the bank. As soon as the bag's on the riverbank the fish skip in the air, flicking their tails, gasping, trying to get out. And it kind of makes me feel bad. Cos that's them dying, isn't it? I did that to them.

I try and grab them up and they slip from my hands. But eventually I manage to get them all back in the bag at the same time and tighten the toggle, so they can't get out and I can't see them die.

And I think about the clips on The Screen. I need a fire to cook the fish and to keep me warm, don't I? Cos that water was cold and now my teeth are clacking against each other and my skin feels numb. So I start squizzing around for wood to make the fire, and a few minutes later I set to work with the firelighting kit. I've watched this so many times on The Screen. I sit cross-legged, place a small ball of cotton wool on the ground and bend over it, striking the metal key against the stone over and over again, sparks flying off it. Only it isn't as easy as it looked on The Screen, cos although I can feel my hands and fingers again, they're so cold that they're clumsy and won't do exactly what I want them to.

It takes a while. But eventually a spark flies off and lands in the cotton wool ball. Immediately it starts to burn and smoke. I pick the cotton wool up, bring it towards my face and blow on the smouldering spark. The ball glows, then releases a great cloud of smoke when I stop. I blow again, until I feel dizzy and I can see spots dancing in front of my eyes. The spark glows brighter. I blow again until – *WOOF* – there's a small flame.

I place the cotton wool ball carefully amongst the leaves and twigs at the base of the fire and watch as the flames start to take hold. I feed the fire with tiny sticks and then bigger branches. And when the fire's burning and it doesn't look like it's about to go out, I grab the blanket from the ground and wrap it around myself.

Gawping at the blaze, I remember how I used to stare at the clip of a fire for ages, watching the flames flicker, and how I'd start to feel sleepy. But what I saw on The Screen is nothing compared to the real thing – the heat coming off it, warming my skin and my bones. The smell as the wood burns. The sound as the fire crackles and spits. It's amazing.

I go back to the bag, open it up and the sight I see is horrible. Dead fish – glazed eyes, mouths open, bodies stiff and lifeless. Only I'm too hungry to feel bad for them. This is the only food I've got, isn't it? If I don't eat, I'll end up as dead as the fish.

The clip I saw on The Screen, the first thing they did to the fish before cooking them was they cut them open and took their guts out. Then they put them on sticks and cooked them over the fire.

And that's exactly what I'm gonna do.

I grab the knife, flick up the sharp blade and start on the biggest fish, slitting its belly open and looking inside. Blood leaks out right away, and the air fills with a stink. I grab on to the most likely-looking thing inside the fish – something slippery and pink and tiny – and I pull. A whole load of shiny, slippery, bloody stuff comes flopping out and the stink gets ten times stronger.

When the first fish is ready, I start on the next one and the next one and then the last tiny one. I give them a quick wash in the river. And then I find some sticks and sharpen them with the knife, before sticking them right through the middle of the little dead fishes.

Not long after I've put the fish over the fire, they change colour and shrivel. I watch the dead eyes of the fish as they dry out and harden and don't look like eyes any more. The air fills with the kind of food smells that make my belly feel like it needs feeding. And I can't wait any longer; I have to eat them now, so I take them off the fire and lay them out on a rock.

The skin peels off and the flesh comes easily away from the tiny bones. I grab up all the flesh, cram it into my mouth and scoff like I've never eaten before. One fish. Two fish. Three fish. Four fish. And it tastes better than any food I've ever had in my life. Juicy and meaty and smoky and hot and delicious. Almost as soon as I've started, it's all gone. Just bones and skin and the heads and the tails remain. And even though I'm still hungry, I'm not eating that, so I toss it all on to the embers of the fire and watch it shrivel and blacken and slowly turn into ash and dust and smoke.

I put my bag to dry on a branch over the fire and stare at the clouds of steam that rise from it. And as I'm staring I realise that maybe I can do this. I can survive out here. I can find my own food and cook it.

When the bag's dry, I leave it to cool for a while. And then I pack everything back into it and head north-west.

Carina

The wagon trundles along potholed roads right out to the edge of town. We stop when we reach two rows of bombed-out houses facing each other. The houses have been that way since New Dawn seized control. The people who lived here are either long dead or else they learned to shut up and agree with New Dawn and were housed elsewhere.

We jump down from the wagon.

'You all know what to do,' Father Muller says as we stand around on the road. 'Carry on working in the property you were in yesterday.'

He claps his hands twice and everyone hurries off, taking gloves and saws from the back of the wagon and moving to a building.

Everyone except me. I was working in the kitchens yesterday, so I stay where I am until Father Muller points me in the direction of the closest house on the right-hand side, with the instruction: 'You'll work with Hans. Make sure there isn't a scrap of wood left inside that house. Load it all on to the wagon, then we take it to the power station.'

Inside the house, I see evidence that someone's stayed here recently – a scorched mark on the floor where they had a fire, and a few discarded items of clothing. I shift the clothing aside with my foot to inspect it. But then Hans calls me. 'Come over here and help me with this.'

I look over. He's struggling to lift a large wooden beam that was once part of the roof and is now wedged across the room.

'Grab the other end.'

I rush over and take hold of the other end and together we lift. The beam is heavy and pretty much wedged in place. We lift and we turn, over and over again, until eventually, between us, we manage to move it and bring it to rest on the floor.

'I'll saw; you carry the pieces out to the wagon,' Hans says.

To me that sounds like a good division of labour, so I nod. And as he saws and sweats, I pick up the sections of beam and take them out to the wagon, taking my time before tossing them on to the pile that's starting to grow there. I ignore Father Muller's disapproving glance.

On the walk back to the house, after dumping another load of wood, something catches my eye. The wind carries a piece of paper fluttering into my path. I jog a couple of steps and pick it up before it blows away.

I turn it over and my heart races. It's a leaflet, and written right across the top are the words 'The Spirit of Resistance'.

47

My mind immediately fills with memories of Dad. He was leader of the Resistance in our town, a long time ago. New Dawn killed pretty much all the members though.

I look closely at the leaflet. A defaced picture of Commander Brune – head of New Dawn – stares angrily out of the centre. I shiver.

Being caught with a leaflet like this is enough to get me arrested. Or worse. I glance around and notice Father Muller looking my way. I quickly fold the leaflet, put it inside my coat pocket and get back to work.

Jesper

There's a thought that pops into my mind every now and then. I used to think it in My Place, but I thought it was just a crazy thing to think. But as I'm walking through the forest, the thought comes back to me:

Maybe I'm the only person in the whole world.

It makes sense, doesn't it? Cos that would explain why I've never seen anyone else.

When I was in My Place it was just me and The Voice and Feathers, wasn't it? And when I used to think the thought, I used to tell myself that I was wrong, that there were plenty of people in the outside world. Only now I'm in the outside

48

world, aren't I? And there's no one around. Maybe my thought was right all along.

I'm walking along, thinking that thought, when suddenly I see something up ahead.

Amongst all the greens and browns and greys of leaves and trees and sky, I spot stone. Loads of it. Buildings. Like a village or something. I walk closer and find a sign, with the word 'SCHWEILSZELDORF' written on it. And stuck over that sign there's another one – a faded yellow one, same as I saw at that building yesterday. 'WARNUNG. NICHT BETRE-TEN. KONTAMINIERTER BEREICH'. And I'm thinking that Schweilszeldorf sounds like a place name, doesn't it? But the other sign, well, I still don't know what that means. I walk forward cautiously, remembering what The Voice said when he left me in the woods. Stay away from people and towns. But I walk on, don't I? Cos I have to know what's here.

Only, when I get to the buildings, they're just as empty and broken as the other place. Which is strange, isn't it? Cos I thought the idea of buildings is that people built them to live in. That's what The Voice said. So where are the people?

But it gives me an idea. If these buildings are empty, maybe I can stay here tonight. They might look broken down, but they've gotta be better than sleeping out in the open with the animals, haven't they? At least they have walls.

The first building I get to looks like a house. There are metal panels screwed across where the windows should be. Some of the panels have faded writing scrawled on them in big white letters. Things like 'New Dawn' and *'verpiss dich'*. And even though I understand some of the words, I don't understand why they're written there.

I find a window where a big sheet of metal's fallen off and there's a gap which I can get through.

The inside's kind of like the one I was in last night – nothing much except dust and dirt and squawk dung and burnt wood, like someone had a fire in here (or maybe it got hit by a bomb). But there's more stuff in this one. There's carpet on the floor and faded pictures of people on the walls – the same four people in each picture. I walk through into another room and my heart leaps. Cos the room is full of chairs and a little table (busted up and covered in dirt) and over in one corner there's a screen sitting on a table.

Straight away, millions of thoughts fizz around my brain. Cos if there's a screen, maybe I can speak to The Voice. This is what I've been looking for the whole time. And thinking that thought makes my whole body feel light. I'm gonna speak to The Voice and find out what's happening.

I yomp across the room and reach my hand out to the screen. I run my hand across it to wake it. Only nothing happens except for my fingers getting dusty.

I try again – swipe my fingers across the screen and wait.

Nothing but dust.

I try again and again and again. But the screen stays black.

I give it a bang on the side.

50

And I wait.

But nothing happens, does it?

It stays blank. Useless. Dead.

And suddenly something inside me snaps. I've had enough of it all.

I pick the screen up and lift it over my head and smash it to the floor.

And if it wasn't dead before, it sure is now. It's just a mess of broken glass and wires and plastic amongst the squawk dung and dirt and dust.

Straight away I wish I hadn't done that. I feel stupid.

But I can't change it now, can I? It's done.

So I leave it behind me, go to another room.

The next room I find myself in is dark and gloomy and dirty like the others. When my eyes get used to the dim light, I see there's a sink and some cupboards. It's the kitchen. I go straight to the sink, getting my empty bottle out of the bag as I go.

I turn the tap. Only it doesn't really want to turn. And even when I do manage to turn it, nothing comes out except a squeak and then a *thunk*ing sound. I try the other tap and that doesn't work either.

I decide to search for food instead and try the cupboards. Cos there must be some food, mustn't there? The first one I look in is full of cups and glasses and bowls – all broken. The next is the same. And the next too. And in the last cupboard, when I open it, all I see is emptiness.

So I abandon the kitchen and start to climb some steps that lead up to another part of the house. I get the torch out of the bag and give it a wind, counting to a hundred in my head as I do it, and then use the torch beam to light the way.

And as I climb I realise my heart's thudding and my hands feel all sweaty. My body's telling me I should be careful. There could be something dangerous up here.

Except, when I get up there, it's just more of the same. There's a room with a toilet and a sink and a tap in it. So I use the toilet – cos I haven't seen one since I left My Place and I need to go – and it isn't until it's too late that I see there isn't any water in the toilet bowl, and when I flush nothing happens except for a clunking noise. No water. And none in the taps either.

I squizz around the other rooms up here too, but there isn't anything except smashed-up wardrobes and a bed that's collapsed.

I go back downstairs and back out of the window I came in through.

And I search the other houses, finding nothing that works, nothing I can use.

It doesn't make sense – all these houses, filled with people's things but no people. I can't figure it out. And every time I try, my mind fills with that thought again, the one that I know can't be true: *what if I'm the only person left in the world? What if I'm dead and this is me in heaven or hell or whatever, just yomping around on my own forever?*

And I'm yomping around, trying to dodge all the confusing thoughts, when I stumble on something.

An answer.

The first one I've had in two days.

But it isn't a nice one. It's one that sets my heart thudding faster than ever.

It's a man. And he's holding a gun. And beside him there's a great big hound, baring its teeth like it wants to eat me.

Blake

The sensor beeps as I press my pass against it. The lock clunks open. I push the door and enter the building, heading straight for the stairs to my quarters on the first floor. After I've climbed a few steps, I stop though. Voices echo down the stairwell from the floors above, making me suspicious. I take the remaining steps cautiously.

When I reach the first floor, I discover that's where the voices are coming from. The door to my quarters stands open, the lanky figure of Henwood blocking the doorway. He watches as I walk towards him, taking a step to his left to block my way.

'What's going on, Henwood?'

'I can't let you in.'

'Why not? These are my quarters. I need to get in.'

He sighs. 'I'm sorry, Blake. Mr Huber's instructions.'

I run my hand through my hair. 'What? Why?'

'Boy 23's disappearance. They're carrying out searches of everyone's quarters.'

I stand for a second, saying nothing, thinking what to do. Demand to be let in? Barge past Henwood?

No.

I turn on my heel and head back down the stairs, taking them two at a time.

At the main facility, armed men still stand guard. I scan my pass and the doors swish open, and then I hurry along the corridors to Huber's office. His door's closed. I open it and walk inside.

He looks up, surprised. 'Ah, Blake. I didn't hear you knock.'

'Could you explain why my living quarters are being searched?'

Huber breathes in deeply. 'Have a seat, Mr Blake.'

I shake my head.

He shrugs. 'As you wish. Blake, Boy 23's still missing.'

'I know.'

'We've been through the entire secure facility with a fine-toothed comb, Mr Blake, yet nothing has been found. We've been searching within an eighty-kilometre radius of the facility, and as yet there is no sign of him.'

'So?'

'So we have to try another tack. All the signs point to the

probability that Boy 23 didn't do this alone. He knows nothing beyond the four walls in which he's lived his entire life. How could he have known about our security systems? How could he have known to remove his tracking chip? It seems logical that he received help.'

'Why the search of *my* quarters? Do I take it you suspect me?'

He shakes his head. 'We're throwing the net wide to gather as much information as we can, as quickly as we can. Everybody's a suspect at the present time, Blake.'

I shake my head and sigh. 'I don't like this.'

'Nobody's above suspicion, Blake. Everyone's quarters are being searched, including my own. We've started with yours, Mr Blake, as you worked directly with Boy 23.' The office falls silent as Huber surveys me, eyebrow raised. 'You were his donor.'

I nod. 'Even if I wanted to break him out of Huber, what would be the point? He wouldn't survive a day in the real world. He's probably lying dead somewhere as we speak.'

'Possibly so.'

A few awkward moments pass silently.

'You broke with procedure and taught him in English rather than German, Mr Blake.'

I nod. 'English is my first language. It comes more naturally. What difference does that make?'

Huber ignores my explanation. 'You gave him a name.'

'I couldn't call him Boy 23. It was demeaning. I'm sorry.'

'It was against procedure though.'

'But it doesn't mean I let him out of the facility ...'

'No, it doesn't.'

Huber stares, watches me. The room's silent for what seems like an age.

'So, in your opinion, who might have helped Boy 23 escape?' he says eventually.

I shrug. 'I don't know. It could have been anyone.'

Huber raises an eyebrow.

'All I know is I'm worried for the boy, but I had nothing to do with his disappearance, as you will discover in your search of my quarters.'

'I do hope so. The search will be complete soon enough, and you can return to your quarters,' says Huber. 'And if what you say is true, you have nothing to worry about.'

Jesper

I stand exactly where I am, gawping, pulse racing, brain struggling to work out what's going on, wondering whether this is one of the people The Voice said was after me.

The hound strains at the rope it's attached to, barking '*Ruff ... ruff ...*' and showing its enormous teeth. The man yanks at the piece of rope, shouts something at the hound that I don't hear properly and the hound shuts up. In the man's other hand is his gun, still pointing directly at me.

The man is old, with grey straggly hair that looks like it's never been washed. He has a beard as well, long and tangled. Across one eye he has a patch. His clothes are torn and ragged and dirty. He's thin too. He looks unwell. Except I don't spend too long looking at him, do I? Because most of my attention is on what's in his hands – the rope that's attached to the hound in one and the gun in the other.

The hound rears up on to its back legs, showing its teeth, making a *GRRRRRRRR* sound at me, ready to tear at my flesh. I stumble backwards.

'*Wer bist du? Was machst du hier?*' the man says, and his voice sounds like a growl, just like the hound's.

But I don't understand any of what he says cos it wasn't even words, was it? Just sounds. I gawp nervously at him and he gawps back, waiting for an answer I can't give him.

The hound tries to lunge for me, nearly pulling the old man off his feet. The man yanks the rope forcefully back and the hound makes a funny strangled yelp sound. The old man squizzes angrily at the hound, kicks it in its skinny ribs and says something else I don't understand.

Only as he's talking the man starts coughing, and he takes ages before he stops and spits into a dirty rag he takes from his pocket. When he's done coughing and spitting, he looks at me. '*Wo kommst du her?*'

I still don't understand. Why can't he talk properly?

'*Ich habe nichts zum stehlen. Ich bin ein armer, alter Mann,*'
he says, before coughing again.

But I say nothing, cos I have no idea what he means.

Neither of us speaks for ages. We just gawp at each other.
The wind blows, making me shiver. Slowly the old man
lowers his gun and tucks it into the waist of his dirty trousers.

'*Hast du hunger?*'

I keep my mouth closed.

'*Komm mit …*' he says, turning his back and starting to
walk away. He gestures with his free hand like he wants me
to follow him. For a few seconds I do nothing but gawp as
he disappears towards one of the buildings. I think about
The Voice's letter in my pocket, about staying away from
people.

Just before he gets to the building, the man stops, turns and
beckons again for me to follow.

And I do.

Carina

There's an empty bed in our dormitory.

Earlier I tried to find out how Sabine was, but the only
priest I could find to ask – Father Trautmann – simply
shrugged.

Now it's night-time and the lights are out. Sleep sounds drift from the other beds around the room. As usual, though, I have things on my mind. I get out of bed, go to my wardrobe and root around inside until I feel the piece of paper in my hand. I hurry back to bed and unfold the leaflet, straining my eyes in the dim light to read.

The Spirit of Resistance

New Dawn isn't the only way.

They stole power by killing and raping while everyone was busy dealing with Marsh Flu, and at the same time they stole democracy from the people. Some claim evidence exists showing New Dawn engineered and spread the virus.

They control the electricity and the oil. They control the police and the army. They control the food and the money. They control where you go and who you see. They control justice.

They answer to no one.

But you can fight back. Resist their laws and their power.

Together, the people can claim back the power.

A feeling of hope rises in my chest and then in a second it's gone. The Resistance failed when New Dawn swept into power. What use is their resistance now? How can they help me while I'm in here?

I turn the leaflet over and look at the other side. There are directions for contacting them – convoluted, paranoid instructions.

A sudden noise in the dormitory startles me.

Someone clearing their throat.

I jump, then hurriedly hide the leaflet in my nightie pocket. My heart thuds against my chest as I look up to see Father Liebling staring at me. I say nothing. For what seems like a lifetime, neither does he. Then he beckons for me to follow him out into the corridor, so I do.

'The Spirit of Resistance,' he says. 'Your father was a member, was he not?'

I say nothing. I trust Father Liebling, but you can never be sure.

'You shouldn't let anyone catch you with things like that, Carina.'

For a second I think about denying everything, asking what he's talking about, but instead I say nothing.

'There are people in St Jerome's who might inform New Dawn if they knew you had a leaflet such as that.'

I nod. 'Father Frei, you mean.'

He says nothing. He doesn't even nod or shake his head. But I can tell from the look in his eyes that I'm right.

'Would you report me?'

He shakes his head ever so slightly. 'You must be more careful, Carina.'

I nod.

'Give it to me. I'll get rid of it for you.' He holds out his hand.

Reluctantly I pass him the leaflet. He takes it and puts it into a pocket in the side of his robes.

'Do you know what happened to Sabine?' I ask.

'She's in the medical ward. In quarantine.'

'Is she OK?'

Father Liebling shifts his feet around. 'She's very ill.'

'Marsh Flu?'

He shakes his head.

'Then what?'

'They don't yet know. She's had blood tests, but so far they're inconclusive.'

'Will you let me know if you hear anything?'

Father Liebling nods. Then he turns and limps off.

Jesper

The old man coughs, gesturing for me to sit on a chair, so I do. He places his gun on the floor with a clunk, saying more words I don't understand, but I think he's telling me that he won't hurt me. He lets his bag drop from his shoulder on to the floor. The dog immediately sniffs the bag, until the man gives him a whack on the top of his head. The hound yelps.

Then it turns to gawp at me, ears pricked up, like it doesn't like the look of me. But soon enough the dog relaxes and lies down on the floor beside the old man.

The man builds a fire, exactly the way I learned from The Screen. Except the old man's much better at it than me. In no time at all his fire's roaring, filling the room with warm orange light and smoky smells. All the while the hound sits beside him, every now and then opening its eyes to squizz at me.

And as the fire crackles and hisses and spits, the man gawps at me and I look back at him, nervous, wondering what happens now. Cos I've never been this close to another human before. I've never even seen another human before this man except on The Screen, have I?

After a while, he speaks again. '*Lass uns essen.*'

More sounds. They're words, aren't they? Only they're ones I don't know.

He takes the bag from the floor and opens it. The hound stirs once more, sniffing the air. The old man reaches into the bag, and when he takes his hand out again, he's holding a dead hopper – limp and with eyes as lifeless as those of the fish I ate.

He takes a knife with a huge blade that's almost like an axe from outta his bag. He gets up from his seat and places the hopper, belly up, on a table. The hound follows him, tail wagging, slobber leaking from its chops, nose still quivering. The old man lifts the blade of the knife and brings it down

62

with a crack on the back feet of the hopper, snapping them clean off.

I flinch. I saw this done on The Screen once. Seeing it in real life is different though. Seeing a real man and a real hopper and a real hound and real blood and bone and fur.

The old man tosses the feet across the room and the hound chases them, traps them between its paws and tears at them with its enormous teeth.

Meanwhile, the man cuts the hopper's tail off and tosses it away before moving to the other end, using his knife again and this time chopping the head clean off. And even though I've seen it on The Screen before, seeing it in real life, seeing the head roll on to the floor, makes me want to vomit. The old man doesn't even flinch though.

The hound leaves the legs where they are and chases after the hopper's head. As soon as the dog's caught it, it starts crunching it between its teeth and the sound is horrible.

The old man gets a smaller knife outta his bag and makes a little slit in the hopper's belly. Quick and neat, he moves the knife along the belly, cutting right up to the neck. Next he takes hold of the fur and he pulls. It comes away in one piece, like taking off a coat or something. He gives one final yank and then all that's left is the naked fleshy body of the hopper, legless and headless.

Without wasting any more time, the man slits the fleshy belly, just like I did on the fish. He pulls out the guts – and there's way more than the fish had. The guts flop down on to the table, stinky and brown and pink and disgusting. The old man squizzes across at me, smiling, says something else that doesn't make sense to me.

And all the while there are crunching noises coming from where the hound chews the hopper's head, cracking the skull and scoffing the brains.

Soon the old man has the hopper cut into pieces. He picks a black pot off the ground and puts it over the fire. He takes more things from his bag – leaves and a bottle of water and other stuff that I'm not sure about – and he starts cooking, throwing them all into the pot along with the chopped-up hopper.

And soon delicious smells fill the building.

It's night-time and the cooking pot's empty. The old man and the hound lie huddled together on the floor, eyes shut. The old man coughs and mutters as he sleeps.

I can't sleep though, can I? I'm too nervous. Cos even though the man shared his food, I don't like being near him. It doesn't feel right. I'm not doing what The Voice told me.

I get up off the ground and grab my bag. I search inside for the torch. I wind the handle to charge it and then wait a second, making sure I haven't woken the man or his hound. And when I'm sure they're still sleeping, I switch on the torch, put my bag on my back and walk out of the building.

The night is cold and the sky is filled with stars. I take a wander, exploring the deserted village, checking I didn't miss anything useful in the buildings when I looked before. Only there isn't anything useful, is there? And besides, it's too dark to really see inside the buildings with just the beam of a torch. So I think, maybe I should just clear out of here, follow the map on the scroll to the north-west, before the man and the hound wake.

But then I spot something ahead, at the end of the village. A tall shadowy tower stands against the night sky. And I know from seeing them on The Screen that this is a church – the house of God. I walk on until all around me there are big stones sticking out of the long grass. Gravestones, aren't they? Marking where dead people are buried underground. I shiver. I crouch down to look at one of the stones. It's inscribed in fancy old-looking writing, all written in words that I don't know. A green fuzzy plant covers most of the stone.

I get to my feet and keep walking. And soon I see that I'm walking amongst new graves with crosses made of branches sticking out of the ground and mounds of earth that must have been dug recently. As I look at them I shiver again, thinking about who might be in the graves and how they died and who buried them. And I think that I need to get out of here.

Only, as I'm thinking, the beam of my torch picks something else out too, something that sets my heart racing faster than ever.

A pile of bones, almost as tall as me.

65

All I can do is gawp. There are skulls and long leg bones and who knows what else. There must be hundreds of dead bodies piled up. Some of them are animals – I guess hoppers and bushtails and some fish bones. But mostly it's made up of people's bones – some big and some tiny.

And I'm wondering who these people were and how they died and who stacked their bones here.

There's only one logical answer though, isn't there? The old man. I haven't seen anyone else. Maybe he killed them all. And maybe I'm next.

I make the sign of the cross, say a silent prayer, cos the truth is I'm scared and I don't understand what's happening and I need God to help me.

Except, as I'm saying the prayer, I hear a noise that makes me jump.

'Ruff. Ruff.' But it doesn't sound like a dog making the sound. It sounds like a man coughing.

I turn around and I see him walking towards me, coughing. He spits whatever he coughed up on the ground. By his side, straining at the piece of rope, the hound growls like crazy. The old man has his gun with him. It's pointed down at the ground, but I wonder whether in a second he's gonna point it at me. They step closer and closer and all I do is gawp at them, heart thudding.

The man speaks, all in words that aren't words to me. I catch bits of it '… Marsh Gripper …' But it doesn't mean anything to me. Just sounds. I look at the way his face is,

66

trying to work out what he means. Except it's too dark to see for sure. And so what my eye rests on is the gun in his hand and then the hound by his side. I'm sure he's saying he's gonna add my bones to the pile.

Only I have the knife, don't I? So I hold it up, like I'm threatening him. And right away, he takes a backward step. The hound strains at the rope again, barking, showing those big white teeth.

And I start walking backwards too, stepping slowly and carefully, dodging the mounds and crosses, knife still held up, watching the old man and the hound. And as I walk away from him, the old man keeps the gun by his side, watching me.

And I keep backing away until I'm out in the forest, until I'm out of his sight, and I run.

I run and I run and I run, till I hurt so much it feels like my body's gonna break. And as I'm running I realise that I've left stuff in the village – like the coat I had. And that's stupid, cos I'm gonna be cold out here.

But I can't go back, so I carry on running.

And eventually I come out of the forest and into a clearing.

I stop running, cos I'm far away now, aren't I?

And I hear a sound, like *CLIP CLOP CLIP CLOP*.

I stop still and listen to work out what the hell's making that noise.

It sounds like it's coming from the other side of the clearing. I edge closer and pry through. And what I see, well, it's gotta be a road, hasn't it? Hard and grey and straight. Only it doesn't look exactly like roads I've seen on The Screen, cos there's cracks in it where grass grows through. A way down the road, and moving further away each second, there's a horse and a cart with a man in it, steering the horse.

I shrink back into the bush a little.

The horse and cart disappear into the distance.

And it dawns on me that I've just been running, without any idea of which direction I'm heading. I squizz at the scroll and find which way north-west is and it turns out it's to the right, along the road. So that's the way I walk.

I follow the faded white line in the middle of the road, dodging the horse dung. The road's quieter than the forest, cos there's no bushes for animals to scurry around in and no trees for squawks to sit in and call out from and no river to trickle along beside.

There's no more horses or people either. Just me and the stars in the sky above.

Or at least it's like that till I hear a noise which sounds like it's coming from a long way off, up ahead of me, and I look up to see what it is. Only there's nothing there. Just empty black road and sky and darkness. But the noise is there too – like a bee or a fly or something – buzzing, high-pitched.

And after a few seconds I see something appear in the distance. Bright yellowy-white light. A couple of seconds more and I realise there are two lights, right next to each other like eyes. All the time they're getting closer and the sound's getting louder – sort of like the '*RRRRRRRRRRRRR RRRRRRRRRRRRRRRRRRRRRRRRRRRRRRRRRRRRRRRRRRRR RRRRRRRRRRRRRRR*' sound that woke me up the other night.

Cos it's a car, isn't it?

The lights get brighter and closer and the noise gets louder. I stop walking and gawp dumbly at the lights, not knowing what to do.

I could stop the car and ask whoever's inside where I am. Except the thought of seeing another human makes me feel as though I can't breathe and like I want to be sick.

So I turn and run in the opposite direction. And all the while I'm running, the noise and the lights don't stop, they follow me, and I can tell from the way they shine on the road surface ahead of me that the lights are getting closer.

RRRRRRRRRRRRRRRRRRRRRRRRRRRRRRRRRRRRRRRRRRR RRRRRRRRRRRRRRRRRRRRRRRRRRRRRRRR …

And my mind's so scrambled that I can't even think straight. So I just concentrate on running, cos that's easy.

The sound gets louder and the car gets closer and the lights get brighter until it almost feels like I'm inside the noise.

And then I hear a screeching behind me, like some monster wailing, and I know it's the car. It has to be.

Then *THUMP*.

And suddenly I'm in so much pain I can't even describe it. I'm flying through the air, bumping off the front of the car.

And then I'm *SMACK*ing back to the ground and bouncing off the road and into the air again.

And *THUMP*. I land in a heap.

Broken.

Every single bit of me screams in agony.

I lie where I land, stuck to the cold, hard road.

Only something in my head tells me I should get away from here. I try to get up, to push myself up to sitting. But my body won't work. I can't do it. There's pain everywhere. I can feel blood trickling down my face and I can taste it in my mouth.

And somewhere the bright lights are still shining, blinding me. The noise is still going too – *RRRRRRRRRRRRRRRRR RRRRRRRRRRRRRRRRRRRRRRRRRRRRRRRRRRRRRRRRR RRRRRRRRRR ...*

– but it's gentler than before.

Then there's another noise, like something opening and shutting again. Then a clacking sound. And I realise it's a car door and then footsteps, coming towards me. I try to look up to see who it is and what's happening, but the light's so bright in my eyes and I have to shield them with the arm that still works.

There's someone there. A man. Two men. I see their shiny black boots on the road in front of me. One of them leans down, gawks at me. And I see he has something across his face, covering his mouth and nose, like a mask.

For a second I wonder whether this is The Voice, come to find me.

70

Only as soon as he starts talking, I know it isn't. Cos his words are like those of the man in the village – nothing more to me than noises, muffled by his mask.

'*Was machen Sie den hier? Es ist nach der Sperrstunde.*'

And since I can't understand his words, I look at his face and try and read that instead. But it's hard with the mask covering his mouth and nose. I focus on his eyes – angry and small. And I start wondering what he's going to do to me.

'*Haben Sie ihre Personalausweis?*'

In one of his hands he has a long stick and he's holding it like he's wondering whether to hit me. I crane my neck to squizz at the other man, see that he has a stick too and he's gawping at me, his mouth and nose also covered by a mask.

There's only one idea in my mind, to get away, to run. Except I don't think I can do it.

I try to stand. Pain screams around my body, but slowly and unsteadily I manage to move. I push myself up with my hands until I'm sitting. And the man who leaned in close to me stumbles back, fear on his face, looking almost as scared as I am.

He shouts something at me, but it's all words I don't know.

I clamber to my feet, uneasy, falling down and then getting back up and then falling down again and getting back up once and for all. And now I'm standing.

Both the men gawp at me. One of the men makes the sign of the cross in front of himself. And behind them are the lights and the noise, hurting my eyes and my head and my stomach.

I stand up straighter. I feel the crack of bones inside me and I can feel they're crunching into place and healing. I catch sight of the men's faces in the beam of light. They look scared. I feel my skin heal itself, feel the blood seep back inside me. The closer of the two men takes another step away and then he vomits all over the road and his shiny black boots. And as he does it, I notice that the scroll which The Voice gave me lies smashed on the road.

A million pieces.

But I don't have time to just stand here and gawp. I have to get away. So I start running, my whole body screaming in agony with every movement. I run towards the trees, towards the darkness of the forest.

Except that's when I feel something *THWACK* against the back of my head and I collapse to the ground.

And everything goes dark.

Blake

Just as Mr Huber promised, everyone is being watched. Despite this, nobody has any inkling of Boy 23's whereabouts and panic is starting to take over.

But just because they're looking at everyone, it doesn't mean they see everything. It would be impossible for them to.

And so, as I leave my quarters and walk into the grounds of Huber, I check about me and I'm certain nobody notices me. I hurry through the trees, out towards the perimeter fence, towards the disused buildings that once contained the boiler, with their faded warning signs and metal boards covering the windows and doorways. The buildings that received nothing but a cursory search.

The inside of the building is dark – I take a flashlight from my jacket pocket and wind it, before switching it on and shining its beam into the gloom. I head towards the room on the right, where a mess of broken wooden crates is piled untidily against the wall. I place the torch on the floor and move the crates out of the way one by one. Underneath the crates I notice there's a spilt drop of Jesper's blood, from the test tube that contained his blood sample. The sample I took and tested, and found he didn't carry the new strain of Marsh Flu. The bloodstain that proved he could be released into the real world. I spit on it and scrub it away. Next to where the stain was is a small handheld screen stamped with the Huber Corporation logo and the words *'Eigentum von Huber Corporation'*. Property of Huber Corporation.

I stand one of the crates on its side and sit on it. I swipe my finger across the screen to wake it. Right away it shows me what I want to see – a map. On the map is a single red dot. Jesper is in a village called Schweilszeldorf. I tap the screen and bring up a menu of options. I choose **TRACK MOVEMENT** and then, when the next set of options pops up, I choose **LAST**

24 HOURS. The screen refreshes and what I see takes me by surprise. He hasn't moved in the last twenty-four hours. Whatever is in Schweilszeldorf, he seems to have stayed there. I tap the screen again, and this time I zoom in on the town. I keep zooming until I see the exact building he's in and then track his movements in the last twenty-four hours again.

The screen refreshes and I discover he's been in the same building, in the same room, for the last twenty-four hours. He hasn't moved a muscle.

Which could mean a number of things. That he's been captured. That he's sick. That he's sleeping. That he's found a home. That he's dead.

Whatever the reason, I need to do something.

I type a message on the screen, sending it to the scroll I gave him:

Keep moving, Jesper. I'm preparing to come and meet you. I'll be a few days at most. Stay away from other people.

Jesper

I dream. And my dreams are filled with My Place. Of the Waking Sound and getting out of bed. Of letting Feathers out

74

of his cage as I walk over to the hatch to collect my provisions. Of completing tasks – survival tasks this time – as Feathers flaps happily around the room. Of receiving a reward and watching a clip on The Screen.

They're happy dreams.

Cos my life is simple and I know what's going to happen from one minute to the next, don't I?

Only something interrupts my dream, cos somewhere in the distance a bell tolls.

And to begin with I'm not sure whether I'm dreaming any more.

The bell goes on tolling. *DONG. DONG. DONG …*

And it isn't the only sound. There's a howling sound too. '*Aaaarrroooooo.*'

My Place dissolves from my imagination and all that replaces it is darkness. And a pain in the back of my head that radiates out all around, making me feel sick.

And I'm awake. I don't feel good. When I open my eyes they take a second to focus.

And what I see isn't what I was expecting at all.

I'm not in My Place and I'm not in the forest either.

I'm in a dingy room. There are two rows of beds along either side of the room. And in all but one of the beds there are boys. Some of the boys lie in bed silently, and others cry or rock backwards and forwards on top of their beds, moaning. The only bed that doesn't have anyone in it is the one opposite mine. The sheets are on the bed, all made up as though no

75

one's slept in it. Fastened on to the bars at the end of the bed is a chain that runs underneath it. I can't see what's on the other end. I can only hear it: '*Aaaaaarrrrrrrrrooooooo.*' Cos that's where the howling sound's coming from.

I gulp.

It has to be a hound under there, doesn't it?

And that makes me panic, makes me breathe fast.

I have to get out of here.

A quick squizz around the room tells me there are just two ways out – a window at one end which has bars across it, and at the other side of the room a door.

So I do what I have to do. I jump out of bed and I run to the door, ignoring the pounding in my head and the sore feeling in my legs and my back. Cos the only thing that's important is getting out of here, being on my own again.

But when I reach the door and try the handle, it's locked.

I'm trapped.

I run back to the bed I woke up in and I hide myself under the covers, as the other boys keep making their noises and the hound howls beneath the bed opposite mine.

And it's only when I'm there, beneath the bed, that I start thinking about how I got here. I don't remember coming here. The last thing I remember is being in the forest – running from the old man and his hound. And then the car. Being hit by it. Lying in the road and staring at the bright lights as the men in masks stood over me. Then running.

And then nothing.

Except now I'm here. And I realise suddenly that I don't have my bag any more, nor my clothes. I'm dressed in pyjamas that I don't remember putting on, that aren't even mine.

Where is this?

The words The Voice spoke to me as he freed me come back to me. He told me to avoid people, to avoid buildings. And look where I am now.

I've messed up. I don't even have the scroll.

The bell stops, the last DONG ringing in the air. It's soon replaced by the sound of footsteps coming from the other side of the door. Then jangling metal. Keys in a lock. And then the footsteps sound like they're coming into the room.

Is it the men with masks that knocked me over in their car? Is it The Voice?

I squizz over the top of the sheets.

And what I see is two men dressed in long black robes, strips of white cloth on their collars. Priests, aren't they? Across their faces they wear masks, just like the men on the road. They yomp into the room, pushing a trolley with trays of food on it. Provisions, like in My Place.

My heart races.

I pry on them as they take one tray to each bed, leaving it on the end. And what happens is that on most of the beds the boys take the trays right away and start scoffing like they've never seen food before. But on one of the beds, right at the end of the room, one where the boy's rocking back and forth, the boy sticks out his leg and nudges the tray.

It CRASHES on to the floor.

And that sets the howling off again. '*AAAARRRrrrrrrr-rooooooooo.*'

The boy who kicked the tray places his hands over his ears and rocks faster than ever, humming. '*MMMMMmmmm.*'

The priests ignore it, go on delivering trays. And in no time they get to the bed opposite mine, the empty one. This time, rather than placing the tray on the bed, the priest leaves the tray in front of the bed, on the floor. 'Michael,' he says. '*Frühstück.*'

Instead of prying at the priests handing out the other trays, I gawp at the tray and the empty bed and the chain. Waiting to see.

But nothing happens. The priests hand out all the trays (including mine) and then they leave the room, locking the door behind them. The tray on the floor stays where it is, untouched. And in the end I get fed up of waiting and prying so I look at what's on my tray instead, cos I'm hungry.

A cup of water. Some bread, some cheese and a couple of slices of something looking like meat. It doesn't look like the best food I've ever eaten, but my guts are gurgling and telling me I'm hungry. So I scoff it. As I'm swilling my food down with the water, I hear a sound that makes me stop what I'm doing.

It's the sound of a chain dragging across the floor.

And I can't stop myself from gawping across at the empty bed. All of a sudden something comes out from underneath – a head. And it isn't the head of a hound or anything like that. It's a boy with long hair and angry, animal eyes. He's completely naked, crouched on all fours. He moves slowly towards the tray of food, sniffing at it. And then he grabs the meat with his teeth and scoffs it.

I don't know what to think. I don't even know what he is. He doesn't look like a hound, but he isn't human either. Is he?

Suddenly he stops eating. He looks up and across the room and my heart stops. He looks directly at me, a piece of meat still between his jaws. He growls, eyes fixed on me, straining at the chain attached to his neck. The veins in the side of his neck bulge.

Blake

The clock ticks round to seven o'clock and my shift ends. I take my coat and bag and leave the control room. As I get out into the corridor, I fall in step with Jarl, who works in the lab.

'Are you finished for the day too?' I ask him.

He nods.

'Good day?'

Jarl shrugs. 'Not really. Everything's been strange since Boy 23's disappearance,' he says. 'There's so much suspicion and paranoia around. It's difficult to work like that.' And he buzzes us out of the building.

I nod, stepping out into the cold evening air. 'Tell me about it. Try being Boy 23's voice and donor. I feel like my every move is monitored and analysed right now.'

Jarl sighs.

We walk across to the staff quarters. For a while we're silent.

'What are you up to this evening?' I ask.

'Nothing much,' he says. 'I'm exhausted. Eating, washing and sleeping, speaking to the family back home in the Scandi-Countries. You?'

We reach the quarters. I scan my pass to open the door.

'Pretty much the same, I guess,' I say, 'except for the family. I've lost touch.'

We nod goodbye to each other and then Jarl climbs the stairs to his floor of the building. I watch him go before walking along the corridor to my door.

And I figure that tonight is the night.

Jesper

My body aches and my mind's filled with questions about where I am and how I got here and what happens next. But there aren't any answers, are there?

After leaving the room, the priests don't come back. They leave us to our own devices. The boys cry or rock backwards and forwards and the hound-boy howls.

I stay in bed, too scared to move even to go and pee in the smelly bucket at the end of the room where the others do their business.

I watch the sun make progress across the sky through the barred window at the end of the room and I think about getting out of here. Except how are you meant to get out if the windows are barred and the door's locked?

It must be nearly midday (cos the sun is halfway across the sky) when I hear footsteps and keys jangling again. By the time the keys are in the lock, the other kids in the room are going nuts again – howling and humming and rocking and crying. I sit where I am, prying as the priests open the door and walk back in.

Only this time they're not pushing a trolley. Instead, one of the priests carries a brown leather bag. And once the door's been locked, the Father with the bag looks around the room before his eyes rest on me. With horror, I realise he's heading straight for my bed.

I panic. I pull the bed sheets higher, trying to hide myself, but it's useless, isn't it? He reaches my bed and speaks – sounds that don't make any words I've ever heard.

I say nothing. I squizz around the room looking for a way out that I already know isn't there.

He speaks again. More words that aren't my words, too fast for me to catch them.

I look at his eyes – blue and sparkling, looking at me, boring into me. He places his bag on the end of my bed and opens the metal clasp at the top.

I gawp nervously at the bag, wondering what's inside.

And then he speaks slowly. '*Sprechen Sie deutsch?*'

I say nothing.

'English?'

And I sit up a little in bed, lower the sheets from my face and gawp at him, cos I'm sure I understood that word.

'English?' he says again. 'You speak English?'

I nod.

And he nods too. He takes a small bottle filled with a clear liquid out of the bag.

'I speak English a little,' he says. 'What is your name?'

I open my mouth to speak, only I can't force the words out.

'You can't speak?' he says as he takes more things out of his bag.

'I'm Jesper,' I say croakily.

He smiles. He starts to put together some of the things that he got from the bag. 'I'm Father Lekmann. You're in the medical room at St Jerome's Children's Home,' he says. 'You were brought here after a bad accident. Miraculously you don't seem to have sustained any lasting injuries.'

I gawp at him, then at the equipment.

'I need to give you an inoculation, Jesper.'

I watch as he continues to put the things together and I realise he's making a needle. A memory from My Place flashes into my mind. A needle going in my arm and then darkness. At least I think it's a memory.

I feel nervous. I shake my head. I squizz around the room again. Except there's nowhere to go, is there? And he has the needle in his hand. He pokes the sharp end into the bottle and fills the needle with liquid. And then he's reaching for my arm. And I realise that I have to do something quick, so I let the bed sheets drop and I grab hold of his arm and I sink my teeth into it.

'*AAAARRRGGGGHHHH!*' he yells, pulling his arm away.

The needle clatters down on to the floor.

And then, before I even have time to react, he slaps me right across the face. He grabs my arms and another priest rushes over to hold me down on the bed. And it all happens so quickly I don't have time to do anything about it.

Father Lekmann grabs the needle off the floor and stabs it into my arm. 'This is for your own good,' he says. And then he presses the plunger and the liquid goes into my arm.

I'm expecting the jab to make me start to feel sleepy.

Only the sleepiness doesn't happen.

All that happens is that time drags slowly past and more provisions arrive so I scoff them. The other boys in the room, they spend their time rocking and humming and crying and howling like always. All except for the boy in the bed beside mine. Cos he's been lying in bed the whole time, eyes closed, tossing, turning, coughing, moaning.

Eventually, after the sun's gone down and the bell has tolled again, the light in the centre of the room goes out and all the others close their eyes and sleep. I try to do the same.

Only my brain won't switch off, will it? All the same questions keep bouncing around my mind.

A new thought is bouncing around in there as well. Cos I've been thinking about how I don't have my bag or the scroll any longer. I don't have any way to know which way I'm meant to be going (not that I can go anywhere while I'm locked in this room). And that makes me think about how The Voice is going to find me. He said he'd come and find me, didn't he? But how will he know I'm here?

Another question I don't have an answer for.

Questions isn't all I'm filled with, is it? Cos I've been in this bed all day long and I haven't been to the toilet the whole time, not while the others are awake. And now that the rest of them are sleeping, it seems like the best time, doesn't it? So I peel back the sheets and I cross the room to the bucket which serves as a toilet. And what I find is that doing my business wakes up the horrible stink of everyone else's dung and pee. It makes me feel so sick that I have to cover my nose and mouth with my hand.

When I'm done, I creep over to the window and squizz outside. Beneath the inky star-filled sky, there's a building, right next to this one. A church. It's lit up and shadowed and creepy-looking. It must be where the bell was tolling.

The church makes me think of God, makes me realise I haven't prayed for ages. So I say one in my head, facing the church, eyes closed, hoping God can hear me, even though I'm sure He can't. And what I pray is that He gets me out of this place, that He sets me free, puts me back in the forest or, even better, guides me to where The Voice is.

But God can't hear me, can He? He doesn't even know where I am.

I decide to test it. If God was listening, He'll have done something to help me escape. He'll have unlocked the door, or provided a key or something. So I creep across the room to the door and try the handle. Only what I find is a locked door.

I'm trapped here and there's nothing I can do.

So I go back to my bed and I wait for the sun to come up again, listening to the kid in the bed next to mine as he groans and whimpers in his sleep.

Blake

It's three o' clock in the morning. There are four hours until I'm due on shift again. The building where my quarters are located is entirely silent. I'm dressed head to toe in black, stepping silently along the corridors, sticking to the shadows. I have a gun in my right hand. What I'm about to do is risky.

But it's necessary to get the cure out of the hands of the Huber Corporation and into those of the Spirit of Resistance.

I creep to the end of the corridor, past four shut doors on each side, behind which the men and women who staff the Huber Corporation sleep. I reach the stairwell and climb up to the next floor, gun at the ready. The only sound I hear is the soft shuffling of my own footsteps.

I head straight for door number 11. I stop and check around me, making certain I'm alone. I reach inside my pocket, take out the picks and then work on the lock – turning and listening as the lock clicks and clunks and eventually unlocks.

I take a careful step into Jarl's quarters. Right away I can hear that he's inside, sleeping in the bedroom. I push the door closed behind me. And I wonder where he'd keep it.

The layout of his quarters is identical to mine. I decide to try the living room first. I step carefully through the hallway, stopping after each step, listening for Jarl's breathing from the bedroom to check I haven't disturbed him. Eventually I reach the living room – and what I find is nothing. A sofa the same as my own. A table with a dirty plate and a glass on it. A few pieces of paper on the floor, which I pick up and check, discovering they're nothing more than letters from Jarl's family back in the Scandi-Countries.

I step through to the kitchen area. More glasses and plates lie around, filling the sink and covering the sideboards. I open the cupboards and look around, moving food and crockery aside. But no sign of what I'm looking for.

Which leaves only two rooms to check – bedroom and bathroom. I choose the bathroom first as it's closest and there's less chance of waking Jarl. Lying across the floor of the bathroom, I find his clothes. My heartbeat quickens. I pick up his suit jacket and check the pockets. And there it is – in the front pocket.

Jarl's pass.

I pocket it and leave the bathroom, pausing outside the bedroom to listen in, checking Jarl's still sleeping.

And then I leave his quarters and slip back into the shadows of the corridor.

I fasten the scarf across my face, pull my hood up and step out of the shadows and on to the path leading to the building. At the entrance, I scan Jarl's pass. The glass front door slides quietly open. I hurry inside and through the dimly lit corridors, past the control room, heading for the laboratory.

As I arrive outside the lab, I take a look through the window. The lights are out. The place is empty. I scan Jarl's pass and the door buzzes. I slip inside.

For a second I stand at the entrance, looking around as my heart thuds. I spot the computer on the far side of the room and head straight for it. I swipe my finger across the screen and it lights up, showing a login page.

```
Login Name:
Security Code:
```

And this is the point at which I have to bluff it. I don't know Jarl's login name or security code. But I know that my own is based upon my personal information. I look at Jarl's security pass and enter his first initial and last name as his login name. And then I try his employee number as the password.

Immediately the screen changes. I read the information.

```
First stage complete. Answer a security
   question.
What is your place of birth?
```

And again I can't be sure. But I have a vague recollection that he once mentioned to me that he was from Aarhus, so I type that in.

The screen glows green.

I'm in.

I scroll through the system, searching until I find a folder named '*Zweiter Stamm – Impfstoff-Entwicklung*'. In English, Second Strain – Vaccine Development. Inside I find just what I'm looking for – diagrams and rows of numbers and chemical equations and scans of untidily handwritten notes. I plug a blank scroll into the computer and download it all, deleting from the computer as soon as it's copied.

As soon as the last file has copied, I log out of the computer, put the scroll in my bag and look around the lab once more. There's a freezer with a warning sign on it. A light comes on inside as I open the freezer door. There are racks and racks of test tubes with substances inside them. I look through the labels, until I find a whole batch labelled '*Zweiter Stamm*'. I open up my bag, carefully take the test tubes from the freezer and place them inside my bag alongside the files. I'll need to get them into a freezer as quickly as I can.

As I turn, I catch sight of the window in the door, see someone walk past the laboratory. I freeze where I am, switch off the flashlight.

I watch the window, waiting in case whoever it was returns. Seconds pass slowly. My heart pounds. But nobody comes back.

When I'm sure the coast is clear, I hurry from the lab and then from the building.

Jesper

When I hear the bell tolling, I open my eyes. The sun's already flooding in through the barred windows. The others are waking as well, all except the boy in the bed beside mine. In no time at all the room fills with the sounds of growling and crying and moaning again. That isn't all the place fills with though, cos one of the boys goes over to the bucket and pees, waking the smell.

Time passes slowly until there are footsteps outside the door. All the others go loopy, cos they know food's coming.

As the two priests come into the room, I pry on them. Cos, as I lay awake last night, a thought came to me. The only chance to get out of this room is when the priests come and go, and that's mostly at mealtimes. Those are the only times the door is open.

I watch as one of the priests pushes the trolley into the room. The other stays right by the door, locking it as soon as they're both inside.

Could I get out? Could I charge at them and run out of the room when the door's open?

I think it over while the priests hand round the trays.

One of the Fathers brings a tray to the bed next to mine where the boy still hasn't woken, is still mumbling. When he gets to the bed he gawps at the boy, moving close, adjusting his face mask. He says something urgently to the other priest, who immediately puts down the tray he's holding and rushes over. Both of them lean over the boy, speaking to him in their words, repeating the same word: 'Andreas.'

But the boy doesn't say a word back. He just tosses and turns and moans and coughs, eyes closed, like he did all night.

The priests speak quickly to each other, nodding, and then hurry from the room, leaving the trolley here, not even handing my tray to me.

Blake

I take my coffee to the cafeteria table where Franks is already sitting. He nods as I take my place.

'You've heard the news about Jarl?'

My heart races, but I try not to let it show. I shake my head. 'What news is that?'

Franks takes a deep breath. His eyes dart around; he leans in closer and lowers his voice. 'He's been detained by Huber.'

I take a sip of bitter coffee. 'Really? What for?'

Franks shrugs. 'I don't know for sure. The rumour is that he let himself into the lab late last night and took the development information on the vaccine for the second strain of Marsh Flu – all the samples and vaccine trials too.'

I take a long, deep breath and blow it out slowly. 'Wow. You're sure?'

'It's just a rumour. But I've heard it from various people.'

I run my hand through my hair, giving the impression of taking the information in, thinking. 'Why would he have done it, though?'

Franks takes a gulp of coffee, then wipes his mouth with his hand. 'I don't suppose anyone knows for sure at the moment – like I say, it's a rumour. But some are saying he knows where Boy 23 is, that he might be the one who helped him escape. There are rumours he also stole a blood sample from the lab a while back. This might be part of his plan.'

'Why though?'

Franks shrugs. 'Maybe he thought he could develop and sell the vaccine himself. Do that and he could make himself millions ...'

I shake my head. 'But Jarl? Really? I never would have suspected him of doing something like this. I can think of others, but ...'

Franks nods, draining the remains of his coffee. 'It's always the ones you least suspect,' he says. 'Anyway, I've got to go. See you around.' And then he leaves the table.

Jesper

Hardly any time passes before the door's unlocked again and the priests rush back into the room. But the boy's gone quiet now. Silent. No moaning. No thrashing about. He just lies there.

And when the priests come in, I see that as well as their mouths and noses being covered, now their hands and hair and everything is too. They push a trolley into the room. Only this one isn't like the provisions trolley; it's more like a bed. It's long and has a white sheet draped over it. They push it over to the bed beside mine where the boy lies still. And when they stop, they make the sign of the cross in front of themselves.

They speak to the boy, but his eyes stay closed. Both of them lean over him, speaking to him, sounding desperate, repeating the same word, 'Andreas'. And I wonder whether that's his name.

But the boy doesn't answer and he doesn't move.

And when the priests touch his face and neck, then try to lift him up, to sit him up in the bed, his whole body is limp.

Like the hopper in the bag. Like the fish. Cos he's dead, isn't he?

He died in the bed next to me. Just now, while I was thinking about my provisions.

That's why he was moaning and whimpering last night.

That's why he didn't wake up properly this morning when the bell tolled.

And no one did anything to help him.

The blankets are nowhere near my face now. I'm just gawping as the priests lie the boy back down, cover him right over with his sheet and cross themselves. And when they're done with that, they lift him from his bed and on to the trolley they wheeled into the room. I watch one of the priests adjust his face mask with his gloved hand, making sure it's completely covering his mouth.

Around the room, the other boys have stopped making their noises and rocking and whatever else they do, cos they're all prying like I am, aren't they? The priests make the sign of the cross again and then wheel the trolley out of the room, taking the boy away.

As soon as the door's locked again, the whole room goes madder than ever – rocking and moaning and crying and bouncing and growling. And I've missed a chance to get out.

Blake

Hersch catches me as I walk through the corridor. 'I'm surprised to see you're still here,' he says.

'What do you mean?'

'Haven't you heard?'

'Heard what?'

Hersch looks furtively around, then leans in closer. 'They think they found him.'

'Who?'

'Boy 23 of course.'

For a second a paralysing feeling grips me. I take a few seconds to process the information and what it means. 'How? Where?'

Hersch shakes his head. 'That I don't know. Maybe it's something to do with Jarl.'

'Is the boy alive?'

Hersch shrugs. 'I don't know. All I heard was they found intelligence as to his whereabouts this afternoon and left right away. I guessed you'd be with them.'

'Who's "they"?'

'I'm not sure,' Hersch says. 'Henwood, I think.'

'Right. Thanks.'

And I hurry through the corridor.

Back in the outbuilding I make my way across the room to the pile of crates beside the wall and take them down one by one until I can reach the handheld screen. I drag my finger across it, and as soon as the screen wakes up I see the map and the red marker which shows he still hasn't moved. He's in the same room he's been in for days, in the village of Schweilszeldorf. If he's been in one room for that length of time, the chances are he's dead, or ill, or he's been captured and whoever has him has got in touch with Huber. He still hasn't responded to the message I sent him either.

I'm starting to fear the worst.

What I know for sure is there's no time to waste. I have to get to him before Henwood does. I put the screen under my arm and hurry back towards my room to grab what I need.

Jesper

There's even more of a reason to get out of here after what I've seen. Cos I've thought about what happened to the boy and the jab that they gave me when I got here. It started me thinking about diseases. That's got to be what the boy had. And I'm scared that if I stay here I'll get the disease too.

But I have a plan, don't I? I know the habits of the priests. I know when to expect their visits to the room, and I know exactly what they do when they get here. And I can use that knowledge and the element of surprise to get out of here, can't I?

And that's the reason I've been watching the sky and waiting since I finished my morning provisions. Waiting for my chance. And it's nearly here. Cos right now the sun's getting towards the highest point in the sky. The lunch provisions will be here any minute. And I'm ready. I block out all the other sounds in the room and I listen until I hear footsteps in the corridor.

And that's when I pull back my sheets and get out of bed.

On the other side of the door, there's jangling as the priests search for the correct key. I hear the sound of the lock turning and I step towards the door.

As soon as the door swings open, I run, barging past one of the priests, knocking into him, sending him sprawling, while the other one looks on, shocked.

And before they've realised what's happening, I'm out of the room.

Blake

The area where Jesper's been for the last seventy-two or so hours is right in the middle of a 'no-man's-land', not far from the landing site. For eighty or more kilometres around, the population was decimated, first by the impact, then by the fever and finally by New Dawn's clearance operation when they sprang to prominence in the wake of the pandemic. The only people who stray into this area now are New Dawn patrols and the desperate.

And Jesper.

As I race along the two hundred or so kilometres from the Huber Corporation facility to Schweilszeldorf, the road is empty. No patrols, no wild children. The only other living soul I see is a deer that stands in the middle of the road, dumbly watching my van race towards it, before darting away at the last minute.

In the back of the van is a small portable freezer, keeping the strain frozen.

From time to time I check the screen to see if Jesper's moved, to see whether they've found and taken him. The red marker remains unmoved in Schweilszeldorf, which could mean a number of things. Perhaps Henwood's information was wrong and he's searching the wrong place. Maybe he found Jesper and shot him, leaving his body where it fell. Or perhaps he was already dead.

As I reach the outskirts of Schweilszeldorf, I pull off the road into the trees and switch off the engine. Another look at the screen indicates Jesper still hasn't moved.

I must be careful. If Hersch was right, Henwood is probably here now, or at least on his way. I take my handgun from its holster underneath my jacket. With a click, I release the clip. I refill it with bullets and then push it back into the handle of the gun.

I reach over and put on a breathing mask and then I leave the car.

There's silence, but for the rustle of leaves and the chattering of birds. The area's deserted. I walk along the overgrown road towards the village, gun held out in front of me, eyes darting around. I reach the village sign, covered by a biohazard warning, and pause for a second, looking around at the ruins.

The coast seems clear. I pick out the building that the tracking device suggested Jesper was in and hurry towards it. As I get close, I see immediately that it's been used recently – someone's had a fire here. There are animal bones scattered around the room. I start to hope that this could be a sign that Jesper's survived out here, that the clips I played on The Screen gave him enough information to survive.

Then I notice something screwed up next to a wall. It's the coat I dressed Jesper in, the one he was wearing when I dropped him off in the forest. I reach down and grab it. I feel along the hem of the coat until I find something hard and square – the tracking chip I inserted in there. I go through the pockets of the coat and find a slip of paper – crumpled and stuck together. The letter I left him with. I hide it in my own pocket.

I check the rest of the rooms in the building and find no sign of him, so I head back outside, searching from building to building – prising boards off doors of some buildings to get inside.

But Jesper is nowhere.

It's in the gap between two houses that I finally stumble across something.

Two bodies.

An old man – bearded and dirty and looking like he's been living out here alone these last twenty years.

And beside him a dog – all skin and bones and matted fur.

A bloody puddle surrounds the dog. It's been shot through the head. There's no obvious sign the man's been shot, but when I bend down and check his pulse, I discover he's also dead.

But no sign of Jesper.

Could he have had anything to do with the deaths?

But before I can even think that through, I hear a click behind me. I turn slowly around, clutching my gun.

Henwood stares back at me, wearing a face mask, pointing his gun at me. 'What are you doing here, Blake?'

Jesper

I find myself in a dimly lit corridor. And I have a decision to make – left or right?

But I can't just stand here deciding which way to go, can I? If I do, they'll catch me. So, as the priest I knocked down gets back to his feet and the kids in the room go berserk, I head left and run along the corridor.

My bare feet slap against the wooden floor. Behind me I hear the clacking footsteps of the priests, running after me. I don't stop to look over my shoulder though; I run as fast as I can. I have to get away from this place.

I run until I see a closed door up ahead – one with glass panels so you can see through to the other side. I race towards it and then, as I reach it, push it with my shoulder.

Only the door doesn't open.

And when I try to pull it instead, it stays closed.

I push and pull at it frantically, trying to get it to open. Cos this can't be the end of it, can it? I have to get away. But as hard as I pull and push, the door stays closed.

Locked.

And I have nowhere to run. Cos, when I turn, I see the two priests stalking towards me, sticks in their hands, just like the ones the men in the forest had. I hear the howls and shouts from the room I've come from.

I squizz around, searching for an escape.

There are two options: a barred window set high into the wall to my right, which is too high and too small for me to fit through, or to run back past the priests.

And that's what I choose to do. I run straight at them, barging into them again, covering my head with my arms in case they batter me with the sticks. And in a second, I'm past them and charging back along the corridor, past the door of the room they've been keeping me in. I keep running, praying that this way there's another door to the outside and that this one is open.

And soon I find there is another door, same as the one I ran into at the other end of the corridor. I push against it, pull it, rattle it so hard that it feels like it must fall down. But the door doesn't budge an inch either.

And in another two seconds the priests grab me by the arms and take me back to the room.

Carina

Today I work outside – taking vegetables from the fields and packing them into sacks, ready to be stored for winter. It's hard, dirty work, but it isn't the worst. The fact the sun's shining makes it bearable.

As I go to wash my hands for lunch I spot Father Liebling standing by the cabin, handing out water. I walk over, past the children lining up to be served.

'Father Liebling, can I speak to you?'

He turns to me and nods his head, but I can tell from the look on his face that he doesn't want to be speaking to me. 'What is it, Carina? I'm busy, as you can see. There's a queue.'

'I just want to know about Sabine. It's been a few days. How is she?'

Father Liebling stops what he's doing and looks at me. He shakes his head ever so slightly. He doesn't say a word. Then he goes back to serving water to the children.

And even though I know from that small shake of the head what the answer to my question is, I want to hear it from him. 'She's dead, isn't she?'

Father Liebling says nothing, doesn't even glance at me.

'Was it Marsh Flu?'

But Father Liebling ignores me.

Blake

'I asked what you're doing here, Blake?' Henwood says, gun still aimed at my head.

'Looking for Boy 23. Same as you.'

'How did you know to come here?'

I pause before answering. 'The gossip around the canteen was that Boy 23 had been tracked to Schweilszeldorf. I needed to see for myself.'

'Gossip?'

I nod.

'Who did you ask for clearance to come here, Blake?' he says, still pointing his gun at me.

I say nothing.

'Does Mr Huber know you're here?'

I shake my head. 'Listen, Henwood, do we need to have this conversation at gunpoint? You're making me nervous.'

Henwood slowly lowers his gun.

'Thank you.'

But although the gun might have been lowered, his suspicion and thinly veiled dislike remain. 'You were about to tell me whether Mr Huber knows you're here ...'

I shake my head. 'Huber was busy interrogating Jarl. I took the decision myself. I was Boy 23's voice, his donor. I want to be the one to find him. I want to be the one to take him back to Huber. It looks like I was too late.'

Henwood raises an eyebrow.

'I take it he's dead now, like the dog and the old man?'

He shakes his head. 'Boy 23 wasn't here, just the man and his dog.'

'Did you kill them?'

'The old man was already dead when I got here,' Henwood says. 'My guess is the new strain got him. The dog was by his side, barking like mad when I turned up. I had to shoot it.'

'Are there any clues to Boy 23's whereabouts?'

Henwood shakes his head. 'Just footprints. They don't belong to the old man, so I'm guessing they're Boy 23's. They lead back into the woods and then they stop.'

I sigh. 'He probably won't have got far.'

'We'll track him down,' Henwood says.

Jesper

They didn't beat me with their sticks, but they brought me back here, didn't they? Back to this room where the boys howl and rock and cry. I'm back to passing the time by sitting on the bed watching the sky through the window so that I don't have to look at the other boys.

I'm starting to give up hope. There isn't a way out of this room. The Voice will never find me. I don't know what I can do to help myself.

When the night-time comes, I drift in and out of sleep, dreaming of running away and finding myself trapped.

* * *

I wake when the morning bell starts tolling and the others in the room stir. I stay in bed, waiting for the footsteps and the keys and the trolley with trays of provisions to arrive.

And soon enough they do.

Except when the priest comes over to my bed – Father Lekmann, the one who speaks English – he's brought a pile of grey clothes as well as my tray. And after he puts them on my bed, he doesn't just go away again like usual. Instead he speaks to me, and it makes me flinch because it's not what I'm expecting.

'How are you feeling today?' he asks.

I shrug.

'What you did yesterday, Jesper, was unnecessary,' he says. 'Your time in the medical ward is coming to an end. You'll be allowed out of this room later today.'

I squizz at him, hoping I just heard him right. 'What? Really?'

'Yes. You'll join the rest of the children in the home, work-ing, attending church and sleeping in an open dormitory.'

I nod. And I'm already thinking that maybe I will get out of this place after all. Maybe I'll get to go and find The Voice.

'Tell me, Jesper,' he goes on, 'how have you felt since we gave you the injection the other day?'

I shrug. 'OK.'

'You haven't felt ill at all?'

I shake my head.

'Interesting,' he says. 'That would seem to indicate that you're already immune to Marsh Flu. Otherwise you would have contracted a very mild form of the disease by now. Have you been inoculated against Marsh Flu before?'

I don't know what he means, but I don't ask. I shake my head.

'Interesting,' he says again.

'You'll be moving out of here in a little while, Jesper. Put these clothes on. We'll come and fetch you.'

Time passes more slowly than ever.

When the priests come back to the room in the middle of the day, I'm already changed and waiting. Before the provisions are even handed out, Father Lekmann comes over to my bed. 'Time for you to leave,' he says. 'Are you ready?'

I nod.

'OK,' he says. 'Father Frei would like to see you before you join the others. Come with me.'

And he leads me out of the room and into the corridor. As soon as he's out of the room, he removes his face mask.

We walk through the building, out into the sunshine (and it's good to feel the warmth of the sun on my skin and the breeze in my hair) and towards the church that I saw from the room, towards the big wooden front doors.

He opens one of the big doors and holds it so I can get through before he lets it close with a *thunk* that echoes all around the empty church. And my heart beats fast cos I've never been in a church before. The house of God. And I wonder whether God can read the thoughts going through my head right now, whether it's true He knows everything I've ever done. Cos that's what The Voice used to say. Back when The Voice was there.

And for a while I just stand where I am, gawping all around me, taking everything in – the size, the smell of burning and dust, the enormous coloured glass windows showing pictures of stories from the Bible. Jesus. And Mary. And Moses.

Rows and rows of wooden seats fill the church, for people to sit and listen to the priest as he leads them in prayer. Only right now there's no one here except me and Father Lekmann. And I realise that he's prying at me with a sort of smile on his face. 'You look like you've never seen a church before,' he says, making it sound like that's a weird thing.

I shake my head.

'Well, this is it. This is St Jerome's church.' And then he gestures. 'Come, we must go and see Father Frei.'

He yomps down the centre of the church towards the end, where I can see a huge golden cross. Just in front of the altar, he leads me off to the right, to a little wooden door set into the stone of the church wall. On the other side of the door, we climb stone steps that wind round and round and round until we come out on a landing with a door. Father Lekmann knocks on the door and waits for an answer.

From the other side of the door I hear a voice calling, 'Come.'

Father Lekmann opens the door and we walk in. I feel sick with nerves.

An older-looking priest sits in a chair that creaks as he moves, behind a great, dark wooden desk. He smiles at me. 'Jesper,' he says, 'I've been waiting for you. I'm Father Frei.'

And he says it all in my words. But I don't know what to say or what to do, so I just gawp back at him.

'Father Lekmann, you may leave us,' Father Frei says to the other priest.

And that leaves just Father Frei and me. He gawps at me without saying anything and I don't like it, so I squizz around the room instead. There are stone walls, hung with pictures of Jesus and Mary and a man who I think must be St Jerome. Behind Father Frei there's a coloured window in the stone wall, and the glass in it has a picture of Mary holding Jesus as a baby. On another wall there are some clothes hanging up – white priest's robes. On the last wall there's a fireplace, where a fire crackles away, glowing and making the room smell of woodsmoke. I breathe it in, remembering the forest.

'Sit down, please,' Father Frei says.

When I'm sitting, he speaks again. 'So, how are you, Jesper?'

I say nothing. I turn my head down and gawp at the floor.

'You were hit by a car in the uninhabited area before you were brought here?'

I nod.

'It seems you were lucky; you were unharmed. New Dawn brought you straight here as you had no identity card, no papers.'

I say nothing, don't even move.

Father Frei adjusts himself in his seat with a creak. He places his hands on the desk. 'So tell me about yourself, Jesper. Where did you come from?'

I shrug, saying nothing. Why should I tell him anything?

'Where's your home?'

I shrug again.

'England?'

And what else can I do except shrug?

'You don't know where you lived?'

I shake my head.

Father Frei raises an eyebrow. 'Who did you live with?'

This time the answer is out of my mouth before I can think. 'No one.'

'You lived alone?'

'Yes.'

'Always?'

'Yes.'

'No mother or father to look after you?'

I shake my head. 'No one.'

'Did your parents die of Marsh Flu?'

I shake my head. 'I don't know what you mean.'

'Did they have Marsh Flu?'

I shake my head. 'I don't know what that is.'

A look of confusion crowds Father Frei's face. 'Really?'

I look away from him.

'How interesting,' he says. 'I can't believe anyone's managed to avoid knowing all about Marsh Flu.'

I don't know what he wants me to say to that, so I say nothing.

'Did your parents die in the uprising?'

I shake my head again. 'I told you I didn't live with anyone.'

He nods slowly, thoughtfully. 'So who looked after you? Who got you food?'

'My food was just there,' I say.

Father Frei sits back in his chair with another creak. 'I see,' he says. 'You lived in a room, alone. But you were provided with food. There must have been someone leaving it for you ...'

I shrug. 'There was no one. I never met anyone before I came here.'

Father Frei makes a face like he doesn't believe me. 'So how did you learn to speak English?'

'The Voice,' I say. And as soon as it's out, I know I've said too much. The words The Voice spoke to me when he left come back to me. Avoid people. Say nothing. Why did I say anything?

'The Voice?'

I say nothing. I don't even move.

'Did you meet this person?'

I shake my head. That's hardly even lying, is it?

Father Frei looks puzzled. And for a while he gawps at me, waiting for me to say something, before he smiles and says, 'Fascinating.'

The only sound for ages is the crackle and spit of the fire and the *tick-tock* of a clock.

110

'Jesper, you were hit by a car belonging to New Dawn out in the forest. How did you get there?'

'I walked.'

'From your home? Is your home in the forest?'

I've said too much already. I shake my head. 'I don't know. I woke up in the forest.'

Father Frei leans forward, his forehead creasing. He clears his throat before speaking. 'You were found without an identity card or a medical card. Did you lose them?'

I shake my head. 'I don't know what those are.'

Father Frei raises an eyebrow. 'You also had a bag, Jesper.'

I nod.

'There were a lot of things in the bag, Jesper. A torch, a knife, a telescope.'

Silence.

'Where did those come from?'

And I don't know, do I? So I shrug. 'I found it in the forest.'

'You didn't steal any of it?'

'No.'

'You realise it was all very high-specification equipment. Not the kind of thing a boy like you would usually own ...'

I don't say a word.

For a few seconds Father Frei says nothing too. His eyes examine me, and it makes me uneasy because I don't know what he's thinking. 'You've been brought to the best place, Jesper. St Jerome's is a children's home. You won't be alone here. We have a hundred children like you – wild children,

111

orphans, refugees. Here we give them a new chance to be worthwhile citizens through work and prayer.'

I have no idea what that means but I say nothing.

'You'll be given a bed and food, and in return we expect you to attend daily Mass at church in the morning and the evening, and in between to work. Do you understand?'

I nod. I think I do.

'St Jerome's is full of sad stories, Jesper. Some of the saddest are to be found in the medical ward you were in until just now. Many of the boys there are locked inside their own minds. Some of them are wild children, abandoned and left to fend for themselves, no more than savages or animals.'

I nod, thinking of the hound-boy.

'Let us pray you're not to be another sad story. God willing, yours will be a story of hope and redemption.'

I nod, even though I don't have a clue what he means.

Carina

The corridors are quiet as I carry a crate of cauliflowers to the kitchens. Suddenly I feel an arm on my shoulders, and I'm so startled that I let out a squeak of surprise and almost drop the crate. I spin round to see who's there. Staring back at me from the shadows is Father Liebling. He puts a finger to his lips and then pulls me into the shadows.

'What is it?'

'I want to talk to you,' he whispers, eyes darting around to see if anyone is listening in. 'I couldn't talk in front of the others.'

'Is it about Sabine?'

'Yes.'

'What is it? She's dead, isn't she?'

He nods. 'I'm sorry, Carina.'

I feel tears coming. I fight against them.

'Medics did all they could, but she was too ill. She died peacefully, Carina. I gave her the last rites.'

Despite my best efforts, a tear leaks from my right eye and I feel it run down my cheek. I quickly wipe it away. 'Was it Marsh Flu?'

Father Liebling shakes his head. He looks around again before leaning in closer. 'It was very much like Marsh Flu,' he says in a whisper, 'but Sabine had been inoculated when she first came to St Jerome's, as everyone is.'

'Then what was it?'

His eyes dart around furtively once more. 'I shouldn't tell you this. Blood tests indicate it wasn't Marsh Flu, and there have been similar cases. It seems like it might be a new disease, Carina.'

He stops talking because the sound of footsteps starts to echo through the corridors as children come in from the fields. Father Liebling looks around and then slips away and I join the stream of children carrying vegetables towards the kitchens.

Jesper

I'm taken to a room bigger than any I've ever been in. It's filled with hundreds of dirty-looking children sitting on rows and rows of benches, set out either side of wooden tables. All of them are wearing the same grey clothes as me. And what they're doing is stuffing their faces with food – spooning some brown slop from bowls into their mouths.

And the noise in the room is something else. It makes me panicky, cos it sounds like every single one of them's talking at the top of their voice or laughing or shouting or crying, all of them using their words that I don't understand. That isn't the half of it though, cos there's the smell as well – so thick and meaty that I can almost feel it on my face as I walk through the room.

It's too much. Too many people. Too much noise. My brain tells me to run, to get away. Only that isn't gonna happen, is it? Cos right next to me is another priest – Father Liebling – and he's hobbling through the gaps between the rows of benches, leading me along.

I flinch at every movement, jump at every shout or burst of laughter from the children as we squeeze past them. But Father Liebling keeps limping on, taking me to the front of the room, where two other priests stand behind a table, spooning food into bowls. As we reach the front table, Father Liebling talks to them in his words. The priests fill a bowl with the brown lumpy stuff and put it on a tray for me together with a hunk of bread and a glass of water.

Father Liebling nods to me, looking at the tray, and I work out that means I should pick it up, so I do. He leads me back across the hall, until we stop at a table where there's a space.

He speaks to the children already sitting there in the words I don't understand. They say nothing to him, just go on stuffing their mouths.

The priest looks at me. 'I've asked these children to look after you,' he says in my words.

I nod. I look at the children. The hard looks on their faces make me think they don't want to look after me.

'You sit here,' Father Liebling tells me. 'I'll get you when you're finished and take you to your dormitory.'

I watch as he hobbles off again, until he's gone out the door.

And I'm left here, all on my own. Except I'm not on my own, am I? Cos I'm surrounded by other children, who sit and stuff their faces, who gawp at me like I'm the weirdest thing they've ever seen. And maybe I am. I know I'm not the same as everyone else.

115

And all I can do is squizz down at my food, at the brown slop and the bread. I start to scoff, not looking up, not wanting to see any of the other children. And as I'm eating, they talk to each other and I don't understand. It's me they're talking about though. I know that cos they gawp at me and laugh and sometimes say things to me.

I don't answer. I keep my eyes down, keep scoffing, trying to get this over as quickly as possible, so I can get out of here, go to my room and be on my own.

Only when I'm finished, Father Liebling doesn't turn up, does he? And the kids sitting at the table keep on and on and on so much that I have to put my hands over my ears and squeeze my eyes shut to block them out.

When he finally does come and get me, Father Liebling puts his hand on my shoulder and I let out a scream, like an animal. I open my eyes and see that it's him and he's holding the bag I had in the forest. He passes it to me and tells me to follow him. He hobbles right through the room where everyone's eating and out of another door into another huge room. On either side there are wooden stairs. Father Liebling leads me towards the set on the right and hobbles up them, and I follow.

At the top of the stairs we pass doors on either side of a dark corridor until eventually we stop by one. Father Liebling pushes the door open. And it takes me by surprise, cos I didn't think that the door would be unlocked. Through the door there's another big room, with rows of beds and wardrobes on either side. Loads of them. Twenty on each side probably.

And I get a churning feeling in my guts, cos I'm not getting a room on my own, am I? This room's for all the boys. Including me.

We walk into the room, between the rows of furniture, until halfway along the room we stop.

'This is your place,' Father Liebling says.

I squizz at it – a bed and a wardrobe and a little table next to the bed with a drawer in it.

'You can put your belongings in the wardrobe and your drawers,' he says. 'The lights go out at nine o'clock exactly. Prayers are at five in the morning and five in the evening. You'll be assigned work tomorrow. Sleep well.'

He hobbles off again and leaves me in the empty room.

The room doesn't remain empty. Soon enough it fills with boys; some of them I recognise from the room downstairs. And the first thing they do when they come into the room is gawp at me and talk and make noise. And I can't handle it. I just want to be left alone. So what I do is, I close my eyes and curl into a ball on my bed and I wait and I wait and I wait. And eventually the noise quietens. I figure it's safe to open my eyes and I see I'm alone in the room again. I get down from my bed, kneel beside it and say a prayer:

Dear God,

Please keep me safe from temptation and evil spirits. Help me find the patience to choose the right time to get away from this place, to find my way back to My …

Only my prayer's interrupted by noises. Footsteps approaching. Voices close by. A shushing noise and laughter. I open my eyes, squizz around to where the sound's coming from.

And what I see is a group of boys.

They've been prying on me, haven't they? One of them – a tall boy with blond hair – points, says something to the others in words I don't understand and laughs. My guts tie themselves in knots.

They yomp towards me, laughing, saying words I don't understand. And I realise that my hands are still together in prayer, so I quickly put them by my sides and get up from the floor.

And before I can do anything, before I can even think, they're surrounding me. Five of them. Laughing and gawping and talking.

'*Was machst du?*' says a smaller boy with brown hair. '*Betest du?*'

I stare at him, not understanding his words, but knowing, from the look on his face and the way he and the other boys are laughing at me, that he doesn't like me.

He speaks again, more violent-sounding words. And then he nudges me in my side with his knee and I fall over on to the floor.

Inside me, embarrassment and anger start to build. But I try not to look at the boys cos maybe if I ignore them, they'll ignore me.

Only that doesn't work, does it? Cos they stay near me, laughing and saying things and nudging me while I'm on the ground. And anger keeps building up inside me so that I feel like I'm going to explode.

I try to get up from the floor and I feel a foot in my side and I fall again. They laugh. And when I try again to get up, the blond boy kicks me in the guts.

And something inside me snaps. Before I can even think about what I'm doing, my body makes a decision and I get up from the floor and I lunge at the boy. And as though my body knows what to do automatically, my fists fly, clouting him round the face, knocking him straight to the ground. And I think he can't have been expecting it cos he just lies there for a few seconds, shocked. And I stand over him, panting, tears springing from my eyes.

For a second or two no one does a thing, like we're all too shocked to act. But then they close in on me. I'm surrounded. I try not to look at them, except I can't help it, can I? They gawp at me as though they're gonna do me harm.

Slowly the boy I knocked over props himself up on his elbow. Blood leaks from his lip. He puts his free hand up to it and touches the blood, squizzes at it. And then he gawps at me, and there's a look in his eyes like he wants to kill me.

He gets to his feet and takes a step towards me and the others close in on me as well, so there's nowhere to run, and I realise I've made a mistake. The blond boy bunches his fingers into a fist. And I know it's coming so I brace myself.

WHUMP.

His fist hits me in the stomach, folding me in two, making me feel like all the air's been knocked out of me, like I'm gonna vomit. Another fist smacks into me, lands on my cheek, and I feel the pain surge across my face. And then a kick to the legs and I'm lying on the floor again.

I gasp for air. I feel tears running down my face. A second passes and I'm hoping they're done – that they're gonna leave me alone now. But I feel a kick in the guts and another and another and all I can do is curl into a ball to try to protect myself.

The kicks keep coming, thudding into my side and my legs and my neck and my head. And there's pain all over me now. I start to think that they're not gonna stop, that they're gonna keep kicking me until all the breath has left me, till I'm dead.

Only then there's a voice.

And it's the blond boy, isn't it?

And he says, '*Hören Sie auf.*'

Which must mean stop, cos that's what they do.

But I stay curled in a ball. I'm not moving till I know they've left me alone.

And then someone leans in towards me. I feel a face coming close to mine, smell the bad breath.

A voice hisses something in my ear.

I don't say anything. I stay curled up.

There's another kick, in my side, and another surge of pain. Hands grab me, pulling me up to standing, and there's nothing

120

I can do. So I stand there, feeling sick and dizzy and sore, but I don't look at him.

'*Wie heißt du?*' he says.

And I know what he's asking me, even though it's in his words. I open my mouth and speak: 'Jesper Hausmann.' It comes out sounding broken and croaky and like I'm gonna cry.

And it makes them all laugh.

He speaks again, saying things fast in his own language so that I don't understand.

I stay silent, gawp at the floor. I squizz up at his face, at the blood leaking from his lip, drying on his face. He turns to the others, who are waiting either side of him, all gawping at me, and he gives a command.

They all start moving, going through my wardrobe and the little table beside my bed. One of them finds my bag and tosses it over to the blond boy. He smiles at me, then opens the toggle at the top of the bag. I lunge forward to get it from him, but two of the other boys grab my arms to stop me.

So I just gawp as the blond boy goes through my bag. He sniffs my blanket and screws his face up, letting it drop to the ground, tosses the water bottle and the notebook across the room. He takes out the firelighting kit and looks at it, opens it up, turns it round and then finally hits the metal against the stone and sends sparks flying. He does it a few more times, sending the sparks flying in my direction, so they land on my skin. He pockets the kit, then looks again. And one by one he takes the rest of the items out of my bag.

When he puts his hand in the bag for the final time, his eyes light up as he discovers my knife. He opens out all the blades, and chooses the longest and sharpest. He lunges at me as though he's gonna stab me, only stopping at the last moment. He tucks it in his pocket and then throws the empty bag at me, so it hits me in the face and drops to the floor.

'*Ich heiße Markus,*' he says.

The boys let go of me with a shove and they all move away.

The light went out ages ago. Everything's still and silent. All the other boys are in bed, have been for ages. And I'm as sure as I can be, without checking on every single one, that they're all asleep.

All except me.

Because now is the time to get out of here, isn't it? How is The Voice going to find me in here? I need to get out and find The Voice.

I throw back the covers of my bed, still in my clothes, cos I never changed into pyjamas like the others, did I? I grab what's left of my stuff – bag, stuffed with bottle and blanket and notebook and pen – and step across the room, in the direction of the boy's bed, ignoring the soreness and pain from the kicking I got earlier. Markus, he said his name was. He was the one that took all my things – the firelighting kit, the knife, the torch and the telescope. And they're things I'm gonna need when I get back into the forest.

The floor creaks and I feel nervous as hell. But no one wakes and I make it across the room to his wardrobe. Only there's a problem, isn't there? Cos on his wardrobe he has padlocks. Even in this dim light I can see the doors are shut and locked and there isn't any way I'm getting in there unless I find the key or smash the doors in. And if I do that I'm gonna wake everyone, aren't I?

What do I do? I need those things. I need to be able to light a fire and cook food. But I also don't want to wake anyone up and get found out.

A wave of panic washes over me.

So I do what I have to do, and that is I creep across the room, towards the door Father Liebling brought me in through, which no one locked. I reach out, turn the door handle and in a second I'm out of the room, free, walking along the corridor which echoes as I creep along it. I pass rows and rows of doors and I don't see another person. It sends a tingle of something right from the top of my head all the way down my neck and my back, cos in a few minutes I'll be out of here and on my own. And that's the way I want it.

It takes me hardly any time to sneak along the corridor to the stairs. I take a squizz around me before I step down them, carefully and quietly, thinking there could be someone hidden, prying, listening.

But I get to the bottom and I see the doors to the outside, and there isn't anyone. Just shadows and darkness and silence and me.

So I make a dash for it, across the wooden floor, eyes focused on the doors, my way out of here. And then I'm reaching my hand out, putting it on the door handle and turning. Only it won't open, will it? I shake it, try and budge the door, but it won't move at all.

It's locked.

I squizz around the room. Still no one there. But there are other doors, aren't there? There's the one that led to the church for a start. I rush across the floor towards it, and when I get there I try the handle and I find that's locked too. I try all the others and find it's the same story. I'm trapped. Locked in.

And then, when I look up, thinking about what to do next, I see I'm not alone after all. Father Frei stands in front of me, arms folded, a smile on his face, and he says, 'What are you doing, Jesper?'

Carina

The morning bell stops tolling. We sit in rows like every morning and evening – silent, heads bowed as if this means something. As if anything matters except what you can see in front of your own eyes. As if there's a God.

And while Father Frei leads everyone in prayer – murmuring and crossing himself and wafting his incense around – my lips move but I remain silent, as I do every day. A million thoughts go through my mind that definitely have nothing to do with God or Jesus or Mary. I stopped believing the day I asked for God's help, the day I really needed it, and He wasn't there.

As I think thoughts that would see me burn in hell, someone comes into the church late and sits down beside me on the pew.

He's a new one. There's something wild and animal-like about him. The way his wide, wide eyes dart around, terrified, nervous as hell, not staying on any one thing for more than a second. I hear his short, shallow, panicky breathing above the sound of all the mumbled prayers of Father Frei and the children. The boy looks up and across at me, sees me looking back at him, and straight away he flinches, as though he thinks I'm going to hit him or something. He shifts as far as he can go to the edge of the pew and looks down at the ground. His whole body shakes.

He's not the first one I've seen in that state. Sometimes when they first come in they're like that: nervous and trembling and strange-looking. It's how I looked when I got here, I'm sure.

But this one's worse than any of them. He's so edgy, he looks like he'd have a heart attack if I so much as spoke to him. And every time something happens in the Mass – every time the organ starts or they parade the cross and the candles around the church – he jumps out of his skin and the look in his eyes is pure fear.

He's one of the wild ones, that's for sure.

I sit and pretend I'm praying, make the sign of the cross at the right time, open my mouth in time to the music as we sing a hymn, but I think my own thoughts. And as soon as it's over, Father Liebling comes and grabs the boy, and I walk off to the gardens to start work.

Jesper

'Follow me, Jesper,' he says.

We leave the church – the whispering and the smell of dust and burning and whatever that smoke stuff was – and we walk around the outside of the building. I feel relieved to be out of there.

'What happened to your clothes, Jesper?' Father Liebling says as we walk away from the church. 'These aren't the clothes I gave you yesterday.'

I squizz down at what I'm wearing, cos he's right. This morning my clothes had gone. I had to search for what I could find and all I got was other people's dirty clothes that had been left on the floor and they don't exactly fit me like they should.

I gawp back at Father Liebling and shrug.

'Did the others take them? While you slept.'

I nod even though I don't know for sure.

'You have a lot to learn, Jesper. I'll find you a lock for your wardrobe.'

'Thanks,' I say.

'You'll get used to St Jerome's soon enough. The others will leave you alone if you try not to react to them.'

We walk on, not stopping until we come to a field with bare earth and fifteen or twenty boys working in it, digging the earth, taking things out of the ground (and I think the things are potatoes) and putting them in sacks. Around the edge of the field on two sides is an enormously tall wall. I gawp at it, wondering whether I could climb it and escape. Only I think it's too tall, and besides, there are two priests standing beside the wall, prying on the boys working. They'd stop me, wouldn't they?

Father Liebling speaks to the two priests in their words. As they talk, I squizz across the field at the boys working. And I spot the blond boy from my dormitory. Markus. He's crouching on the ground, picking potatoes from the soil and putting them in his sack.

'You'll work in this field,' Father Liebling says to me. 'Take a fork and a sack and go and work on the row next to Markus. He'll show you what to do.'

The other two priests give me the equipment I'll need, and I trudge across the dirty ground to start work.

As I get close, Markus stops work to gawp up at me. He says something (I think it's an insult) and then he spits on the soil between us. And I decide not to ask him to show me what to do.

Cos it doesn't look difficult. I dig the soil, then pick up the potatoes and put them in my sack, then move down the line. Easy.

For a while it's just me and the soil and the potatoes. No one bothers me and I don't bother anyone. And before I know it, hours have passed and the priests are whistling at us. When I squizz around the field, I see the rest of the boys are yomping over to a little wooden hut to wash their hands under a tap and then queuing to get into the hut before coming back out with cups of drink and plates with big hunks of bread.

My guts rumble. I put my tools down and follow the tide of boys over to the hut, where I wash my hands under the trickle coming out of the tap. I join the line for bread and cheese and water, then take it outside, where all the boys are sitting around on a patch of grass, scoffing food and talking and laughing.

When I get close some of them stop talking and squizz my way. And soon their squizzes become gawps and I don't like it, so I keep my eyes on the ground and walk till I find a place away from them all, right on the edge of the grassy patch.

I tear into the bread with my teeth, swallowing it down without hardly chewing, cos all that work's made me hungry. The bread's horrible, just like the provisions they gave me in

128

the medical room – it's dry and hard – but that doesn't stop me from scoffing it down. And as I'm eating, feeling sunshine on my skin, just for a second everything's calm. Cos I'm filling my belly and the work wasn't too bad, and right at this moment no one's asking me questions or hitting me.

It doesn't last though, does it? Cos I hear a soft kind of pattering sound, like something falling or being scattered. I hear it again and again. And then I feel something small and wet land on me. Then more of the same, and some of it falls down the back of my shirt. I grab at my head and my shirt where it landed. And what I see is soil. As I'm reaching for it, more soil lands on me, showering down on me. I turn around, squizzing to see where it came from. It doesn't take long, cos just a little way from me is Markus with his group of friends. And while his friends are laughing at me, I see that Markus has a look on his face like he hates me. And as he realises that I'm looking at him, he says something angrily in his words. His friends aim more soil at me and some hits me in my eye.

I turn back around so I'm not looking at them, and for a few stupid seconds I sit there doing nothing except getting embarrassed and angry and covered in dirt. The anger builds inside me, the way it did yesterday just before I hit him.

And that's when I catch myself, remember what Father Liebling said. I get up from where I'm sitting, take the rest of my food and I just yomp away from them, don't even squizz in their direction.

Even when a big wet lump of soil hits me in the face, I keep walking. And soon I'm away from them and back near the field. And sitting just in front of the wooden hut, there are girls.

Carina

It's the new boy from the church earlier.

He eats his bread and cheese, tearing at it with his teeth like a starved animal, barely even chewing it before he swallows. He avoids looking at me, at anyone. But every now and then he sneaks a furtive, nervous glance from underneath that heavy brow of his, head remaining bowed, eyes darting madly around for a few seconds and then staring back at the ground.

And it reminds me of when I was brought here. I remember how no one did a thing to help me. I remember how angry and scared I was. I spent the whole time running away and being punished for it.

I catch his eye – just for a second – and my heart races because it's like making eye contact with a wild animal. Scary and unpredictable and thrilling. Just as suddenly, he looks away again.

And I decide to say something to him.

'*Hallo. Du bist neu, nicht war?*'

The boy turns to look at me, scared, staring dumbly. He's stopped chewing the food in his mouth.

'*Wie heißt du?*'

He doesn't answer, doesn't even look like he understands. I wonder for a second whether the fever got to his brain but didn't kill him. Usually the ones like that don't survive. They don't make it to the home. They're shot or they starve or the animals get them.

The boy looks away from me, resumes chewing his food. But I can see he's sneaking looks at me out of the corner of his eye, trying to work out whether I'm safe.

'*Ich bin Carina.*'

He hears it, I can tell that, but he doesn't say a word or even look at me for more than a second. He puts the last of his bread and cheese in his mouth and then picks up his drink as though he's gonna wash it down. But he looks at the brown water and decides not to drink it, like there's something wrong with it.

'*Ich weiß nicht, wie sie erwarten, dass wir das Zeug zu trinken überleben,*' I say.

He still doesn't say a word, but he looks at me. So I smile at him. '*Ich bin Carina,*' I say again.

At first he does nothing. But then he nods his head. 'I am Jesper,' he says. 'Jesper Hausmann.'

It takes a second for his words to sink in, for me to realise the words are English. I haven't heard anyone speak English for a long time.

'You're English?'

He looks back at me, saying nothing, looking like he doesn't understand.

'You speak English?'

He nods.

'I speak a little English as well. My dad was born in England.'

He doesn't say anything more. He nods, stares at me, glances at the food in my hand.

'Are you still hungry?'

He nods. I tear my bread in half and hold it out for him. He shuffles closer and grabs it from me, crams it into his mouth, looking at me suspiciously like he thinks this might be a trick. I hold the cheese out for him and he grabs that too.

'Do you come from England?'

He shakes his head, shoving the cheese into his mouth.

'Where did you come from then?'

He shrugs. 'My Place.'

'Where's that?'

And he shrugs again, chewing.

'Is that where they took you from?'

He shakes his head again.

'Where then?'

'The forest.'

'Same thing happened to me. Were you on your own?'

He nods. He stares at the rest of my food and I hold it out for him to take.

'What happened to your parents then? Did the militia get them?'

He shakes his head, swallows the last of the bread and cheese.

'Marsh Flu?'

He shakes his head again.

'What then? You ran away?'

'I don't have any parents.'

'You must have parents. Everyone does. Do you mean you never knew them?'

He looks at me like he doesn't understand. He says nothing.

'Did you know them?'

He shakes his head. But he still looks confused.

'So now you're here?'

He nods ever so slightly.

'It's a shitty place,' I say. 'That's for sure. The work is hard. The food is inedible. The Fathers are mean.'

'Why do you stay here then?' he says. 'Why don't you escape?'

I shrug. 'It's possible to get out of here. But staying out is the difficult part. There's hardly any food in the woods. And if you're on your own, there's no one to look out for you.'

'It's got to be better than here though,' he says.

He's right about that. I nod. 'It's not that easy though. New Dawn always find the escapees. They pick them up and they beat them. Then they bring them back here and the Fathers beat them some more and give them the worst jobs.'

And before he can say anything to that, Father Henning blows his whistle and everyone stands up and gets ready to go back to work.

Later, after work has finished and I'm walking through the corridor back to my dorm to wash, I find my way blocked by Sabine's brother Markus and his gang.

'My sister – you were in the same dormitory as her, weren't you?'

I nod. 'I'm sorry to hear about what happened to her.'

'They're saying what she died of was something like Marsh Flu.'

I nod. 'I heard that.'

'The thing is though, she had the vaccine when we came to St Jerome's in the first place. So it can't have been Marsh Flu, can it?'

I shrug.

'People are saying there's a new strain of the disease,' he says. 'That's why people are getting ill again. That's what killed Sabine.'

I say nothing. I gulp. I heard the same thing too.

'The word is, a new boy from the forest brought the disease to St Jerome's. Jesper Hausmann. He was found by New Dawn near the meteorite landing spot. He must be the carrier. He killed my sister.'

The news hits me with a jolt. That's the boy I ate with at lunchtime.

'I saw you with him today,' Markus says.

I say nothing. My stomach knots up.

'If you want my advice, you should stay away from him,' Markus says. 'God knows what disease he's carrying. You don't want to be associated with scum like that.'

I stare at Markus. Can this be true? My mind races with thoughts that maybe I've already contracted the disease.

'They say there's no cure. He could be infecting all of us, and there's no way of making us well,' Markus says. 'He's a danger. Pass it on.'

Jesper

The bell tolls as I follow the crowd of hurrying boys and girls into the church. A hum of noise fills the air, even though no one seems to be speaking. Candles glow in their holders at the ends of the pews and on the walls, filling the air with soft light and the smell of burning.

I find an empty pew at the back of the church and sit. Children continue streaming inside, finding somewhere to sit, filling up all the pews. Only no one comes and sits at my pew. Children come near, but when they see me, they all of a sudden look shocked and go to sit somewhere else.

And I don't mind.

I don't want to sit next to them, do I?

I'd rather be on my own.

Except in the end, when all the other pews are filled, the priests *make* people come and sit on my pew. The children sit, warily, staying as far away from me as they can.

Eventually the service starts and Father Frei comes out wearing robes and starts doing all the same stuff he was doing this morning – the prayers and the smoke and the chanting. And I watch what the children do and try to do the same.

After the final 'Amen', the children all get up again, start walking back out of the church silently and I follow, trying not to catch anyone's eye.

Only, as I'm about to walk out of the door, Father Liebling limps towards me. By his side he has Markus and Carina.

'Come with me, Jesper,' Father Liebling says. 'Father Frei has chosen you three to clear away.'

Carina

The church empties of people in a few moments. Only Jesper, Markus, Father Liebling, Father Frei and I remain. Our footsteps echo around the church as we follow Father Liebling to the altar, where Father Frei is standing. Markus's words bounce around my head, and I keep my distance from Jesper.

136

Father Frei starts to tell us what to do, like we don't already know – snuff out the candles, collect the prayer books, sweep the floors, take the extra chairs and store them down in the crypt, etc. etc. It's like a double punishment – first we have to do extra work, and second we'll be last in the food hall and we'll likely get the dregs or nothing at all.

After he's done telling us what to do – in English as well as German – Father Liebling hands us brooms. We set to work, sweeping along between the pews, silent but for the scraping of the brooms' twigs on the stone floor.

And still I stay my distance from Jesper, wondering if it's true. I watch him though, trying to catch his eye. He keeps his gaze fixed on the floor, as though he's in another world and he doesn't want to be reached. So I concentrate on getting this done as quickly as I can, so I can get out of here.

When the floor's swept and the candles are snuffed and the prayer books are stacked, all that's left are the chairs to be taken to the crypt. I sigh. The crypt is dark and dirty and dusty. There are bats and rats and graves and secrets. Being down there gives me the creeps.

I end up picking a chair up and folding it closed just as Jesper does the same, unable to avoid being close to him this time. My heart beats quickly. And this time he gives me a glance. I smile at him, but his eyes dart away and he follows Markus towards the stairway down to the crypt.

Our footsteps echo along the spiral staircase as we walk down into the gloom. In the crypt, Father Liebling lights a torch and hangs it on one of the stone walls, shedding a dim light across the nearest pillar, casting shadows, making the rest of the room dark and unseeable. I shiver.

Father Liebling points to where he wants the folded chairs stacked, and we leave them there before going back up for more.

The three of us work at different speeds, and each time I take a chair down the steps, I end up waiting for either Markus or Jesper to climb the steps before I can go back downstairs. I notice that every time Markus passes Jesper at the top of the steps, he gives him a filthy look and his lips move like he's saying something, no doubt about Sabine. Jesper looks away and tries to ignore him.

I grab another chair, fold it and make my way over to the top of the staircase, where Markus is already waiting to go down. I rest the chair against my leg, listening to Jesper's footsteps climbing up and out of the crypt. As he gets near the top, I hear Markus speak to him in English:

'Get out of my way.'

And then I see him step into Jesper's path and shove him with his shoulder. At first there's no noise, just a look of shock on Jesper's face as he loses his balance.

And then there's a THUMP, followed by another and another and another. Because he's fallen. And I'm certain Markus did it on purpose.

Jesper

My hands go out automatically to break my fall, but there's nothing to grab on to. I fall backwards, end over end, thumping against steps all the way to the bottom and it's all so quick I barely even know what's happening.

It takes a few seconds for everything to stop moving around me, for me to work out I've stopped falling and I'm lying in the crypt, in the dust and the spiders' webs and bat dung. And that's when the pain starts – like every single part of me is smashed and hurting and crying out for help.

I try to move, but I can't. Nothing works. I know my brain's sending signals to my neck and my hands and arms and legs and feet, but nothing moves and I just stay there, slumped.

Broken.

I hear feet hurrying down the steps and a voice saying words.

And at first I'm so disorientated I don't know who it is. But slowly my brain recognises the voice. Markus. He pushed me. And now he's standing over me with a look on his face like he's seen something horrible, like he's seen a ghost or a monster.

But it's me he's looking at, isn't it? He's seen me, and he looks like he's ready to vomit.

Me, lying in a heap, where I landed. After he pushed me. Me, in so much pain that I can't even describe.

Next to him is Carina.

I hear more footsteps. And another voice.

'What's happened? What happened here, Markus?'

It's Father Liebling.

I manage to move my neck and my head to see him gawping at me the same way Markus and Carina are – horror on his face.

'*Oh, lieber Herr,*' he says, crossing himself. He looks upwards for a moment. His lips move but he makes no sound. He's praying, talking to God, asking Him to save me. His lips stop moving and he makes the sign of the cross again.

I move my head and it hurts so much I want to scream – only when I open my mouth no noise comes out. I manage to look at myself and what I see is just a tangle of bits of my body. There's blood everywhere, mixing with the dust and the bat dung. My leg's pointing in the wrong direction.

'What happened?' Father Liebling asks me.

I say nothing because I'm in too much pain to talk and also my brain is too scrambled.

'It was Markus,' Carina says. 'He ...'

'Jesper fell,' Markus says quickly. 'I tried to catch him, but I couldn't.'

'Run and fetch Father Frei, Markus,' Father Liebling says. 'And tell him we need a medic.'

Markus nods and turns, squizzes at me one more time and then runs back up the steps. I listen to his footsteps echoing as he climbs and my head starts to feel weird, like I'm floating.

'Jesper, where does it hurt?' Father Liebling asks me, bending down.

The answer is everywhere. Only when I open my mouth to say it, I find I still can't even make a noise.

Father Liebling looks around him and I think he's trying to work out what to do, how to help.

'We should stop the bleeding. Make a bandage,' Carina says. 'Your robe – tear off a strip of material.'

Father Liebling gawps at her for a second before he pulls his white robes up and over his head and then off. And right away he and Carina start tearing until they've ripped them into strips. Carina takes the strips of cloth and she ties them around me, everywhere the skin's broken. I look at her face, see her wince as she does it, trying not to look at the mess that my legs and arms are in.

'You'll be OK,' she says. 'It should help stop the bleeding.' And then she strokes my hair.

'Markus has gone to get help,' Father Liebling says, just sort of standing there and trying not to look at me. 'Stay still. Don't move.'

Only quite suddenly I don't feel like staying still. My body tells me to move. And I have to do what my body is telling me. I have to try to stand.

Carina

He's completely busted up. Blood everywhere. One leg and one arm bend in directions they shouldn't. His face contorts in pain. And for the first time since I've known him, his eyes have stopped darting around. Instead he stares at us, willing us to help. But all I can do is crouch next to him, stroking his hair, feeling helpless and useless. We've bandaged what we can to stop the bleeding, but that's not going to fix him. What he needs is a medic. Or a miracle.

He glances at me for a second, but then looks away as an expression of concentration suddenly appears on his face.

And then there's a cracking noise – CCCCRRRIIICCCKKK.

It makes me jump back. I look around into the shadows for where the noise is coming from.

CCCCCRRRAAAAACCCCCKKKK.

CCCRRRUUNNNCCCHHHH.

But I don't need to look in the shadows for the source of the noise, because it's right in front of me. It's Jesper. It sounds like his bones are cracking and crunching together. And I don't understand. How can his bones be doing that?

The sound makes me feel sick. I watch as one of his arms, which until now was bent and facing in an impossible direction, starts to move back into place. I watch as the blood that leaked out of him starts to bleed back *into* him. I watch his skin repair itself, so nothing more than a faint pink mark is left.

142

CCCRRRIIICCCKKK.

CCCCRRRRAAAACCCCKKKK.

CCCCCRRRRRUUUUUNNNNNCCCCCHHHHH.

I haven't seen anything like it in my life. I've seen people die, seen people killed and mangled and maimed. But never this. Never.

'Dear Lord,' Father Liebling mumbles, making the sign of the cross.

I hear footsteps approaching, clacking and shuffling down the steps behind me. I turn to see Father Frei and Markus. Father Frei makes the sign of the cross as he steps down the last stair.

'Jesper, are you OK?' he says. He looks at Jesper's leg, seeing as clear as anything that he's not OK. 'Help's coming. Stay still.'

But Jesper doesn't listen. As we watch he pushes himself up to sitting, his leg still a twisted mess.

And then the *CRACK*ing and the *CRUNCH*ing start again.

Father Frei jumps back, gasping, crossing himself again as the bones in Jesper's leg crack back into place, straighten out, realign themselves, as blood seeps back inside him and his skin mends.

And then Jesper stands.

This can't be happening.

'Jesus,' says Markus, and he bends over and vomits on the floor.

Everyone stares at Jesper, brains not believing what eyes and ears are saying. Jesper stands a little unsteadily, looks down at his legs and his arms and then at the floor. He takes a step forward. Father Liebling gasps and takes a frightened step back.

The Fathers cross themselves once more, utter more useless prayers.

'It's a miracle,' Father Liebling says. 'He walks.'

Father Frei steps forward. The expression of shock on his face slowly gives way to a smile. 'Yes. A miracle,' he says. 'In front of our eyes.' He touches Jesper – his arms, his legs, his face – as though he's checking to see whether they're real. 'Truly a miracle. Praise God. We're blessed.'

Jesper

Father Frei leads me away from the church and back into the building. All the while we're walking, he's turning to me, checking I'm all right, asking if I'm in pain.

And I say I'm OK.

Cos, I am OK, aren't I? Of course I am. I hurt and I ache and I feel sore. But I've healed. I'm OK. I'm walking and everything's fixed.

But every so often Father Frei looks up towards heaven, speaking to God in his words, smiling, making the sign of the cross over and over again.

'We'll give you your own room, Jesper. I'll arrange for the medic to attend to you there, to check you're well.'

And sure enough, we go up the stairs and Father Frei shows me to a small room with a window, a bed, a small table and a wardrobe. Through a door at the end of the room there's a toilet and a sink. It's almost like My Place, except there's no screen and no Feathers.

'Make yourself at home, Jesper,' Father Frei says. 'I'll have food sent up and the medic will come and see you.'

I nod and Father Frei leaves me alone, closing the door behind him. I hear him locking it before he goes.

Four walls and no other people.

I lie down on the bed and close my eyes.

And for a while there's nothing but silence and darkness and me.

The darkness swallows me. Empty and warm and silent. But it doesn't stay dark forever, nor silent. The darkness gives way to light and I hear a sound – the cock-a-doodle-doo *of the Waking Sound. It's far away and muffled at first. But the longer it goes on, the louder and clearer I hear it. And before I know it, I'm somewhere else.*

I'm in My Place. And it's the start of the day and I'm back in my own bed. I sit up, look ahead of me and I see The Screen on the far wall.

'Good morning, Jesper,' The Voice says.

I mumble a 'good morning' back to The Screen and then get out of bed, yomp over towards the door, to the hatch, where my provisions are waiting. Water. Juice. Cereal. Toast. I take the tray over to my table and sit and scoff it all down. And when I'm done I set the empty bowls and plates and glasses back on my tray and take it to the hatch. I open my wardrobe, grab a pile of clothes and go through to the shower room. I take off my pyjamas and put them into the dirty clothes chute. I turn the shower dial and the water comes on – warm and fast and steady.

When I'm done and I'm dressed, I go back through to the main area of My Place. I let Feathers out of his cage, and while he's flying around the room, I pull up my seat in front of The Screen, waiting to find out what's happening today.

A film. One of my favourites: a meteorite speeding towards Earth. And as it flies through the dark starry deepness of space, bits of it whizz off in all directions. But the main part of it keeps heading towards Earth and eventually it passes into the atmosphere. And it's moving so fast that in seconds it crashes into the Earth, into some buildings and people and some trees. And in the second it lands, the buildings and the trees disappear and all that's left is fire and smoke and the meteor. A meteorite.

It's showing because of yesterday – because I did all my tasks well yesterday. Top marks, nothing wrong. I earned two rewards, but I only had time for one of them before lights out.

The film ends.

'Good morning again, Jesper,' The Voice says, taking me by surprise.

Pictures appear on The Screen – first a field of grass with a mountain behind it, then a city with tall buildings, then a lake …

'Good morning,' I say again.

'How are you feeling today, Jesper?'

'Good.'

'Do you have any problems? Any questions?'

I shake my head.

'OK. Good.'

There are new pictures appearing on The Screen all the time. Animals. People. Fields.

And then something else appears. A picture of a horse with a saddle on and a man on his back. The horse looks like it's running fast, like it's racing. It has the number four on it. This picture stays on The Screen.

'We'll start with some logic puzzles, Jesper.'

I smile. Logic puzzles are one of my favourite things.

'Here's a warm-up question. On the screen you'll see a picture of a horse taking part in a race. Now, have a look at the problem on the screen and think about it.'

And as soon as The Voice says that, the picture of the horse disappears and words appear on The Screen:

There were five horses in a race: Jake finished ahead of Rodney.

Jake finished after Misty.

Rum beat Misty but finished after Gordon.

Where did Rum finish?

Straight away I reach for The Scroll, take out the stylus and use it to try to figure the puzzle out, writing down the names of the horses, putting them in order.

'Second,' I say aloud.

The Screen turns green, which means I'm right. My time flashes up on The Screen – 10.32 seconds.

But I'm feeling kind of peed off with myself, cos that was an easy question and a rubbish time. If I want a reward, I've gotta be quicker than that. I squizz down at The Scroll and press the button to clear it. And I make sure I'm concentrating properly before the next puzzle.

All the letters of the alphabet appear in a long line across The Screen. Black letters on a light yellow background.

And then a whole load of words appear on The Screen, but before I even get a chance to read them, The Voice is saying them out loud, like:

'This test involves letter sequences. For each question, look at the sequence and work out which of the five letters below it is the next in the sequence. You'll need to speak your answer aloud. The alphabet is given below to help you.'

I take a moment to let all the information sink in, read it again to myself, thinking, understanding what I gotta do.

'Are you ready, Jesper?' The Voice says.

I finish reading and nod. I gulp, feeling nervous. The timer starts and the first question appears onscreen. My heartbeat quickens.

A B ? D E

It takes me less than a second to read it and answer 'C', and for The Screen to flash green.

Immediately the next question is up.

Z ? X W

It takes a little longer, but not much, before I have it worked out and I say the letter 'Y' out loud. The Screen flashes green once more.

Right away the next one is there:

A A Z B B ?

And this time I panic the first time I read the sequence. So I read it again. The answer is Y, isn't it? Has to be. So I say it. And I'm rewarded by a green screen.

The sequences appear on The Screen one after the other, getting more and more difficult every time. And as each one comes up, I get a sinking feeling that it's too difficult for me and I won't be able to do it. But each time I calm down and work it out logically, make notes on The Scroll, look at the alphabet on The Screen and then solve it.

X T C G P L K ?

I scribble on The Scroll, circling numbers, counting the jumps, and it takes ages and ages. But it has to be O, doesn't it? It's the only letter it can be.

'O,' I say.

The Screen flashes green. And The Voice speaks back to me. 'Thank you, Jesper. That's the last question.'

My score flashes on to The Screen. Twenty-three out of twenty-four and a total time of five minutes and fourteen seconds. And I know right away that's a good score, even before The Screen turns green and The Voice says, 'Excellent, Jesper. You've earned a reward of a video clip of your choice.'

The Screen changes again and this time there are nine little video clips and an arrow at the bottom. I scan the rows of clips: building shelters, firelighting, wild animals, cars, home, war, and so on and so on. I press the arrow and look at the second page too: animals, a cartoon, fighting and loads more. There are so many of them I want to see. Most of my favourites are there.

'Home,' *I say eventually.*

Immediately the rows and rows of little clips disappear and The Screen fills with Home, *a grey and black and white picture – kind of grainy just like all the* Home *clips – and it's like I'm looking down from the ceiling. It's set in a room that looks a lot like My Place, only I'm not sure if it is. This one's a clip I've never seen before.*

A woman sits in a chair similar to the one I'm sitting in right now – the same woman that's always in the Home *clips. She has long, dark hair and she's tall. She's dressed in plain clothes – a shapeless jumper and a skirt and shoes. And even though I want to see her face, to see who she is, I can't cos her hair's kind of falling across it, covering it, as she bends over the little kid who sits on her lap. The kid can't be older than two. He's smiling, saying something to the woman, and even though I can't see her face to prove it, I'm sure she's smiling back at him. She lifts him above her, so it's like he's flying through the air. And just at the moment when I think I'm gonna see her face, she brings the boy through the air towards her, getting in the way of my view.*

There's movement somewhere else in the room, and I look away from the woman and the boy and see there are other people there. A girl who looks older than the little boy. In her hand she carries a toy – a wooden horse, which she's making fly through the air as she skips along. And it's my wooden horse, isn't it? There's another boy as well, who looks even older. He walks towards the woman. And I see his face. And it's familiar. I know the face. Only how can that be?

'Jesper.'

Everything goes blank. Black. The room and the people in it all disappear.

But there's sound. A voice.

'Jesper. Jesper, wake up.'

And I feel something on my shoulder. A hand?

I jerk awake. Eyes open. Squizzing around.

And beside me, crouching down at my level and gawping at me, I see one of the priests, the one who put the needle thing in me the other day. Father Lekmann. And I can see that this time he's brought another priest with him – Father Liebling, standing over by the door.

'Hello, Jesper.'

I say nothing. I gawp back at Father Lekmann, suspicious.

'How are you feeling?'

And I hadn't had time to think about it until he asked. But come to think of it, I feel stiff and sore and tired. I shrug.

'I need to have a quick look at you, Jesper, to check you're OK after your fall.'

And I still don't say anything.

'That was a nasty fall you had, Jesper. Father Frei said that one of your legs and one of your arms was broken.'

I look down at my arm. It's mended just the way it ought to be.

'Can I check you over, Jesper?'

I shake my head.

'You'll make this much easier if you do as I ask. I won't hurt you.'

And I stare back at him. 'There's nothing wrong with me.'

'Well, in that case it shouldn't take long. Could you lift your arms?'

Reluctantly I lift my arms like he asks and I watch his face as he looks surprised.

'What about your fingers? Can you use them?'

I stare back at him cos I don't know what he means.

'Can you wiggle them?'

And of course I can, so I show him.

'Your legs ... Can you move them?'

I nod. I move them about under the covers.

'Can you walk?'

And I can do that as well, can't I? Of course I can. I walked to this room with Father Frei. I swing my legs out of bed and I stand up, and at first I feel kind of unsteady but then I just walk. One foot in front of the other. Exactly the way it's meant to be.

The priest gawps at me, mouth slightly open, eyebrow raised, like he can't believe what he's seeing. And I don't know why. Why wouldn't he believe what he's seeing?

'Quite amazing,' he says quietly. 'Could I have a look at your leg, Jesper? The one that broke …'

I roll the leg of my trousers up and the priest bends to look closely at it, at the lines of pink scar tissue that still criss-cross the skin, muttering to himself. I squizz down to see him extend a finger and touch my leg. And it makes me jump, makes me flinch and move my leg away from him.

And right away he squizzes up at my face, still kneeling down. 'Is it painful?' he says.

I shrug. 'A little. It's sore.'

He scratches his head. 'Well, I have to say I'm confused. There seems to be nothing wrong with you, Jesper. Your body seems to have healed as good as new.' He crosses himself. 'Perhaps Father Frei is right. Perhaps this is a miracle.'

Carina

Just after the evening meal, I pass Father Liebling in the corridor outside my dormitory. He smiles momentarily as he sees me and then his head goes down and he carries on walking.

But I have questions I know he'll be able to answer, so I go after him.

As he becomes aware I'm following, he checks around the corridor before stopping to speak.

'Father Liebling, there's a rumour spreading about the disease Sabine died of. People say Jesper Hausmann brought it into the home. Is that true?'

Father Liebling doesn't say anything straight away. He checks the corridor again, makes doubly sure we're not being watched, before he takes a step backwards into the shadows. 'Where did you hear this rumour, Carina?'

I shrug. 'Sabine's brother – Markus.'

Father Liebling sighs. 'I thought you knew better than to trust the word of someone like Markus.'

'You haven't answered my question.'

Father Liebling nods. 'As you know already, Carina, there does seem to be a new disease. But at present nobody knows where it originated.'

'So could it be Jesper?'

Father Liebling shakes his head. 'No. It couldn't be Jesper. It wouldn't add up. Sabine never met Jesper to my knowledge. And more importantly, she contracted and incubated the disease long before Jesper was even brought to St Jerome's.'

'So it came from somewhere else?'

Father Liebling nods. 'It must have.'

'So why has Jesper been locked away from everyone?'

'That has nothing to do with the disease,' he says. 'Jesper's being kept on his own to recover after what happened in the crypt.'

I nod. 'Markus pushed him,' I say. 'He did it because of the rumour.'

Liebling nods. 'I suspect you might be right, Carina.'

'Then why is he still walking around the home? How come he hasn't been punished?'

Liebling shrugs. 'You'd have to ask Father Frei about that, Carina, although I wouldn't advise it. Father Frei spoke with Markus yesterday evening. He's convinced it was nothing more than an accident.'

I sigh. 'So does anyone know where the disease came from then?'

'No. And we'll probably never find out. There are conspiracy theories of course.'

'Really? Like what?'

Liebling shakes his head.

And as voices approach along the corridor, he walks off without answering me.

Tonight is one of those nights. I won't sleep; I already know that. I'm too tired to walk the corridors. So instead I lie in my bed, amongst the shadows and everyone else's sleep sounds, and I close my eyes and let thoughts come to me.

And this is the thought that comes first:

Me and Greta. In the kitchen at home. Greta's fifteen and I'm seven. The low winter sun pours in through the kitchen window, where we're making bread – Greta in charge and me helping. The table's covered in bowls and spoons and cups and ingredients, but it's an organised mess. The smell of wood burning in the stove fills the air. It's the smell of home, the way life is meant to be.

Although I know that, even in this scene, life isn't really like that. Because neither Mum nor Dad is there. It's just me and Greta looking after the house. Well, Greta looking after the house, and me helping.

Someone else shuffles into the room. Even before I see her face, I know it's Mum. She squints against the sunlight, takes small exhausting steps into the room and then lowers herself awkwardly into a chair near the table. She's wearing her dressing gown. She looks like a bag of bones with a head.

'Hey, Mum,' Greta says. 'How are you feeling?'

Mum smiles. 'Better,' she says. But I can tell from the stiff way she's moving, the way her skin looks grey and sallow and clammy, that she's not telling the truth.

She watches Greta and I set to work. 'Are you making bread?'

'Yes,' I say.

'Why don't you wash your hands and you can help us?' Greta says.

But Mum shakes her head and sits where she is, looking drained and tired and weak.

I grab a cup from the table to start pouring out five cups of flour on to the table top. When I've finished, Greta takes the cup, measures out some oats, adds those to the flour and then a

156

handful of caraway seeds. I make a little crater in the middle of the flour mixture with my fist, the way Mum taught me to.

'Where's your father?' Mum says croakily.

'Out,' Greta says. 'The men left in the middle of the night. Dad didn't want to wake you.'

Mum frowns. She says nothing.

I take the lid off the pot with the sourdough mixture in it and pour some into the crater I've made in the flour. Greta adds sour milk and yoghurt.

Over on her chair, Mum coughs – a deep rasping cough that sounds like it'll tear her in two. The coughing goes on and on, gradually getting weaker as she runs out of energy. She takes a few deep breaths, steadies herself and her eyes close for a few seconds, like she's too tired to go on.

Greta catches me watching Mum, catches the scared look on my face. She smiles, trying to distract me. 'Do you want to mix, Carina?'

I nod, rolling up my sleeves, and then I mix everything together, working the dough until it's a sticky ball and my hands are covered in tendrils of bread mixture. Greta and Mum watch in silence.

The sound of dogs barking outside the house shatters the peace in the kitchen. We all look up to the window. The dogs must have seen something.

'Could be the men returning,' Mum says.

Greta nods, then takes the dough, starts to divide it into smaller balls which she rolls out, ready for plaiting.

Sure enough, as we watch Greta work, watch how quickly and skilfully she gets the dough to do what she wants, the sound of hoofs approaches, then the snort of a horse outside in the road.

A minute later the door opens and Dad comes inside, looking tired.

'Peter, you're home,' Mum says. 'Are you OK? Are you hungry?'

Dad goes straight over to Mum, kisses her on the top of her head, running a hand through her straggly hair. 'I'm OK. Hans is feeding the horses. How are you feeling?' He gently places the palm of his hand on her forehead, feeling her temperature. He frowns.

'I feel a bit better, I think,' Mum says. But this time even she doesn't sound like she believes it.

Dad goes over to the cupboard and gets a cup, takes it to the sink and tries the tap. He sighs when all he gets is a clunking sound.

'The water supply's off again,' Greta says. 'There's a container by the back door.'

He sighs, nods and goes over to the container, pours himself a cup and drinks it down in one go before pouring another.

'Where did you go?' I ask.

'Grubingen,' he says without looking at any of us.

'Why?'

'New Dawn,' he says. His voice sounds tired. 'They've been clearing the surrounding villages. Last night they moved in on Grubingen itself. The Resistance tried to evacuate people.'

'Did you succeed?' Greta says.

158

Dad shrugs, staring out of the back window. And I can tell that he's thinking, reliving what he's just seen. 'We got some people out in time. But New Dawn were quicker than we thought. We couldn't stop them. They wiped the whole town out. Every man, woman and child they found – even the animals – slaughtered. We had to flee before they got us too.'

None of us says a word. Greta and I exchange a look. We both know it could be us next.

'They've got everything,' he says, still looking out at the land. 'The power station and the water pumping station. The whole lot.'

No more electric, no more fresh water. It's going to be even more of a struggle.

Dad goes over to a cupboard and searches it for food. There's almost nothing there though. Our supplies are running out. Not much food is getting through at the moment, unless you know the right people. He takes out some smoked sausage and crackers and puts them in his bag.

Mum coughs again. Deep and hacking. It goes on and on and on. She bends double. The colour drains from her face. Dad looks at her. He takes the cup he drank from, goes to the back door and fills it from the container. He takes it to Mum, who is still bent over, her coughing getting weaker and weaker. She sips from the cup. Some of it dribbles down her chin.

'You should lie down,' Dad says. 'You need rest.'

He helps her up and Greta and I rush over. I take Mum's arm, feeling how frail and skeletal she's become. We walk her back

159

through to the bedroom, where the curtains are drawn and the
room smells of illness. And no sooner is she on the bed than her
eyes close and she's sleeping, drawing shallow breaths.

We go out of the room in silence, each thinking the same
thing.

'Listen, girls,' Dad says. 'I'm going to have to go out again. We
need to make the village secure. New Dawn will be here before
long. It could be today or next week, but they'll come and we
need to be ready to resist them.'

'Can we do anything to help?' Greta asks.

Dad nods. 'Look after your mother. Make sure she's comfort-
able,' he says. 'And pack a bag. Pack one for your mother too. Just
in case. We should be ready to leave if we need to. Greta, make
sure the wagon's ready.'

And even as I lie in bed at St Jerome's, remembering, I start
to feel the panic and the chaos welling up inside my chest
and my head. I open my eyes, sit up, heart racing.

I don't want to be alone with my thoughts. I can't be.

I drag my tired limbs out of bed and I start walking.

Jesper

I'm taken from my room to Father Frei's warm and comfortable office.

'We have many children like you here, Jesper: children with no past; wild children abandoned in the forests, parentless; children who've had to learn to fend for themselves.'

I listen.

'But you're different, aren't you?'

I say nothing.

'You're special.'

I shrug.

'You are, Jesper. I'm convinced.'

I squizz down at my feet.

'I believe we witnessed a miracle the other day in the crypt.'

There's that word again. Miracle. Like in the Bible. He said it over and over on the night I fell.

'I saw with my very own eyes. Your leg was broken, twisted, bloodied. And right before my eyes, it healed in a way that just isn't possible.'

What else does he think is gonna happen to your body when you get hurt? That it should stay broken?

'I would like to share your story, Jesper,' he says, smiling at me. 'Miracles are rare indeed. And yours will bring light and hope to millions of people in a time of hardship. Reading your story in the newspaper will help strengthen the faith of any who might be losing theirs.'

I say nothing. And after a few seconds Father Frei walks over to his desk. I hear him open a drawer. He takes something out. And when he comes back over I recognise it as a camera. I've seen them on The Screen.

'For the newspapers,' he says, and he holds the camera up and presses a button.

I just stand there.

'Excellent,' he says, gesturing to me to sit down on the chair facing his desk. So I do. He sits too. For a while he says nothing, just gawps at me. The clock ticks. The fire crackles and spits.

'So tell me more about yourself, Jesper …'

But all that follows is silence, because I don't know what to say, do I?

'You told me you lived in a place all on your own. Did it have a name?'

And before I've even thought about what I'm doing, I've said, 'My Place.'

Father Frei smiles. 'My Place. Hmmm. And you're certain you were kept alone?'

'I wasn't "kept" there; I lived there.'

'Have you ever thought why, Jesper?'

I don't understand, so I say nothing. And besides, The Voice wouldn't want me telling him this information, would he?

'It sounds like your upbringing was quite unique. It's peculiar that you never saw another human but that there was always food for you.'

I say nothing. He knows too much.

'Why do you think somebody went to the trouble of feeding you, clothing you, keeping you warm and safe?'

I shrug. The truth is, I never thought about that before.

Father Frei opens his desk drawer again. 'When you were discovered in the woods, you had with you an electronic device,' he says. And he places the broken remains of the scroll on the table.

'Jesper, do you realise that this kind of technology is incredibly rare? Very few people have electricity in their houses, let alone anything like this.'

I shake my head. Although when I think of the buildings I saw in the forest, I suppose that makes sense.

'Where did you get this device?'

'I don't know.'

'You must do, Jesper.'

I shake my head.

'What does the machine do?'

I shrug.

'Can you show me what it does?'

'No. It's broken.'

For a few moments the office is silent. Then Father Frei clears his throat. 'Whoever kept you in My Place must have been wealthy, Jesper.'

I shrug. What does that mean?

'They must have had a reason to keep you safe, to keep you away from the rest of the world.'

I say nothing.

The fire crackles. The clock ticks.

'You must be intrigued, Jesper ... You must wonder who kept you in that place, who let you free in the forest, aren't you?'

I think of The Voice, of all the things he taught me, of how he talked to me when I was unhappy or unwell. I think of how he left me alone in the forest to fend for myself, how he gave me the scroll to guide my way.

I think of how he said he'd come and find me. Only he hasn't, has he?

'I know I want to find out,' Father Frei says. 'The newspaper article might help that to happen.'

For a while neither of us speaks.

'When we find who kept you, Jesper, we can perhaps answer the question of why.'

I gawp back at him.

'I have my suspicions though. You're special, Jesper. You're different. Clearly you're important.'

The clock chimes half past the hour.

'We must make sure we take the best care of you here,' Father Frei says. 'I'll see to that personally.'

Blake

'Things have become complicated,' Henwood says, getting back into the car, holding a newspaper in his hands. He sits in the driver's seat and lays the newspaper in the space between our seats so I can see. A picture of Boy 23 stares out from the

164

front page. 'He's been taken in by priests near Manburg,' Henwood says. 'They think he's some kind of miracle child.'

'He's safe though. And we know where he is. That's something, isn't it?'

Henwood sighs. 'I suppose. Although our job would be much easier if he'd been eaten by wolves in the forest.'

I read the article as Henwood stares out of the windscreen.

'I don't think they have any real idea of who he is,' I say.

'They know the name you gave him – Jesper Hausmann.'

'That won't get them anywhere. He has no papers. There's no official record of Jesper Hausmann. He can't be traced back to the Huber Corporation through his name alone.'

'But he might talk to them.'

'He can't tell them anything,' I say. But I'm concerned too. The article's nothing but speculation, but still, I need to get to Jesper. 'He has no concept of his place in the world. He never met any of us. He doesn't know who he is or what he is or where he comes from.'

Henwood nods. 'True. But it seems they've already discovered his physical qualities. They know he heals differently.'

'It says here they think it's a miracle. They think he's sent from God. No mention of Huber or the Sumchen project.'

'But realising he's different is halfway to knowing what he is and where he comes from. If they run blood tests on him, they could discover his secrets. Huber's secrets.'

'Now we know where he is, we can get him back before that happens.'

165

Henwood folds the newspaper and puts it in the back of his car. 'This will only make it more difficult. He's become famous, for the time being at least. People are interested in him. If we decommission him now, people will notice. We'll have to tread carefully.'

'So what do we do?'

Henwood gets his scroll from his pocket and swipes his finger across the screen to wake it. 'I'll make contact with Mr Huber,' he says. 'And then we'll travel to Manburg.'

Carina

Today I work at the landfill. The sky is grey and miserable as I leave the building. Rain falls in tiny drops and a wagon trundles off down the road. Mine waits for me, already loaded. Father Trautmann sits in the front seat, impatiently holding the reins. One of the horses tosses its head and whinnies, like he's waiting for me to get there too. I pull up the hood of my coat and walk the last few steps to the wagon.

'You're late, Carina,' Trautmann says as I reach the steps at the back of the wagon. 'Hurry up.'

As if I care what he says. I'm in no rush.

'You think any of us want to be doing this?' Trautmann says. 'You think I want to spend my day at the landfill?'

I climb the steps as slowly as I can, then sit beside Ralph, a young boy who never says a thing and looks terrified the whole time.

Father Trautmann whips the reins and the wagon heaves into motion, creaking and groaning as it trundles along the road.

We're pulled through the outskirts of town, past ghostly skeletons of buildings and piles of rubble. We roll past the power station and into countryside – fields at first and then through woodland.

I smell the landfill before I see it. The rain seems to stir the smell up and reinvigorate it. We climb down from the wagon reluctantly. The ground is waterlogged and muddy. Father Trautmann puts on a gas mask and beckons for us to follow him, so we do, heads down, silent, wanting the day to hurry up so we can be back at St Jerome's or anywhere but here.

He leads us through the landfill, passing the enormous vehicles that dig and lift and move the rubbish on either side of us. We stop at site 3, where a New Dawn officer in a gas mask stands guard and teams of children are already working. They dig out the smelly trash and sort it, ready to be taken off so it can be cleaned and sold and reused. We stop beside our heap, which one of the digging machines has scooped out of the ground – a small mountain of stinking rubbish.

Trautmann lifts the gas mask from his face, wrinkling his nose at the smell. 'You work here,' he says. 'Dig the things out that can be reused: metal, glass, plastic and wood. Put what

167

you find on the trucks. The rest of the rubbish stays here. If you unearth anything of value, you hand it over. Understand?'

It's always the same: you start the day thinking you'll be careful not to get covered in dirt and shit and mud, but within minutes it's everywhere – smeared across clothes and faces and arms and legs and in your hair. The stink gets so ingrained it takes days of scrubbing to shift.

In amongst all the trash, there are animals. Mice. Rats. Foxes. Crows. Gulls. Some of them are dead, but most are alive and scurrying around and they aren't scared of humans. They dive-bomb or bare their teeth. They bite.

And if *they* don't get you, you can be sure you'll plunge your hands in and there'll be something sharp that'll tear your skin – glass, metal, plastic. It happens every time, no matter how careful you are.

This is the worst of the bad jobs.

But, just occasionally, even this job has an upside. Sometimes there's something that makes sifting through all this shit worthwhile, and that's because, years ago, people used to throw everything away. That means, buried amongst all the garbage, there's treasure. I've found all sorts before: money, jewellery, pictures.

It's after lunch and the rain's still falling when my spade moves a moulding old cushion aside, and underneath I see something that makes my heart jump. Not a rat this time.

A black handgun.

Just lying in the trash.

I look around me, make sure no one's watching, and then I bend to the ground and pick it up. I hide it in my pocket before getting back to work.

Blake

I wait in the car. From here I can see the children's home where the newspaper claims they have Jesper. I watch Henwood as he approaches a blond-haired, grey-uniformed boy and speaks with him. The boy looks shifty. Untrustworthy. I'm not even sure he's supposed to be outside the home at this moment.

As Henwood speaks, the boy nods.

Their conversation lasts no more than two minutes, and when they're finished the boy looks furtively around him before slinking back into the building.

Henwood hurries back to the car, his long black coat billowing as he walks.

'We're in luck,' he says as he gets in. 'That boy's called Markus. He says he knows Boy 23.'

'OK. Good.'

'What's more, he holds a grudge against him. There's been an outbreak of the new strain at the home and Markus's sister

169

died. There's a rumour circulating that Boy 23 brought the strain to the home.'

'Really?'

Henwood nods. 'I'm not sure if it could complicate things further or whether maybe it could work to our advantage.'

'How?'

'Markus wants Boy 23 dead. He made that very clear. We could use him to do our dirty work.'

I nod, but a nervous feeling washes over me.

'Markus also told me that Boy 23 used to be in his dormitory, but since the accident that was reported in the newspaper he's been kept in a separate room. I've asked Markus to find out where and report back to us.'

Carina

By the time the sky's starting to get darker and Father Trautmann's telling us it's time to stop, the truck we've been loading with reusable rubbish is almost full and we're stinking and wet.

We trudge silently back across the landfill, earth movers and diggers and trucks still doing their jobs under floodlights which are just starting to blink into life. I put my hand in my pocket, feeling the cold metal of the gun.

Eventually we reach the wagon and climb aboard, finding everything's soaked and we have to sit on wet seats. Father Trautmann stops to talk to one of the New Dawn men. Shivering on top of the wagon, none of us children says a word. We just want to get home, so we can get clean and warm and dry.

I sit beside little Ralph, who's covered head to toe in dirt, smeared right into his skin. His clothes are soaked and he's frozen. His teeth clack together as he sits and waits to start moving. I give him a nudge, and when he looks my way I smile.

Father Trautmann climbs up to the front seat and at a flick of the reins we roll homewards. Which is when I notice something.

On the front seat of the wagon, beside Trautmann, is his bag. A newspaper sticks out of it and the picture on the front cover catches my eye. Even though it's upside down, I can clearly see the person in the picture is Jesper. And beneath it, there's a headline: SAVAGE BOY RESCUED FROM FOREST IS A MIRACLE.

I glance around me, check nobody's watching and then snatch the newspaper. I hide it inside my coat immediately. Beside me I see Ralph's face. He looks at Father Trautmann's bag and then at my coat. For a second I fear I'm sunk, but Ralph holds a finger to his lips and smiles. I nod back at him.

The wagon rolls through open countryside, then forest and then past the piles of rubble near the home. Close to St

Jerome's, I see something that makes me do a double take – a shiny black car waits in a side road. It has windows you can't see in through. I can't help but wonder what it's doing there. I can't remember the last time I saw a car, let alone one as new as that. And I wonder who it belongs to and why they're there. Could it be an important New Dawn member?

A couple of seconds later, we turn in to the gates of St Jerome's, where a small crowd has gathered. But all I care about is getting out of my stinking clothes.

Jesper

'Word has spread quickly,' Father Frei says as we sit in his room. 'People have heard of your miracle. People have begun to visit St Jerome's in the hope of seeing you.'

I say nothing, because my mouth is full of food and because I don't know what to say anyhow.

'Powerful and influential people are taking an interest in you, Jesper.'

I nod.

'Many of them are interested in seeing you. Meeting you. Looking after you even,' he says. He leaves a pause, but I don't say a thing. 'Your story seems to have struck a chord.

People say you're a symbol of hope for our times. This could make us both rich, Jesper. Both of us.'

Still he gawps at me with that mad look in his eyes and the grin on his face. There's something about it I don't like.

But after a while he squizzes down at his desk, opens a drawer and takes something out. A book. 'The Bible,' he says. 'A book filled with miracles. Do you have a copy?'

I shake my head, swallow the mouthful of food.

'This is for you then.' He holds it out to me.

I take it. It has a leather cover and '*Die Bibel*' written on it in swirly golden letters. That has to be their words for the Bible, doesn't it? I open the cover and flick through. I don't understand a word.

'As you learn to speak German, you can discover the Bible, Jesper.'

I nod, still flicking through. As well as the German words, there are whole pages taken up with pictures. I stop on one: a picture of a man with long hair and a beard gawping at a bush which is on fire. Appearing out of the flames there's an angel, speaking to the man.

'You know this story, Jesper?' Father Frei asks.

I squizz up at him and nod my head. Moses. I heard this story in My Place. I watched it on The Screen. The angel speaks to him, tells him to lead the Israelites out of Egypt.

'There are many unexplained things in the world, Jesper,' Father Frei says. 'Many things we cannot understand. Many things we're not meant to understand.'

I nod my head. Right at this moment, the whole world seems full of things I don't understand.

'Sometimes these things are God's way of sending us a message, of renewing our faith in Him.'

I say nothing.

'Many years ago, Jesper, I lived a life which I'm not proud of. But then, one day, a miracle occurred. God spoke to me. My life turned around from that very instant.'

I say nothing.

'The miracle of my faith is nothing compared to you though,' Father Frei continues. 'God has sent you to us as a sign. We must spread the word.'

He gets up from his seat and crosses the room towards me. 'And now, Jesper, I must prepare for evening prayers. I'd consider it an honour if you'd help me.'

Carina

I stand at the cracked sink, turn on the taps and wait for the basin to fill. While I wait, I stare at the faded sign above the sink, the one you find everywhere:

KILL THE VIRUS, NOT YOUR FRIENDS.
WASH YOUR HANDS

It always made me think of Mum. Today it makes me think of Sabine too.

I turn the tap off and scrub at the filth on my hands. No matter how hard I scrub, no matter how much soap I use, the stink clings to my skin though.

And sure enough, ten minutes later, when I get into the church for evening prayers and sit at the back, the boy next to me screws up his nose and shuffles away. I do my best to ignore him, looking around the church instead, trying to spot Jesper. Because I need to see him. I want to show him the newspaper I found.

As I stare around the church, fruitlessly searching the sea of dimly lit heads, Father Frei steps out from the side of the church in his robes and stands in front of us all. He makes the sign of the cross.

'Please be ready for prayer.'

So we all get up off the pews and we kneel.

'*Dear Lord,*

As we gather in your presence this evening …'

I lift my head, trying again to locate Jesper. But with everyone kneeling and their heads bowed, it's even more difficult than before. So I bow my head and close my eyes again. And in my pocket I feel the newspaper I took from Father Trautmann's bag. I wonder whether Jesper has any idea what's happening out there. I wonder whether he's locked up some-where in the home. Since he fell down the stairs, I haven't seen him. Not in the dining hall. Not in church. Not in the dormitories or at work.

All the while, Father Frei calls to his flock, murmuring some prayer or other, and everyone else bleats back to him.

'Amen,' I hear him say.

'Amen.'

'Please be seated.'

So we all get up from kneeling and sit back on the pews. Father Frei stands in front of the altar, making the sign of the cross, talking excitedly. I tune back in to what he's saying, because normally when he stands there, all he does is murmur, going through the motions, but right now he's more animated than I've ever seen him.

'Today, children,' he says, 'I have physical proof of God's power and divinity to lay before you. I have something wondrous to show you, something miraculous which will renew the faith of even the most fallen amongst us.'

I swallow the urge to laugh. If he shows me anything that could convince me of God's greatness, it really would be a miracle.

He extends his arm and looks to the side of the church, into the transept. And slowly a figure emerges from the gloom.

Jesper.

He stands beside Father Frei, staring down at the ground, so nervous he's shaking.

'Here is our miracle,' Father Frei declares.

And I wonder why on Earth he's doing this.

Jesper

All I know is Father Frei says loads of words in German and everyone listens, but I have no idea what he's saying. And all the time I'm standing there, my whole body shakes with nerves, cos there are hundreds and hundreds of people there, and every single one is gawping at me.

Even when it's done and everyone's filing out of church again, my heart's still racing and the church feels like it's spinning around me.

I walk, taking small steps, not knowing where I'm going or what's happening.

And then, suddenly, I feel a hand on my arm, grabbing me, and I jump.

It's Carina. She squizzes nervously around and says, 'Follow me.'

I don't have much choice except to do as she says, do I? Cos she has hold of my arm and she pulls me along the aisle and out of the big wooden doors. Outside in the darkness and cold, she pulls me round the side of the church, to a place where there's no one around.

'What is it?'

She reaches into her pocket and brings out a piece of paper. 'Look at this.'

But I'm already looking. Cos right in the centre of the paper there's a picture of me standing in Father Frei's room. It's the photo he took yesterday. All around the picture are words in German.

'What does it say?'

'It's about when you fell down the stairs and broke your arm and leg. It says Father Frei prayed over you, and that because of this a miracle happened – your bones and skin started to heal in front of him.'

'But why? That's not what happened,' I say. 'Is it? You were there …'

Carina squizzes at me, nodding.

'Father Frei wasn't even there when it started. He didn't heal me.'

'I know.'

'It wasn't even a miracle. It was just my body repairing itself. What does he expect to happen? For my leg to stay broken?'

Carina's expression changes, like she's confused. 'I don't understand what happened down in the crypt, Jesper. I don't know how your body fixed itself like that. I've never seen anything like it in my life. But I don't think for a second it was a miracle. And even if it had been, Father Frei had nothing to do with it.'

'So why does it say Father Frei healed me?'

Carina shrugs. 'He must have spoken to the newspaper. He wants to make himself seem important. If you ask me, he's trying to use you to make himself rich and powerful.'

I say nothing. But I'm wondering whether the newspaper could be a good thing. Cos maybe The Voice will see this and he'll know where I am. Maybe he'll come and find me.

'Someone must have told them about your past, Jesper. It says you have no mother or father. That you have no ID or papers; that you didn't have a medical card. It says you were kept in isolation, with high-specification technology at your disposal. That you never met another human being before you came to St Jerome's. That you were left for dead; that you were at death's door before Father Frei took you in and nursed you back to health.'

I say nothing. I squizz at the German words on the paper, gawp as though staring at them for long enough will make them make sense.

'Is that true?' Carina asks.

'Most of it, yeah.'

We hear footsteps approach. Carina hurriedly hides the newspaper away.

A second later, Father Frei walks towards us with an expression on his face like he's caught us doing something we shouldn't.

'Jesper. Carina. What are you two doing here?'

Carina

It's night-time and I'm wide awake, so, to save me from memories I don't wish to revisit, I get up. I creep across to my wardrobe and open the drawer that contains my under-clothes. I rummage beneath the bras and vests and pants, until my hand grasps the gun I found at the tip.

My heart races as my skin comes into contact with it. I look around the dormitory, checking no one's watching. Everyone's sound asleep though. Nervously I lift the gun from my drawer and I hold it. I've held guns before, of course. I've used guns. But I've never had one of my own. The metal feels cold and heavy. It feels solid. Deadly.

My head fills with images of what this gun could do, the devastation it might cause. And the images it creates are almost exactly the same as the memories I was trying to escape.

I turn the gun round in my hands, open up the chamber to see that it's empty. No bullets.

I think of Father Frei, of what this gun could do to him if it was loaded. What I could do to him, if I chose to.

I know where his room is. I could take the gun, hide it in my nightclothes and creep through the dark corridors. Then when I found him, I could shoot him as he slept. I could be back in bed, asleep, before they found the body.

I could.

If I was as bad as him.

I wipe the handle of the gun clean with an old vest and then carefully place it back in the drawer.

Blake

Henwood's scroll beeps. He takes it from his jacket. His right eyebrow arches as he reads the message.

Across the street, a wagon driven by a priest rolls past us. It's laden with ragged children leaving the orphanage, going out to work. It passes the crowd which has gathered outside the gates.

Henwood puts his scroll back into his jacket pocket. 'That was from Huber. There's a change of plan. He's worried about the newspaper article and the crowd. He says we need to act quickly, but we can't risk going into the orphanage ourselves.'

'Right,' I say.

'Instead, we'll get Markus to do the dirty work for us.'

'The boy from the orphanage?'

Henwood nods. 'He wants you to pay Markus and give him a gun,' he says. He reaches into his jacket pocket and gives me a handful of banknotes and the weapon.

'Of course.'

'Make sure he knows that a bullet through the heart is the only way to kill him. That or smashing his brain in.'

I nod. 'Why me, though?'

Henwood straightens in his seat. He looks out of the windscreen. 'Huber's coming to Manburg as we speak. There's a function at the town hall this evening, which Huber and I will attend. The priest who took Boy 23 in will be there.'

'Right,' I say, putting the gun and the money inside my jacket pocket.

Carina

It's my third straight day at the landfill.

Today, just after the break for lunch, there was a loud explosion. We all jumped out of our skins and then stopped work and looked up. At first we couldn't see anything at all. But then, coming from site 1, we saw smoke rising. We all knew what had happened. Everything but the earth-moving machines went quiet.

It's rare, but sometimes, if you're unlucky, moving some rubbish uncovers a pocket of trapped gas. It mixes with the air and then, *BOOM*, it explodes. Usually it's the earth-moving machines that disturb the gas, because they're the ones that shift most of the rubbish around before we sort through it. But not always. Sometimes it's a person. And sometimes they die.

For the rest of the day I worked carefully, nervously lifting and turning and digging things.

But now I'm on my way home. The horses' hoofs *clip* and *clop* on the hard road as we pass the ruined buildings and St Jerome's comes into view. I'm starting to think about getting out of these clothes, about soap and water.

But those thoughts are driven from my mind for a second. Because for the second day in a row I spot a car – the same black car, sitting in the same side street.

Jesper

I flick through the pages of Father Frei's Bible as I lie on my bed, trying to figure out what the words mean. And I think I must be starting to understand German a little, because I can work out some of it. There are whole sentences I can just about guess.

Footsteps approach my door as I stare at the words underneath a picture of Jesus healing a blind man. Seconds later, Father Liebling limps in carrying a pile of clothes, rather than the tray of provisions I was expecting.

'Father Frei has asked me to bring you these,' he says.

They're not like any clothes I've ever worn before – there's a black suit and a white shirt that looks stiff and uncomfortable.

'What are these for?'

'You're Father Frei's guest of honour this evening. He's taking you to meet some of his important friends. He wants you to look smart. Get changed and I'll be back in a few minutes to pick you up.'

Father Liebling seems nervous as he leads me from my room and along the corridors. Just before we get to the stairs, he stops and turns to me. 'Jesper, you must be careful tonight,' he whispers, leaning in so close that I can smell his breath.

I gawp at him, expecting him to say something more. But he doesn't. He limps on along the corridor and I follow him, down the stairs, into the big wood-panelled entrance of the building, where Father Frei waits.

Blake

I sit in the car while Henwood and Huber attend to their 'business'. I hide the gun Henwood gave me beneath the passenger side seat.

As afternoon turns to evening, Markus appears out of the shadows and comes to the car window. I hand him half the money and the message to kill Jesper. But I don't tell him how. And I certainly don't give him the gun. He slinks back into the shadows, leaving me with an uncomfortable feeling.

Is this a risk too far?

I sit and stew on what could happen.

Carina

I'm alone in the dormitory – a moment of peace before church. I open the drawer where I keep the gun and take it out.

I stare at it and I think how pointless it is me having it. I know I'll never use it. I might have the opportunity and the motive to use it a million times, but I don't have what it takes to pull the trigger and end somebody's life. Not any more.

It was different before. There was a clear choice between losing my life and keeping it. I chose to keep it. I didn't hesitate for a second to do what I had to.

No regrets.

So why have I kept hold of this?

I don't have an answer.

I could have sold it. It would fetch a good price. Maybe that's what I should do.

Maybe.

A sudden noise from the other end of the dormitory startles me.

I hurriedly fumble the gun back into the drawer and leave the dorm.

'Jesus, what's that smell?' Markus says as he sits at my bench in the food hall. 'Did something die?'

I sigh. 'Go away, please.'

But he doesn't. He wrinkles his nose. 'They shouldn't let you in here, you know. You're putting everyone off their food.'

I'm not going to give him the reaction he's after, so I look down at my plate instead of at him.

'Have you seen Jesper Hausmann recently?'

'What's it to you?'

'You're his only friend, aren't you?'

I shrug. 'Hardly. I barely even know him ... Why?'

'Nothing. I just need to see him, that's all. I figured you might know where he's kept.'

I shake my head. 'Ever since you pushed him down –'

'He slipped.'

'Ever since then, he's been kept away from everyone.'

Markus smiles. 'If you ask me, we're all better off with

him locked away. At least this way he can't infect anyone else.'

I'm tempted to argue with him. But what's the point? You can't ever win an argument with someone like Markus.

So I change tack. 'If you're happy he's locked away, why are you so keen to see him?'

Markus shrugs. He picks an overcooked potato from my plate and shoves it in his mouth. 'No reason,' he says with his mouth full. 'I just want to say hello.'

I look at him, raising an eyebrow. I don't trust him.

'If you must know, I have a new friend who's very interested in him. From Huber. If you can let me know where Jesper is – which room he's in – there'll be a little reward for you,' he says, and he puts his hand in his pocket, brings it back out with a banknote in it.

'Where'd you get that?'

He shrugs. 'None of your business.'

He reaches over and takes another potato from my plate and shoves it in his mouth. 'You know, Carina, maybe you could use the money to get yourself some soap,' he says, waving his hand in front of his nose.

'If I was going to take advice on body odour, it wouldn't be from you,' I say.

Markus raises an eyebrow. 'Funny,' he says. He gets up from the bench. 'Remember – help me find Jesper and I'll pay you.'

Jesper

I can't help gawping at the man driving us. Cos the clothes he wears are the same as those the men driving the car that hit me had. It's not the same man, I'm sure, cos his face is different and he doesn't wear a mask. But as I gawp at him I can't help remembering, and that makes my heart thump.

Father Frei talks as the car glides down the roads. He sounds excited, asking me what I know about cars. Only I don't know anything about cars, do I? All I know is I woke up in the back of one before I was left in the forest. And another car ran me over. A car like this one.

That's all I know.

So as Father Frei talks, I gawp out of the window at the town, lit by dim yellow gaslights on poles on the pavement. In the distance a bell tolls and people rush through the streets, hurrying into buildings.

'The curfew,' Father Frei says, squizzing over at me. 'But not for us this evening.'

Before long the car stops outside a tall building which has the word '*Rathaus*' written on it. Big, stone steps lead to an enormous front door.

'We're here,' Father Frei says, opening the car door. 'This is the building from which New Dawn runs the land for two hundred kilometres around.'

Carina

As soon as my head hits the pillow the memories come to me.

Me in bed at home. Seven years old. Hearing a voice and waking up.

'Carina, come quick!'

It's Greta's voice coming from another room – panicked and loud and desperate.

My heart races. The seven-year-old me opens her eyes. It's the middle of the night. The room's pitch black but I can make out that Greta's bed is still made, unslept in. I look over at the bedroom doorway. A strip of light leaks into my room from the crack between the floor and the bottom of the door.

The hairs on the back of my neck and on my head and my arms prickle. I have a feeling I know what's going on. And I don't want it to be happening.

I pull on my robe and walk slowly out of the bedroom, following the dim light and Greta's voice to Mum and Dad's room, saying a prayer in my head.

My heart thuds against my chest as I get to the doorway. I know what I'm about to see in there. I can hear Mum's voice, cracked and tiny-sounding; I can hear her moan and Greta whispering to her, reassuring her.

I peek my head round the door. Mum's in bed, grey-faced and sweating, eyes closed, moving her head jerkily from side to side, mumbling and making all sorts of noises. On her knees beside the bed, Greta mops Mum's brow with a cloth. She turns as I creep into the room.

'What is it?' I ask, my voice sounding small and scared.

Greta gets up from the side of the bed, walks over to me and then puts her hand on my shoulder, guiding me out of the room and into the hallway.

'Mum's really poorly,' she says.

I say nothing, but I can't stop myself from gulping.

'She asked to see you, Carina.'

I nod, even though I have butterflies in my stomach. We walk back into the candlelit bedroom without another word. Greta gestures for me to kneel down beside the bed.

Terrified, I reach my hand out and place it on Mum's forehead.

'Mum?' I say.

'Is that you, Carina?' Her eyes stay closed.

'Yes. How are you?'

'I'm fine, dear,' she says.

And I want to believe her.

Jesper

We're met at the top of the steps by a man wearing the same black uniform I've seen before. On his arm is a badge that says 'New Dawn'.

I follow Father Frei in through the big wooden doors at the front of the building. And the room we walk into is the tallest and longest room I've ever seen. I squizz all around it, gawping at pictures hanging on the walls. The high ceiling is painted gold, carved with patterns and pictures and faces and shapes. Huge, fancy electric lights hang from the tall ceiling, making the room bright and warm.

The room's packed with people, most of them men wearing the black uniform with the New Dawn badge on it. Except their uniforms have gold braid on their sleeves, like maybe they're the ones who're really in charge. There are women here too, though none of them wear the uniform. They wear dresses and necklaces and earrings and rings on their fingers.

And the noise they all make – talking and laughing in German – makes me feel nervous and dizzy and sick, like the room's spinning around me.

I feel a hand on my shoulder and I jump.

'Jesper, are you OK?' Father Frei says, handing me a drink.

I nod, even though I don't feel OK. I finish the drink in two gulps.

'In that case, I'll introduce you to some of my friends. They've heard a lot about you. They're eager to discover more.'

He guides me through the crowd. I shudder every time I brush past someone. And when I squizz around, trying to take everything in, what I find is they're all prying at me.

Every single one of them. And I don't like it. Only there's nothing I can do to stop them gawping, is there?

We stop in front of a man with a big moustache and more gold braid on his New Dawn uniform than anyone else in the room. He towers over us both, squizzing down first at Father Frei and then at me.

'Commander Brune,' Father Frei says, 'this is Jesper Hausmann.'

And the man looks down at me with his mean face before speaking in German to Father Frei in a deep, deep voice. The two of them speak so quickly I don't understand. And then all of a sudden Commander Brune turns to me and speaks and my heart thuds.

'So you're the miracle child?' he says.

I'm too terrified to say a word. I nod.

'You're very welcome here, Jesper. Eat and drink as much as you like. Later I would like to find out more about you.'

Blake

When the curfew bell tolls eerily through the empty streets and the lights go off in all the buildings, I make a decision. Now's the time to act. This is my chance to break Jesper out of there. I leave the car and make for the orphanage building,

192

sticking to the deepest shadows. The only other soul about is a fox, who rattles through some bins and then, when he spots me, stops and stares before disappearing into a hedge.

At the front door of the orphanage I ring the bell and wait.

There are no lights on inside the building, no sign of life. And for a long time nobody comes to the door. I begin to wonder whether I'm going to have to break in, to search for Jesper myself. But finally I see movement. A shadowy figure hobbling down a flight of wooden stairs and then across the large entrance hall to the door.

The door unlocks with a clunk. The hobbling figure – a priest – steps into the moonlight.

And with a shock, I realise his is a face I know.

'Gerd?' I say. 'Gerd Liebling?'

For a second there's incomprehension on his face and he says nothing. He looks like he's seen a ghost. 'Is that really you, Blake?' he says eventually.

'It is. Listen, Gerd, I don't have much time. I need your help.'

He nods.

'You've got a child here. Jesper Hausmann. I need to see him now.'

Liebling's eyes narrow. 'What do you want with Jesper?'

'He's in very serious danger. He's on the run from the Huber Corporation.'

Liebling's eyes widen. He nods.

'They were planning to end his life,' I say. 'I had to set him free. I need to get him to safety, to the Spirit of Resistance.'

Liebling clears his throat. 'OK. I see. Why is he important to them?'

I take a deep breath. 'It's a long story, but there's a new disease,' I say. 'A new strain of Marsh Flu.'

Liebling nods. 'I'd heard rumours. I didn't know whether to believe them. So is Jesper a carrier?'

I shake my head. 'But Huber don't want anything out in the real world that could set a trail back to them. As they see it, Jesper must die. He isn't like everyone else. He'll draw attention.'

'I noticed. Father Frei thinks he's some kind of miracle.'

'So, can I see him?' I ask.

Liebling shakes his head. 'Jesper isn't here at the moment.'

'What? Are you sure?'

'Certain,' he says. 'Father Frei has taken him to meet some of his friends in New Dawn.'

'Then your help is even more important.'

Liebling nods. 'You'd better come inside.'

Carina

Greta left a few minutes ago to find Dad. Now I'm alone with Mum and I'm scared. I watch her sleep, watch her breathe. Each gap between her breaths makes me nervous, in case the next breath doesn't come.

I say nothing because I don't know what I should say. Instead I stroke my hands gently against the side of her head.

Slowly her eyes open. She tilts her head to look at me.

My heart thumps. 'Mum.'

A smile so small it almost isn't there forms on her face. 'Carina,' she whispers.

I smile back, thinking maybe this means she's beaten the fever. It's the first time she's spoken in days.

'How are you, my beautiful flower?'

I gulp. 'OK. How are you feeling?'

She reaches her hand shakily towards mine. We hold hands. 'I have something to say to you, Carina.'

I nod.

'You've always been strong. Now you need to be even stronger for me.'

I nod. My stomach is tying itself in knots.

'You must take care of your father and Greta for me. Can you do that?'

'Yes.'

She smiles again. 'I can rely on you, Carina. You always do what you think is right.'

There's silence in the room. A breeze disturbs the candle, making the light flicker.

'Promise me you'll continue to do what you think is right.'

I nod, even though I don't really understand what she means. 'I promise.'

She smiles. Slowly she turns her head back. Her eyes close. I watch her breathe, slow shallow breaths.

The gaps between each breath seem to stretch.

She's fading.

I wait for the next breath. I wait and I wait.

But the next breath doesn't come.

I close my eyes, feel tears spring up and course down my cheeks.

She's gone.

And I need to be strong for her.

I open my eyes, wipe away my tears. I kiss her hand and lay it across her chest, just as I hear the front door rattle and Dad and Greta rush into the room.

My eyes open with a start and for a second I don't know where I am. I look around me, feeling the thud of my heartbeat in my chest, and I see the dark dormitory.

And rather than close my eyes again, rather than remember any more, I get out of bed and I walk, past Sabine's empty, stripped bed, out into the corridor.

Jesper

I stand near Father Frei as he talks to New Dawn members. In my hand I have a plate of delicious-looking food. It's untouched though. At this moment I don't feel hungry.

Standing here, I've been thinking about running away. Cos this is a place where there don't seem to be any locks on the doors. I've decided that I'll wait for a moment when no one's looking at me and then just yomp straight through the room and out of the door and into the night. I'd be in the forest in minutes. Alone and free. Only finding a moment when no one's looking isn't as easy as it sounds. There are people prying and gawping at me the whole time, squizzing and pointing.

And I've just about given up on the idea, when all of a sudden something happens – another man in a uniform comes over and whispers in Father Frei's ear. And after Frei's nodded and muttered a reply, he turns to me and says, 'I'll just be a few minutes, Jesper. Wait for me here.' And then he yomps across the room with the man in New Dawn uniform.

And I'm alone for the first time.

This is my chance. I can get away. I can yomp straight outta here.

So I start walking through the crowds, rushing, eyes fixed on the doors, blood pumping. I'm gonna do this.

Only, right then, something blocks my way. Two men. Both of them wearing black suits and white shirts, but it isn't the uniform of New Dawn. I try to step around them, but they just move into my way again, gawping straight at me.

And then one of them speaks. 'Jesper. It's good to see you again.' As he speaks, the scar that runs down the side of his face stretches.

The other man – a tall, skinny man – clears his throat to speak. 'We've come all the way from My Place to find you, Jesper.'

And his words almost knock me over. Did I hear him right? 'My Place?'

Both men nod. 'The Huber Corporation,' the man with the scar says.

And I'm too stunned and shocked and scared to speak. I remember the words The Voice spoke to me when he left me in the woods. He said the Huber Corporation would come looking for me, didn't he?

He said they wanted me dead.

And here they are.

Carina

I creep along corridors, past rows of closed doors, sleep sounds drifting from each one. I cross the building and walk the boys' corridor. And as I pass, I wonder which of these doors Jesper's being kept behind.

I walk along both sides of the corridor, listening, turning handles and opening doors so I can peer into the gloom. But the only doors that aren't locked are the dorms, and I'm sure he's not in one of those. He has his own room.

He's behind one of the locked doors. Alone, away from everyone else.

The best chance I have is to knock on the doors, to whisper his name and see if he answers.

So that's what I do.

Jesper

Both of them gawp at me. And I don't know what to do. I look for Father Frei, but he's nowhere to be seen.

'Jesper, it's so good to see you. We've come to take you home with us,' the taller of the two men says. 'We'd like to take you back to My Place.' He holds his hand out like he expects me to take it.

But I don't. Cos The Voice's words buzz around my mind. I shake my head and start backing away from them.

'Jesper, you're not safe out here. We know about you being pushed down the steps at St Jerome's. People are out to get you. We can protect you.'

That takes me by surprise. How do they know about Markus pushing me down the stairs?

'We can take you back to My Place where you'll be safe.'

And I find myself shaking my head again, even though a large part of me wishes I could go back to My Place.

'I think it will be in your best interests to do as we ask, Jesper,' says the other man. He's shorter. The one with the scar down the side of his face that distorts as he speaks.

And again I'm shaking my head. Because The Voice's advice, his words when he left me in the forest, keep returning. I don't trust these two men.

'Come on, Jesper,' the shorter man says. 'You must have missed Feathers. I know he's missed you. We can take you to see him.'

The mention of Feathers makes me squizz up at them. But I shake my head, keep backing away. They're trying to trick me, aren't they?

And now the expressions on their faces are angry, impatient. 'Don't make this difficult,' says the tall man.

'You'll come with us whatever,' the other man says, stepping slowly and menacingly in my direction. His cold eyes glint under the bright lights. 'But it'll be better for you if you do as we ask ...'

I continue backing away, shaking my head. I want them to go away. I squizz around me, wondering where Father Frei's gone.

And all the time the two men are stalking after me, prying, talking.

'Come on, Jesper,' the tall man says. 'Come quietly.'

But I don't. I back away, bumping into people, spilling their drinks. I can't back away forever though, can I?

The taller man makes a lunge for me. I see him coming and dodge out of the way, knocking into a lady who squeals and then says some German words at me.

And then I notice Father Frei and Commander Brune walking through the crowds, heading this way.

The tall man notices them too and he lets go of my shoulders. The questions stop. And as Frei and Brune get close, the two men from My Place disappear into the crowd.

For a moment I'm alone and shaking.

But only for a moment, cos Father Frei and Commander Brune stop beside me, speaking to each other in German words. Father Frei squizzes at me and says, 'Jesper, are you OK?'

I nod my head.

'You look pale.'

Commander Brune clears his throat and then speaks to Father Frei in German. And as he speaks, he points at me.

I watch Father Frei's face. He nods. He listens to Commander Brune.

And the next thing I know, Commander Brune's large hand is on my shoulder. 'Jesper, you come with me,' he says.

Brune and Father Frei take me across the room to a small door. Two other uniformed men come with us. We go through the door, into a smaller empty room.

And when we're inside, I realise everyone's gawping at me – Brune and Father Frei and the two men in uniform. For a second nothing happens, and I wonder why we've come in here, what this is about.

But then Commander Brune takes a step forward, smoothing his moustache with one hand before speaking. 'Jesper, I intend to see your miracle for myself. To check it's real.'

I say nothing. But the panicky feeling's starting to get worse – my head and my heart pound, my stomach turns.

Commander Brune nods to the two men in uniform, saying some German words that I don't quite pick up.

And before I know what's happening, the two men step forward and grab my arms. I try to wrench myself free, but that just makes them grip me more firmly. I'm trapped. One of them pulls something from the belt of his uniform – a long black stick. He holds it up and then brings it down on my arm with a …

CRACK.

And immediately I feel the bone break.

'*AAARRRRGGGGGHHHHHH!*'

The pain's immense.

And when I squizz down at my arm, it's bent and blood is leaking out, my hand hanging limply.

And all four men are just prying at me, aren't they?

Why?

Why are they doing this?

Only I don't think about that for long, because the pain's intense and I feel like I'm going to be sick.

I grit my teeth. I try to breathe deeply.

From the corner of my eye, I see Father Frei make the sign of the cross in front of himself, muttering words. Praying or something. He's gonna pretend he's healing me again, isn't he?

And it isn't long before I get the feeling. My body needs to mend. There's a CRICK sound as the bone starts to fix itself, the two broken ends searching each other out and binding together. The blood which had leaked out begins to seep back inside my arm and my skin mends.

The room is hushed. And when I squizz up, I see all the men's faces, their eyes gawping at me, mouths open, like they're shocked by what they've seen.

'Amazing,' Commander Brune booms to everyone in the room, and he starts clapping. The others do the same, filling the room with applause.

Then Commander Brune steps forward and grips my recently mended arm in his strong hands. And it makes me panic. I try to pull it away, but his grip is solid. 'Let me examine your arm,' he says.

They're all looking at me, gawping. Commander Brune doesn't let go. And I can't handle it. I'm finding it difficult to breathe. It's too much for me. I feel my body starting to shake.

'Jesper,' I hear Brune say, 'I want to examine your arm.'

Only the world's starting to close in around me. Pain pulses around my head.

And still they're prying.

So I do the only thing I can. I open my mouth, and what comes out of it is like the sound of a terrified animal. A roar.

RRRRRR-AAAAA-RRRRRRGGGGGGGGHHHHHHHHH.

Cos that's exactly what I am. A terrified animal.

Right away Commander Brune lets go of my arm and the others take a step back.

And when the roar stops, when I close my mouth again, there's total silence in the room. No talking or clapping.

I drop to the floor, curl into a ball, hoping if I screw my eyes closed tight enough that everyone else will go, that it'll just be me.

We travel back in the car, and even though it's just me and Father Frei and the driver and the only sound's the quiet roar of the engine, I'm still shaking and my heart's still thumping. I gawp out of the window, trying to calm myself. The streets outside are empty; the street lights are off.

'I'm sorry, Jesper,' Father Frei says, breaking the silence. 'I should have warned you what was about to happen.'

I don't say a word.

'Commander Brune's intentions were good, even if his methods were a little brutal.'

But I say nothing. For a while Father Frei's silent too. The car cruises through dark, empty streets.

'Now he's seen your miracle for himself, he seems interested in your story,' Father Frei says eventually. 'This could be a fantastic opportunity for St Jerome's. Commander Brune is bound to be generous towards us if ...'

But I've given up listening. I curl up in a ball on the seat, hiding my head. I think about the men from My Place. I think about The Voice, and Feathers.

After a while I realise Father Frei's stopped talking. I feel his hand on my back and flinch.

'I'm sorry,' he says. 'I think you'll need to get used to other people.'

I say nothing.

'The first step will be to teach you to speak and understand German better.'

I'm silent. The car engine roars.

'We'll start tomorrow.'

Blake

I see Huber's car heading along the deserted main road, watch it approach the side street where I'm parked and pull up alongside me. The driver's window lowers, revealing Henwood's face and, behind him, Huber. I lower my window.

Henwood nods at me. 'Any movement this evening?'

'I saw Markus.'

'Did you make the deal with him?' Henwood asks.

'Of course. He bit my hand off. For that amount of money he'd kill his own grandmother. If he had one.'

From the shadows of Huber's car, I see Huber nod his head. 'Very good. Have you seen anyone else?'

'A militia car came to the orphanage not long after you went and then left again soon afterwards. Other than that, nothing.'

Huber nods, thinking. 'That might have been Boy 23. He was at the town hall this evening.'

'He was? Did you speak to him?'

'We tried to get him out of there,' Henwood says. 'But it wasn't easy. He was taken away from us before we could manage.'

I wonder what they know, what Jesper might have said. 'Was he well?'

'He looked healthy enough.'

'Listen, Blake,' Huber says, 'I think we need to talk over what happens next. Get in with us and we'll go for a drive.'

Carina

I knock gently at another door. I hear no answer but I try again.

'Jesper,' I hiss, 'are you there?'

Still there's no answer, and with only one more door to try on this corridor I'm giving up hope I'll find him.

I move to the last door and knock gently – once, twice, three times. Yet again there's nothing. So I whisper again, 'Jesper, are you in there?'

But just then I hear something and I freeze – footsteps, from somewhere behind me. I turn my head.

Markus walks towards me, smirking.

'Carina,' he hisses. 'What are you doing out of your dorm?'

'Couldn't sleep, not that it's any of your business.'

I can tell from the look on his face that he doesn't believe me, that he thinks he already knows why I'm here. 'You came to find Jesper Hausmann, didn't you? You've been thinking about my deal.'

I shake my head, wondering whether he's been watching, whether he's heard me calling out to Jesper.

'Then why were you knocking at his door?'

I shrug. 'This isn't his door. I told you earlier, I don't know where he is any more than you do.'

Markus raises an eyebrow, but I'm telling the truth. 'I don't have time for this,' I say. 'I'm tired.' And I start walking back along the corridor, towards my room, leaving Markus behind.

Before I've walked more than five paces, I hear a voice. A deep voice that sounds like Father Frei, speaking in English. I hear footsteps too.

If he catches me here, out of bed, I'll be punished, so I race along the corridor, round a corner. Behind me, Markus does the same.

From the shadows we peek out, watching and listening as the voice and the footsteps get closer. Then two figures appear at the other end of the corridor. Father Frei carries a flickering candle. Jesper walks beside him, all dressed up in a black woollen suit and a white shirt. They stop outside a room.

'Tomorrow, Jesper, you begin German lessons.'

Jesper doesn't reply. He stares awkwardly at his feet.

Father Frei unlocks the door.

'Goodnight, Jesper,' he says, handing the candle to Jesper before locking him in. With that, Father Frei turns and walks back the way he came and I listen to his footsteps disappearing.

Beside me, Markus pats me on the shoulder. 'Thanks, Carina,' he whispers. 'I knew you'd lead me to him.' And then he runs off down the corridor.

Blake

We drive out of the town and into the countryside, dark fields and forest surrounding us. No one speaks. There isn't another soul around. I'm beginning to think Jesper must have said something. This won't end well.

'Pull over here,' Huber instructs.

Henwood slows the car and then stops by the side of the road. I put my hand inside my jacket and carefully take my gun from its holster.

'Things have taken a turn for the worse,' Huber says, turning in his seat. 'It seems New Dawn are now well aware of Boy 23. At the moment all they know is he's Jesper Hausmann, a wild boy found in the forest. But Father Frei and Commander Brune took him into a side room this evening. We're not sure what happened in there.'

'Oh,' I say. I don't loosen my grip on my gun.

'They think he's some sort of miracle boy. Or at least the priest does,' Henwood says. 'We don't think they have any idea of who he really is or where he comes from, or that he is linked to the outbreak of Marsh Flu.'

I nod. 'Well, that's good.'

Huber sighs. 'Yes, but knowing New Dawn, it won't be long before they run tests on him to see why he's different from other people. And as soon as that happens, they'll come knocking at our door.'

I nod. 'Of course.'

'We've run out of time,' Huber says. 'We need to deal with Boy 23 immediately.'

'It's already taken care of,' I say. 'I paid Markus half of the money and told him to do it at the earliest opportunity. I told him the remainder would be payable on completion.'

'Good,' Huber says. 'Let's hope he succeeds, and soon. Otherwise we'll need to get in there and take care of this ourselves.'

Carina

As I follow Father Frei through the corridors in silence, I think of my father and give thanks.

Because being the only child in the home who can speak both English and German fluently has secured me the job of being Jesper's German teacher, which in turn has got me out of working at the landfill this morning.

We stop outside Jesper's door. 'Remember, you're here to teach him to speak and understand German. I expect to see a noticeable improvement in his language.'

I nod.

'Otherwise you'll find yourself sorting rubbish again.'

Father Frei puts the keys in the lock and pushes the door open. Inside, Jesper sits on the edge of his bed, staring at me and Father Frei as we enter, eyes darting from one of us to the other.

As Father Frei leaves us, I sit down beside Jesper on his bed and right away I see his nose wrinkle. He shifts away from me. The smell of the landfill lingers on me.

I put down the book and pencil that Father Frei gave me.

'How are you?'

He answers with a shrug and an 'OK'.

'I saw you and Father Frei walking through the corridors last night.'

He looks at me, confused. 'Did you?'

I nod. 'Where did you go?'

'The town hall.'

'What for?'

'Father Frei wanted me to meet his friends.'

The thought of Father Frei's friends brings a sudden and unwanted image into my head. 'Who did you meet there?'

He shrugs. 'I can't remember most of their names. But there was someone called Commander Brune …'

The name just about stops my heart dead. I see my home … I see Dad … I see Greta … before I manage to force the thoughts from my mind.

'Do you know him?' Jesper says.

I nod. 'He's the head of the militia. New Dawn.'

Jesper nods.

'Why did Father Frei take you to meet him?'

Jesper shrugs. 'He wanted to see my miracle.'

'What do you mean?'

He looks down at the floor. 'They wanted to watch me heal. Commander Brune took me to a room and two New Dawn men hit my arm so it broke. They all stood and watched me heal.'

'My God. Really?'

He nods. He rolls up the sleeve of his shirt on one arm and shows where a small, raised pink scar has knitted his skin back together. I reach out my fingers to touch it, but he flinches before I even get close.

'There were some people who said they were from My Place as well. The Huber Corporation.'

'My Place is where you come from, right?'

He nods.

'That's good news, isn't it? Are they going to take you back there?'

He shrugs, then shakes his head. He looks like something's troubling him. 'They tried to. But I didn't let them.'

'What? Why?'

'Because of something The Voice said. He told me never to go back. He said they wanted to kill me.'

We're silent for a moment. I hear footsteps outside in the corridor and I'm reminded of Father Frei's threat to send me back to the dump. 'So, I'm meant to be teaching you to speak German. Do you want to learn?'

Jesper nods and smiles. 'Yes, please.'

'We can start by learning some of the words for family,' I say. Jesper nods.

'Mother is *Mutter*.'

'*Mutter*,' he repeats.

'Father is *Vater*.'

'*Vater*.'

'Sister is *Schwester*.'

'*Schwester*.'

'And brother is *Bruder*.'

'*Bruder*.'

I can tell from the way he looks at me, the expression on his face, that he's got something else on his mind other than German.

And after a while he opens his mouth and he says. 'Do you have a family?'

I nod. 'Yeah. Well, I did. They're dead now. That's why I'm in this place. That's why we're all here, isn't it? Because we have no one to look after us.'

Jesper nods.

I remember what he said to me before, about not having a mum or dad. 'How about you?' I ask. 'Who looked after you before you came here?'

'No one,' he says. And then he thinks and adds, 'Except, there was The Voice.'

'The Voice? The person who left you in the woods?'

He nods. 'He was the person that told me what to do.'

'So you lived with him?'

'No. I didn't live with anyone.'

'I don't understand. You must have lived with other people. Someone must have been with you. You can't just have a voice without there being a person.'

He shrugs.

'You lived completely alone?'

He nods. 'I never met another person till a week or so ago.'

For a moment I say nothing, because I don't understand how what he's saying can be true. And I'm not sure Jesper understands either. 'So what was he like? The Voice?'

'I never met him. I just heard his voice. He was kind and clever and he looked after me.'

I raise an eyebrow. Maybe he's one of those people who hears voices inside his head. Maybe he's mad. 'So where did you live?' I ask him.

'My Place.'

'You said that. But where is that?'

He shrugs. 'I don't know.'

'So you lived in a place where you were alone and you don't know where it was?'

He nods. 'I lived alone. In one room. Just me and my pet squawk. I never met anyone else. I never heard of New Dawn or Huber or Marsh Flu. Not until I was left in the forest.'

I raise my eyebrows. It's astonishing that there's anyone who had never heard of New Dawn or Marsh Flu. And if anyone else told me a story like this, I probably wouldn't believe them; I'd think they were trying to hide something. But Jesper's different. 'So how did you end up here, in St Jerome's?'

Jesper thinks for a moment before replying. 'The Voice took me from My Place because he said I wasn't safe there any longer. He said there were people there who wanted to kill me. The people I saw at the town hall last night. The Voice left me in the forest and told me to head north-west, to find the Spirit of Resistance in the Low Countries.'

My spine tingles. 'The Spirit of Resistance? Really?'

He nods. 'The Voice told me to stay away from people and buildings. He said he'd come and find me when he had completed everything he needed to.'

214

Jesper pauses. I say nothing.

'Except when I was in the forest I found a road. I got hit by a car with New Dawn officers in it. They hit me over the head and I woke up here.'

I nod. What he says sounds far-fetched. But he looks like he believes every word.

And then in the corridor outside I hear footsteps again and keys jangling and we pretend to get back on with the German lessons.

Jesper

The lights have just gone out and my eyes are closed, ready to drift into sleep, when I hear a sound coming from the corridor. A scratching, rattling sound at my door.

I open my eyes, sit up. I squizz through the darkness, wondering what's happening.

The lock clunks.

The handle turns.

The door opens.

And then a dark figure steps into the room, stands in front of the doorway, filling the space up. And even though I can't see the eyes, I know that whoever is there, they're squizzing directly at me.

And I don't know what else to do, so I hide under my bed sheets, peeking out, as the figure moves silently closer. And I see that whoever it is, they're dressed head to toe in black, with even their face covered. They move quietly towards me.

And I know that this isn't right.

I can't just cower in bed; I have to do something.

I jump from the bed and make a run for it.

Only the black figure stands in my way, blocking my escape route.

'Time to die, Jesper,' the figure says. Male. English words, German voice. He pulls something shiny from a pocket.

And it's a knife, isn't it?

It's my knife.

Moonlight flashes off the blade.

'This is for Sabine,' he says. 'From Huber.'

I squizz from the knife to the figure and back again, looking for a way out. But there isn't one. All I can do is lunge at him, try to knock him over before he gets me. So that's what I do.

BLAM. I crash into the figure.

And that's when I feel a sharp pain in my guts.

Cos I've been stabbed.

I collapse to the floor, leaking blood, a puddle forming around me on the floor.

The figure gawps at me for a second, and then turns and flees.

Carina

The lights went out a while ago. I lie in bed and close my eyes.

And what I see is Commander Brune – his heavy brow and his massive shoulders and his big bristling moustache. I see his shiny black boots, splattered with blood. He stands in our kitchen, where I hide, aged seven and terrified. I see Brune lower his gun, pass it to Father Frei.

Though back then he wasn't Father Frei. He was Officer Frei – a militiaman. Dressed in black New Dawn uniform, he grabs hold of the gun.

And then Brune grabs Greta and she squeals. And I see me, aged seven, saying a silent prayer.

I force myself back into the present and open my eyes. I don't want to remember what comes next. I leave the dorm and walk through the still, silent corridors.

And as I walk, the bad memories clear and I think about maybe paying a visit to the kitchens to get myself something decent to eat.

But as I descend the steps from the girls' corridor, I hear a noise that makes me stop still. I hear the sound of footsteps squeaking along the boys' corridor, sounding like someone's running.

I hurry down the rest of the steps and then over to the boys' stairs. I climb the staircase. The footsteps rush in my direction, getting close, so I look around for somewhere to hide, find an open doorway and slip inside. And then, in a flash, someone dashes past, dressed head to toe in black. They're gone in a second.

I stay where I am for a few seconds more, wondering who that was and what they were doing running around the corridors at night. And I decide to investigate. I walk the boys' corridor, creeping nervously along, thinking that maybe whoever just ran past will come back.

But as I turn a corner near to where I hid last night, I see something – someone is slumped on the ground. As I rush closer, I realise that the someone is Jesper and there's a pool of blood forming all around him.

Panic consumes me. I race over and kneel beside him, check his pulse. And with relief I realise he's alive.

'What happened?'

He can't answer though. He looks at me, eyes pleading for help. He holds his stomach and I see that's where the blood's leaking from.

I look around us at the empty corridor and I think a hundred thoughts, trying to figure out what to do first.

'HELP!' I shout. 'HELP!'

I turn back to Jesper and see that his blood is everywhere. 'Did someone do this to you?'

He nods, slowly, pain etched on his features.

If I don't stop the bleeding, he'll die. I take off my dressing gown, rip at the sleeve until it comes free. I move Jesper's hand away so I can look at the wound, but the light's too dim and all I see is a slash in his clothing and blood seeping on to his pyjamas. I hold the torn-off sleeve to the wound.

And still the corridor around us is quiet and empty. Where is everyone?

'HELP US, PLEASE!' I shout. 'JESPER'S HURT.'

Jesper watches me, gritting his teeth, saying nothing.

'Who did this to you?'

He doesn't answer.

'I saw someone in the corridor,' I say. 'Someone dressed all in black.'

He nods, grimacing.

I'm just about to turn and shout for help again, when I hear footsteps. I turn. Little Ralph stands in the corridor and stares, eyes wide and terrified.

'Go and get help, Ralph. Wake Father Liebling or Father Lekmann. Say someone broke into Jesper's room and stabbed him.'

Ralph nods and he runs away down the corridor.

Jesper

There's a gaping hole in my belly – I know cos I felt it with my fingers. Carina holds the bandage to it, trying to stop the blood from leaking out. And all the time, she's whispering to me.

Only my head feels so light and empty that her words just float around me and I don't hear them properly. I force myself to look straight at Carina, to listen to what she's saying.

'… was in the corridor last night.'

'Uh?' I say.

'Markus. He was in the corridor last night, looking for your room. Did he do this to you?'

It happened too fast. It was dark, and I couldn't see a face. But it was my knife, wasn't it, and … I adjust my weight and that sends a surge of pain from my belly around my body. I grit my teeth, close my eyes.

'It must have been Markus,' Carina's saying. 'He asked me at …'

Only I don't hear the rest of what she's saying, because all of a sudden I'm getting that feeling – my body telling me to move, to sit up. Pain surges through me as I force myself upright. But I have to do it, don't I?

'Jesper, no,' Carina's saying. 'You must stay still.'

But my body's telling me to do it.

So I sit up. I move Carina's hand away from the hole in my belly. And then it begins – blood seeping back inside me, skin knitting itself together, healing. It takes little more than a minute.

Carina gawps at me with her mouth open, squizzes at where the hole was, at the floor where the blood was. She shakes her head.

'I don't understand,' she says.

I say nothing.

'It all went back inside you. How did that happen?'

I shrug, because I can't explain it. It just happens, doesn't it?

'Let me look at your stomach,' she says.

I lift my nightshirt up. I run my fingers over the place where the knife went in and the hole isn't there any more. In its place there's just a raised, tender bump. Carina reaches out and touches it, and I watch the look of disbelief on her face.

'It's healed. That's not possible. How do you do that?'

Only before I can answer, there are footsteps along the corridor. And then the boy that Carina sent to get help and Father Liebling are standing over me.

Carina

'What's going on?' Liebling asks. 'Why are you out of bed?'

'Jesper's been stabbed,' I say. 'But the wound just healed before our eyes.'

The colour drains from Father Liebling's face. He makes the sign of the cross in front of his face and whispers some words, as though God had anything to do with what happened. He bends down to Jesper's level. 'Oh no. Jesper, are you OK? How did this happen?'

Jesper nods his head.

'Are you sure you were stabbed?'

Again he nods.

'Show me where.'

Jesper lifts his nightshirt again, shows the dark pink raised line on his belly. Father Liebling stares at it, nervously reaches his fingers out and touches it. Jesper flinches.

'You feel OK?'

'I'm OK,' Jesper says.

Father Liebling brings his fingers away from Jesper, eyebrows raised. 'Fascinating. He's completely healed,' he says in German. 'You're sure he was stabbed?'

'Certain,' I say. 'I saw someone running through the corridor and I came to investigate. When I got here, I saw Jesper collapsed in a pool of blood. He had a big knife wound in his stomach, where the scar is now. I tried to stop the bleeding with the sleeve of my night robe.' I show him the improvised bandage.

He takes it from me, looks at the blood that's soaked into it. Then he hands it back and walks past Jesper, through the doorway into his room. Liebling looks at the door, at the blood-stained floor where Jesper must have pulled himself along, out into the corridor.

'This door was locked,' he says, shaking his head. 'I locked it an hour ago. How did anyone get in here?'

Nobody answers. I put my arm around Ralph, who's staring at Jesper, looking scared.

222

'Jesper, did you see who did this?' Liebling asks in English.

Jesper shrugs. 'He had my knife – so I think it was Markus. He took all my stuff. I didn't see his face though.'

Father Liebling stands where he is, thinking, sighing, still looking around at the floor and at Jesper and at the door.

'Jesper, I think it's best if you come with me, for your own safety. We'll go and speak with Father Frei and find you somewhere safe to sleep.' He turns to me. 'Carina, take Ralph back to his dorm and then go and get some sleep. I'll make sure nobody suspects you were out of bed.'

I start to guide Ralph along the corridor, while Father Liebling helps Jesper to his feet.

Blake

Markus checks around him before hurrying across the street and down the side road to where we're waiting in silence. As he gets close, Henwood lowers the driver's window. Markus checks around him again before coming to the window.

'So?' Henwood says.

Markus nods. 'It's done. I went to his room last night.'

Henwood and Huber both nod. My heart thumps inside my chest. I keep one hand in my pocket, finger on the trigger of the gun which I have there.

'He's dead?'

The boy nods.

'You're sure?'

'As sure as I can be, yeah. I left him in a pool of his own blood. I wasn't gonna stay around and check his pulse, was I? I'd have been caught.'

Henwood sighs. He looks over at Huber.

'I want the rest of my money,' Markus says, leaning in through the window.

'I need to know for sure that Jesper Hausmann is dead before I pay you,' Huber says. 'Bring me proof and then you'll get the rest of the money.'

Markus stares in through the window, disbelieving. 'Of course he's dead. There's no way he could have survived.'

'You'd be surprised,' Henwood says. 'We need proof before you get paid.'

The boy sighs. 'OK,' he says. 'But if I start asking questions, I'm gonna make myself look suspicious. I'll need more money ...'

Henwood shakes his head. 'I don't care if you look suspicious. This is what we're paying you for. Bring us proof, or you get nothing.'

Markus tuts, but then he nods. He looks around once more before hurrying back across the street to the orphanage.

From the front of the car I hear the beep of a message being received by a scroll, and a second later Huber takes his from his pocket and looks at the screen. He sighs. 'I'm needed back

224

at the facility,' he says. 'Girl 16 has contracted the new strain. You two stay here until we know for sure that Boy 23 is dead. You'll need to get his body out of the orphanage somehow, to make sure nobody else gets their hands on it and starts poking around, finding out things they shouldn't know.'

'Of course,' Henwood says.

Jesper

It seems like wherever I go, everyone means me harm.

And so when I hear footsteps approach and then keys in the lock of my new room, I feel nervous.

But it turns out it's just Father Frei.

He asks me a load of questions about what happened. He makes me show him the scar it left. And he asks if I recognised who did it.

And when I say, 'I think it was Markus, cos he has my knife and whoever did it used my knife,' Father Frei nods and goes quiet for a while, staring into space.

'We'll investigate,' he says eventually. 'We'll search his dorm for the knife. We'll ask him some questions.'

And then before he leaves he says, 'You're special to us here, Jesper. Let me reassure you that we'll do everything we can to keep you safe.'

Carina

The first thing I hear is, *'Psst.'*

The sound makes my heart race and my head pound. I sit up in my bed and look around. The rest of the dorm is sleeping. The room is dark.

And then another noise.

'Carina.'

Somebody calling me from the corridor. I can't tell who from the hushed voice though.

Could it be whoever attacked Jesper? Could it be Markus? He could have come for me. Perhaps he worked out that I know what he did to Jesper. Maybe it's my turn.

'Carina, out here.'

I slowly get out of my bed. I open my drawer and grab the gun, put it in the pocket of my nightclothes. And then I head towards the corridor, towards where the sound came from.

And in the darkest shadows of the corridor I see something which makes me jump out of my skin – a cloaked figure, face hidden in shadows and cloth.

I put my hand on the unloaded gun, still tucked into my nightdress. I place my finger on the trigger. 'What do you want?' I ask.

'Carina, don't worry. It's me,' says a voice. The figure pulls the hood of the cloak back. It's Father Liebling. My finger relaxes and I let go of the gun in my pocket.

'What is it?'

'I need to talk to you about Jesper.'

I nod.

'I was visited, the night before last, by an old friend.'

'And … ?'

'He was acting on behalf of the Spirit of Resistance, Carina. He claimed that an organisation called the Huber Corporation wants Jesper killed.'

I take a deep breath. 'Jesper said that name. Was it them that stabbed Jesper?'

Father Liebling shrugs. 'I don't know for sure. But I do know that my friend wants us to help Jesper and the Spirit of Resistance. Are you willing?'

I nod.

'Excellent. In return they'll offer you freedom. A new life away from St Jerome's.'

Did I hear him correctly? Freedom? 'What do I have to do?'

'In the immediate future we must ensure Jesper remains safe from New Dawn and the Huber Corporation. And as soon as we can, we must help deliver him to the Spirit of Resistance.'

I nod. 'But how?'

'I don't know the details yet, Carina. No doubt we'll receive more instructions soon.'

Before I can ask him any more questions, Father Liebling pulls the hood back over his head and hobbles away.

Jesper

Later that day I hear the key in the lock again and I start to panic once more. Before I can even hide though, they're walking into the room.

Three of them.

Father Liebling and two men wearing the uniform of New Dawn, one of whom carries a brown leather bag in his hand.

I stay where I am, gawping as they close the door behind them, lock it and take out the key. The man with the bag places it down beside me on the bed and opens it up.

Father Liebling speaks to the men in German. I don't understand the words, but I can tell he isn't happy with them. His hands make a praying gesture, like he's pleading.

But the men answer him back with one word. '*Nein.*' Which means no, doesn't it?

'What's happening?' I ask.

'Commander Brune from New Dawn has asked for a sample of your blood,' says Father Liebling. 'He's interested in your healing and wants to know more about you.'

I say nothing. My heart thuds.

'I've asked them not to, but they won't take no for an answer. I don't think we have a choice, Jesper.'

And all the while he's talking, the man with the bag is taking things out of it, putting together a needle and then taking out an empty bottle.

I look to Father Liebling to help me, but all he says is, 'Sorry,' and then he gawps as one of the New Dawn men holds me down and the other one sinks the needle into my arm and draws blood.

And even though I scream, they ignore me.

Blake

With Huber still back at the facility attending to the case of the new strain, Henwood and I are once again in charge in Manburg. It's early and we sit in the car. Henwood makes a note as we watch a militia car drive into the orphanage and then leave again ten or so minutes later.

'What do you think that was about?' Henwood asks.

'No idea,' I say. 'Perhaps New Dawn learned of Jesper's death.'

'Hmmm. I'm not sure Mr Huber will be happy about that.'

Markus appears and we watch in silence as he hurries across the road from the home. He comes to the car window, which Henwood lowers.

'What's the news?'

Markus shrugs.

'What does that mean?'

'Jesper survived,' Markus says.

I say nothing.

'How?' Henwood asks.

He shrugs again. 'They're saying it was another miracle. It didn't kill him. He healed himself. Father Frei asked me about the attack. Everyone thinks I did it. I denied it though. They searched my stuff and found nothing. I hid the weapon in the fireplace of my dormitory. They won't find it. Besides, Father Frei wouldn't do anything to me. I know things about him he doesn't want people to know.'

Henwood sighs. 'So where's Jesper now?'

Another shrug. 'I don't know. He's been taken away from the rest of us. The medical ward maybe.'

Henwood runs his hand through his hair, cursing under his breath.

'Can I have the rest of my money now?' Markus asks.

Henwood and I both shake our heads.

Markus swears.

'Did you see a car visit the home just now?' Henwood says.

Markus nods. 'Yeah. Two New Dawn officers were in it.'

Henwood nods, then presses the button that makes his window buzz back up. Markus stares at the glass for a moment before kicking the ground and walking back to the home.

'This is bad,' Henwood says.

I nod. 'What do we do?'

He says nothing for a few seconds, but stares out of the windscreen, thinking. 'I need to speak to Huber. You go and get us something to eat from the town.'

I nod. This is my opportunity. I grab my briefcase and get out of the car.

'I can't let you see him, I'm afraid,' Father Frei says.

'But I must,' I say. 'He's in danger.'

'I'm sorry,' Father Frei says as he sits behind his desk. His fire spits and crackles.

I sigh. 'You don't understand. I come from the same place as Jesper. I brought him up. And now I need to take him with me. He's in imminent danger.'

Father Frei raises an eyebrow. 'You brought him up? Interesting. Jesper has been very reluctant to tell us about his upbringing ... He says he didn't live with anyone, that he had no mother or father, that food was always there, but no people.'

I nod. 'That's true enough.'

'Perhaps you'd care to explain that to me ...'

I shake my head. 'There's no time for that now. I need to get Jesper out of here immediately. There's someone waiting outside this home who wishes to kill him.'

'I assure you, Mr Blake, Jesper is safe here,' Frei says. 'St Jerome's is the safest place for him right now. Nobody will get to him in here, and nobody will take him away. Including you.'

'Then let me see him for a short while,' I say. 'Please. Just a minute with him –'

He shakes his head. 'I'm afraid not.'

For a second I say nothing, but I think this through. By now, Henwood will have spoken to Huber. God knows what course of action they'll have decided on. I have to find a way to get Jesper out of here immediately. 'I have money, if that's what you want.'

Father Frei smiles. 'Don't waste your time, Mr Blake.'

'How much?' I say, pulling a tightly bound wad of bank-notes from my pocket. 'There's enough here to keep your children's home running for years to come ...'

'You're very kind,' Father Frei says, 'but as I've already said, you're wasting your time. St Jerome's has recently accepted an extremely generous donation in respect of Jesper. In return for this, we've agreed to look after him here and keep him safe and healthy.'

'Really? Who made the donation?'

Father Frei doesn't answer. His expression is impervious.

'New Dawn, wasn't it?'

And although he doesn't say anything, I detect a slight change in his facial expression and I know I'm right.

'I can give you more money than they have ... How much?' I say.

But Father Frei simply shakes his head. 'I've made my promises to Commander Brune,' he says. 'And now I think perhaps it's time you left.'

I sense my chance slipping away. I have to do something, so I reach inside my jacket and take out my gun. I point it at Father Frei. For a second he looks surprised, frightened even.

But almost immediately he regains his composure and a look of calm appears on his face.

'I need to see the boy,' I say. 'Now.'

Father Frei opens his desk drawer and calmly brings out a gun of his own. 'We could both play this game, Mr Blake,' he says, 'but I have an idea it won't end happily.'

'I'll shoot you. Take me to the boy.'

He shakes his head. 'Go ahead and pull the trigger, Mr Blake. Take your chances. You have no idea where Jesper's kept. If you shoot me, do you really think the other priests will show you where to find him?'

I say nothing. I adjust my finger on the trigger.

A knock at the door makes us both jump.

'Come in,' Father Frei calls, maintaining my gaze, keeping his gun pointed at me.

A second later the door opens. I hear someone walk in, but I don't look round.

'Ah,' Father Frei says, 'Father Liebling. Just in time. Could you help me to show this gentleman out?'

I lower my gun. Because perhaps there's another way to do this.

Father Frei and Gerd Liebling escort me down the spiral staircase and into the church at gunpoint. I walk in silence, my own gun holstered. Father Frei talks the whole way through the church and into the orphanage, telling me about the interest Jesper has attracted due to his 'miracles'. I let him speak; I don't correct him.

All the while I'm looking for an opportunity to speak to Gerd, to get the message to him, but no opportunity presents itself, and as we near the door I'm starting to panic that I've failed.

But as Gerd unlocks the front door to let me out of St Jerome's, Father Frei hangs back. I reach discreetly into my bag and take the essentials Jesper will need in the palm of my hand. As Gerd opens the door and I leave the building, I shake his hand, passing the items over. He immediately slips them into his robes.

'Give my regards to Jesper,' I say. 'Tell him I came to see him.'

He nods. Behind him, Father Frei checks his watch.

I look directly at Gerd. 'It's time,' I say.

And then the door of St Jerome's shuts behind me. All I can do is hope and wait.

Carina

I'm cleaning the kitchens when Father Liebling finds me.

He taps me on the back and I jump, before turning to see him.

'Carina,' he says. 'The time has come.'

'What? Already.'

He nods. 'Jesper's life is in danger. We need to get him out of here now.'

'OK.'

'You'll be given new documents. New identities. You can start a new life, Carina. Away from St Jerome's. Away from New Dawn.'

He doesn't need to say any more to convince me. 'What do I need to do?'

Life has taught me that there's only one person you can really trust and that's yourself. And in this case, I'm trusting my judgement. I judge that Liebling has Jesper's best interests at heart, not least because he's plotting against New Dawn. And I trust him when he says that Blake – his friend from the Spirit of Resistance – can give me the new start he promised, the opportunity I need.

If I don't trust him, I'll be stuck in Manburg for the rest of my life.

So here I am, following Liebling's instructions, sneaking around deserted corridors with Jesper's bag on my back while everyone else is at work.

I've already been to my dormitory, collected what I need – clothes, the gun – and now I'm on the boys' corridor, which appears empty. I creep inside Markus's dormitory. The room's empty except for a musty smell of stale sweat and dirt. I stand and stare, trying to work out which bed and which wardrobe belong to Markus.

I walk between the two rows. Near the end of the room, something on the floor catches my eye. By the side of the bed, amongst a pile of dirty clothes, I see something that at first glance just looks like a black metal tube. But at either end there are glass lenses – a telescope. It's new and sleek and has buttons on the side. It's unlike anything I've ever seen. It's got to be Jesper's. And that surely must mean this is Markus's place – his bed and his wardrobe.

I look around once more, see that I'm alone. I dash over to the wardrobe beside the bed. A large metal padlock guards the doors. I reach out and try it, hoping it won't be locked, but it is.

I take a hairclip from my hair and start on the lock, working it until it clicks apart. I open the wardrobe door and root around inside. There are piles of clean, folded clothes, like they've come from the laundry room. I put my hand underneath them and feel around. It doesn't take more than a few seconds to find most of Jesper's other things: a torch, and a kit for starting fires.

There's meant to be a knife too though. The knife Markus used to stab Jesper. I search all the way through the wardrobe without any luck. I try his bed instead – lift the sheets and the mattress, get on my hands and knees and search underneath, feel along the edges to see if he's stuck it there. I try the top of the wardrobe, but all I find is dust.

I look around the room, thinking about where I'd hide a knife in here. I try the sinks first, feel behind them, seeing if anything is in the space between the basin and the wall. Nothing.

Then, at the end of the room, I spot the fireplace and rush straight to it.

I reach my hand up it and feel around until I find a ledge, and on it there's something cold and metallic and hard. Even before I've brought it out, I know from the weight of it, from the feel of it, that it's a knife. I take it out of the fireplace and look at it, pull out the largest blade, which has smears of dried blood on it. Jesper's blood.

I put the knife in Jesper's bag and sling the bag across my shoulders, then hurry from the room.

Blake

When I arrive back at the car, carrying bread and coffee, Henwood is staring straight out of the windscreen. He takes his gun from its holster and checks the clip. I offer him his breakfast, but he shakes his head without even looking at me.

'What's the matter? Aren't you hungry any longer?'

Henwood shakes his head. I sit and watch with a feeling of dread as he busies himself, loading the clip with bullets. 'Huber's nearly here. We're going to act today.'

'What? Why?'

'The fact that New Dawn have been into the orphanage, coupled with Markus's failure to kill Jesper – it's forced our

237

hand. We have to get inside and make sure Boy 23 dies. A bullet through the heart.'

'What? But breaking in there and killing him will arouse even more suspicion.'

Henwood nods. 'If we kill him now and dispose of the body, before New Dawn get the evidence linking him to Marsh Flu and the Huber Corporation, the problem goes away. Whatever mess we make by killing him will be easier to clean up than if New Dawn find out who Boy 23 really is and where he came from.'

'This is madness.'

Henwood shakes his head. 'No. Not killing him would be madness.' He puts his gun back in its holster and stares out at the rainy street.

'So, do we do it now?'

He shakes his head. 'We wait for Huber. He'll be here soon.'

I nod and then slide the scroll out of my pocket, keeping it away from Henwood's prying eyes as I send a message.

Jesper

My heart thuds as the keys jangle in the lock. Why is someone coming to my room now? I've had my midday provisions – the tray is still on my table.

I pick up the blunt knife from my tray and stand close to the door.

The door opens.

And standing there is Father Liebling.

He squizzes at the knife in my hands, and then he closes the door quickly behind him.

'Jesper, you must listen to me. I've been visited by Mr Blake.'

I gawp back at him. Who's that?

'From My Place. He looked after you there. He said you know him as The Voice.'

'The Voice has spoken to you?'

Father Liebling nods. 'Yes, Jesper. He's an old friend of mine. He came to set you free.'

'Then where is he?'

'Father Frei wouldn't let him see you. But he gave me these to pass to you. He said you'll need them when you escape ...'

And then he passes me a handful of things. A scroll, just like the one that got broken. I swipe my finger across it to wake it. There are some papers too. A *Personalausweis* with a name on it that isn't mine: Kaspar Hauser.

'You and Carina must get out of here right now.'

I nod, gawping at the things in my hand, thinking about The Voice and how he came to find me, just as he said he would.

'How do I get out?'

Father Liebling lowers his voice. 'Take my set of keys. They open all the doors in the home.' He picks out one key in particular. 'This one's for the front door. Go now. You must get away.'

'But they'll know you let me go,' I say. 'What will happen to you?'

He shrugs. 'I don't know. I'll tell them you overpowered me. By then you'll be far away. What can they do to me?'

I say nothing to that, but what I'm thinking is they'll kill him for sure.

Another sound makes me jump – a quiet knocking. Nervously Father Liebling moves towards the door, pulls it open. He ushers Carina in. She has my bag on her back.

'You have everything, Carina?'

She nods.

'You both have to get out now.' Father Liebling hands Carina a piece of paper. 'Take this,' he says. 'The Spirit of Resistance – find them and they'll help you.'

She glances at the leaflet and then puts it in her pocket.

And for a couple of seconds Carina and I just squizz at each other, not sure what happens next.

'Go,' Father Liebling urges. 'Knock me unconscious and then get out before they find you.'

I squizz around the room for something to hit him with, and all I see is the tray. I pick it up.

'Do it, Jesper,' Father Liebling says. 'It'll make it easier for me to explain.'

I raise the tray above my head, as though I'm going to strike. But I can't, can I? I can't hit him.

'Give it here,' Carina says, grabbing it from me. In one movement she slams it against the back of Father Liebling's head and he slumps to the floor. 'Let's go!'

Blake

Huber's car skids up beside ours. Immediately his door opens and he rushes to our car, opens the back door and gets in. Once in the back seat, he checks the chamber of his gun.

'This is it,' he says. 'We've run out of time and options. Now we need to end this.'

Henwood nods. Hesitantly, so do I.

'Henwood and I will go inside the building and kill him. Blake, I want you to wait here.'

I gulp. 'Wait out here?'

He nods. 'You can keep an eye out for New Dawn. And you'll need to be ready to get us away from here fast. Keep the motor running. Understand?'

I nod.

And that's it. Immediately Huber and Henwood open their car doors and rush towards the building.

I'm left to panic. Jesper and the girl should have got out of the building by now, but I haven't seen them and there's no message either. I take the scroll from my pocket and send another message.

Is there a problem? You need to get out NOW. They're coming inside.

Jesper

We run from the room, through corridors and downstairs. I carry a panicked feeling with me, like this is some sort of trick, that round the next corner someone will see us and shoot.

In the entrance hall we spot Father Brahms. He sees us right away. We slow down. I squizz over at Carina to see what she's gonna do. And what she does is she walks calmly, as though this is the most natural thing in the world to be doing, as though nothing's wrong. So I do the same, walking straight across the entrance hall, towards the door, towards escape and freedom.

'*Carina . . . was machst du?*' calls Father Brahms from behind us.

Carina replies to him in German.

The priest raises an eyebrow and nods.

Whatever Carina said has worked, hasn't it? He's letting us go.

I fumble the key into the lock of the front door. It clunks open as the key turns. This is it. We're free. We're going back to the forest.

Only at the exact moment I put my hand on the door handle, there's a noise from the far side of the entrance hall. I turn and see Father Frei come in through another door. He squizzes around and spots us. *'Haltet sie auf, Vater Brahms!'*

Carina

Jesper freezes. His eyes dart from Father Frei to Father Brahms and then to me. His hand stays uselessly on the door handle.

'Jesper, Carina, stay where you are!' Father Frei shouts, hurrying across the room.

'Now!' I say to Jesper. 'Let's go!'

And that seems to jolt him into action. He turns the handle, pulls the door open and we're outside.

We sprint for our lives, leaving St Jerome's behind us.

'Come back!' Father Frei shouts. 'Jesper! Carina! Don't do this.'

We don't look back but run as fast as we can along the drive. Jesper surges ahead – fast and powerful and strong. But as he reaches the end of the driveway, there's a *BANG* and I don't know where it comes from. A bullet flies through the air, missing him by an inch and thwacking into the wall of the home.

We stop and look around and I see two men running this way, guns held in front of them.

BANG.

Another shot flies through the air, missing us both.

'Quick,' I say, pulling Jesper to the right. 'This way.'

Within a couple of strides he's overtaken me and he's pulling me along. We sprint through the grounds of St Jerome's, the two men following us.

BANG.

Another shot misses us.

This is useless. They'll kill us. They can't keep missing. The gun I found bashes about in my skirt pocket, and I wish it was loaded. Right now I would have a reason to use it. I wouldn't hesitate. And then I spot an opportunity – a low section of wall we could jump. And on the other side of it, bomb sites.

'That way.' I point.

We both leap the wall and I pull Jesper across the road and into the shell of a bomb-damaged building. We dodge between piles of rubble, run around crumbling walls, charge through the weeds and trees that have reclaimed the land. Jesper urges me along. His legs eat up the ground easily while I have to work like crazy to keep up. A glance over my shoulder confirms that they've seen us, that they're chasing us.

And out on the street behind them there's a black car – the same black car I saw waiting outside the home.

And then, all of a sudden, there's a *BANG* that cracks the air as one of the men stops running and aims his gun.

The ground right in front of us explodes in a puff of dust and both Jesper and I dodge out of the way. We stumble, but keep moving.

Jesper

'This way,' she says, pulling me along again. I follow, squizzing quickly over my shoulder. It's the two men from the town hall who are following us, and behind them another man gets out of the car and joins the chase. He lifts his gun and fires.

BANG.

I duck.

But his shot flies miles wide of us. Just another puff of dust.

And if I didn't know better I'd say he missed on purpose. Only we don't have time to stop and think. There's no time for anything except dodging, jumping, scrambling, running for our lives.

We duck inside another ruined house, hurdling broken walls until we come out the other side. And then we run for the next ruined house and then the next and the next. All the time the men are following, but always falling further behind.

By the time we leave the next ruined building, I see they're a long way back, only just scrabbling out of the last building we were in, climbing over the broken walls and squizzing around to see where we are. They stop and aim their guns. We duck down behind a wall.

BANG.

Another gunshot and another puff of dust.

BANG. BANG.

The bullets thwack into the walls of the house and the stone seems to explode and tiny shards and splinters shower down on us. I reach out for Carina and drag her along and we're running again.

And even though the distance is getting bigger between us, they're still there, aren't they? We have to find a way to lose them.

We come out of the last of the ruins on to a road with buildings that look like they're still lived in. A wagon rolls slowly along the road, pulled by a horse. Carina stops for a second, searching for our next move.

'Follow me,' she says suddenly, starting to run in the same direction as the cart. 'We'll lose them in the side streets.'

We run straight across the road, towards the wagon, reaching it and using it to shield us from view. And from there I see the three of them emerge out of the last ruined house we came through, stopping by the side of the road to look for us again. And they must catch sight of our feet underneath the wagon or something, cos at the same time they raise their guns again and shoot.

BANG. BANG.

At first there's the sound of the carthorse whinnying or squealing or screaming or whatever you call it. And when that noise finishes, the horse's legs crumple and it falls to the ground. The wagon smashes down on to the road and scrapes along.

'Jesper, quickly.' Carina pulls me the first few steps, directing us down a side street.

The three men race across the road towards the wagon, guns raised.

And that's when I see it. A house with an open door. I pull Carina inside and slam the door shut behind us.

Carina

We wait behind the door saying nothing in the gloom of the hallway. I try to stop myself from panting out loud as I get my breath back. We both listen, ears pressed to the door, and we hear their footsteps on the street outside. Though I can't see them, it sounds like they're hurrying on to the road, and then they stop. In my mind's eye I see them surveying the empty street, wondering how we disappeared.

Then I hear them speaking.

'Are you sure they came down here?' says a voice.

'I think so. I think we've lost them,' comes a second voice.

Beside me, Jesper's head swivels to look at the door. He has a strange look on his face.

'Well then, where are they?' asks a third.

There's no answer to that question. But from how clearly we could hear them, I know they're right outside the door of this house. Inside my chest, my heart thumps so hard I'm scared they'll hear it.

I hear the clack of footsteps once more, walking slowly, getting closer. I imagine them coming up to the door, barging it down and finding us. The footsteps get closer and closer, clacking on the road, every other noise in the world seeming to fade away. I'm sure they know we're here. I'm sure this door is about to be smashed from its hinges. I put my hand into my pocket and grip the gun.

The footsteps stop. Beside me, Jesper has the same terrified expression as the first time I saw him. His eyes dart between the door and my face.

'Let's take a look at the end of the road,' one of the voices says. 'If we don't see them, we'll go back and get the car. They won't get far.'

There's no answer, but almost straight away the footsteps start to move away. My heartbeat slows, and I start to think maybe we've done it. Maybe we're free. I take my hand off the gun.

I turn to look at Jesper.

But I see that he's looking at something else.

We're not alone.

Because a man has appeared out of another room and he's holding a pistol, aiming it at Jesper and me.

We both stand frozen to the spot.

'Who are you? What are you doing?'

Jesper stares at him, silent, and I wonder whether he understands what the old man's saying.

'There's nothing here to steal,' the man says, his finger moving over the trigger of the gun. 'We're just poor old people.'

'I'm sorry,' I say. 'We didn't come here to steal anything. There are men chasing us, men who want to kill us. We saw the open door and hid from them.'

'Who?' the man says.

'The Huber Corporation.'

'Who's that?'

'I don't know,' I say.

'Why are they after you?'

I point at Jesper. 'They want to kill him. They think he has a new type of Marsh Flu.'

Right away the man covers his mouth and nose with his free hand. He lowers the gun. 'Has he?'

I shake my head.

The man thinks for a second. He doesn't take his hand from his face. 'Get out of here,' he says, sounding scared and angry at the same time. 'Go now, before I change my mind and shoot you both.'

I reach for the door handle, looking nervously at the man and the gun which he holds down by his side. I open the door and start to back slowly out of the house, saying, 'We're going. Thank you.'

And Jesper follows, staring at the old man and the gun, hoping he's not going to pull the trigger.

As soon as we're outside, we look around to check the coast's clear and then we run, through the streets, through the town and out the other side without slowing down.

Blake

The priest – Father Frei – is wandering the streets near to the car when we reach it. He looks panicky. 'What on earth has happened?' he says. 'Where's Jesper?'

'We lost him,' I say. 'He's gone. Him and a girl.'

The priest nods. 'Carina Meyer.'

'We need to find them before anyone else does,' Huber says.

Frei looks suspicious. 'Who are you? What interest do you have in him?'

'We know the boy very well,' Henwood says. 'We run the institution he grew up in. But he ran away a few days ago. We've come to get him back. He isn't safe out there on his own.'

'What was he doing in the children's home?' Huber says.

'He was picked up by New Dawn patrols in the forest,' Father Frei says. 'They brought him to us.'

'New Dawn?' says Henwood. 'What do they know of the boy?'

'They're interested in him,' Father Frei says, turning pale. 'Commander Brune had asked us to keep him safe. He would be most angry if he knew the boy had escaped.'

'Then you shouldn't tell him,' Huber says.

Father Frei nods. 'True. But I need to find him quickly or Commander Brune will discover he's missing.'

Huber stands and thinks for a moment. 'Father, it seems we're both looking for the same thing. Perhaps we should cooperate.'

Father Frei nods. 'We have to bring Jesper back alive, though.'

Huber smiles. 'I wouldn't have it any other way. Do you know where they might be headed?'

Father Frei shrugs. 'They might make for the forest. It's where both of them were found. It's where the girl grew up. I'll bring Markus. He knows the forest as well as anyone.'

Huber nods. 'Come with us. Between us we'll find them.'

Carina

We don't stop until we're in the forest on the other side of town. Alone.

My lungs burn and my legs ache and my clothes feel heavy with sweat. But when I look over at Jesper, sitting on a log, he looks as though he's done nothing more than have a stroll.

'One of those men who was chasing us was The Voice,' he says. 'I recognised his voice when we were waiting in the house.'

'The Voice?'

He nods.

'Why was he chasing us then? I thought you said he looked after you. They were shooting at us. That's hardly looking after you, is it?'

He shakes his head. 'I watched him. He aimed his gun away from us. He's trying to help us. He was the one who set us free. He spoke to Father Liebling. He gave him this to help us ...'

He takes something from his pocket – a little black box which he swipes his finger across. The front of it lights up.

'What is it?'

'A scroll,' he says. 'It's like the one I had in My Place. It will show us the way to go.'

He stares at the screen, moving his finger across it. The machine is black and sleek and new – and on the front of it is a display which shows pictures and writing and maps. Whenever he runs his finger over it, the things on the screen move. I've never seen anything like it.

'He's sent messages,' Jesper says. 'Look.'

He holds it up for me to see. And there on the screen is writing:

Get out now. They're coming for you.

And:

Is there a problem? You need to get out NOW. They're coming into the building.

And:

You're free. I'll keep them away from you. Follow the arrows on the map. Head for the Low Countries, in the north-west. Find the Spirit of Resistance. I'll meet you there.

I sit down beside him on the log to get a closer look.

'Do you trust The Voice?'

Jesper nods immediately. 'Totally. More than anyone else in the world.'

After being shot at, I don't know I have as much faith as Jesper, but what I do know is that I'm free, for the first time in years. Nobody owns me. I'm out of St Jerome's. A smile breaks out across my face. This isn't exactly the way I dreamed of freedom, but it's freedom nonetheless.

I take the Spirit of Resistance leaflet from my pocket and read it and Jesper looks at it over my shoulder.

'That's the man I met at the town hall,' he says, pointing at the picture of Commander Brune.

'Yeah. He's the man the Resistance are fighting back against. The leader of New Dawn. The most evil man I've ever met. And I've met a few.'

'You know who the Spirit of Resistance are?'

I nod. 'My dad used to be a member. Before New Dawn killed him.'

Jesper says nothing, but I can tell that he's thinking.

'You know,' I say, 'we should keep walking. We need to get further away from the town.'

'Yeah.'

'The village I grew up in is an hour's walk north-west of here. We could head there and rest.'

Jesper gets up from the log, putting the machine with the screen away in his pocket. 'That works. The message says to head that way.'

Jesper

It feels good to be out of St Jerome's and back in the forest, free.

It's something I wouldn't have expected I'd think, but I feel better being surrounded by trees and grass and the river and the sound of squawks and the animals in the undergrowth than by the walls of St Jerome's. Even if the forest sounds sometimes make me jump out of my skin.

Only it isn't just the lurking animals that make me jumpy, is it? It's the thought of the men from Huber who want to kill me that makes me squizz ahead and behind and in the bushes and the trees, makes my ears listen out for the slightest noise. The whole time, I'm on alert; ready to run or fight or hide.

254

But we walk for ages and we don't see another human being, just squawks and hoppers. And from time to time I take the scroll from my pocket, looking to see we're still heading in the right direction, checking if I've missed a message from The Voice. And yeah, we are going the right way (and Carina's leading us to the village where she used to live anyway) and no, there aren't any new messages. So we yomp and the sun gets lower in the sky and the air gets colder.

And eventually we arrive somewhere, just as it's getting dark.

'This is my village,' Carina says, and she stops.

I stop too so I can squizz around. It looks like a bomb site, just like everywhere else – piles of rubble and fallen-down walls and trees and bushes starting to cover it all. There are faded signs everywhere, with that same circle symbol with three C shapes coming off it. And there isn't anyone here. Just us.

Carina walks slower and more careful than before, her eyes squizzing nervously around, like she's expecting to see something and it might not be good. And I get a sudden picture in my head of the man and his dog and the pile of bones I saw in the forest. We dodge around the heaps of fallen wall and the trees. And eventually Carina stops outside a building which isn't really a building at all any more – just a few bits of wood where the roof should be and some broken walls. She creeps inside and I follow her.

And inside it's a total mess. Nothing's the way it ought to be. Carina walks slowly around the building, fingers stroking against what remains of the walls, silent, like she's in some kind of dream.

'This was my house,' she says.

'*This?*'

She nods, still squizzing at the walls and the floor and up at the ceiling.

'That was my room,' she says, pointing off to a room that's still a room, almost, except for the fact that it has nothing in it and it has no door or ceiling. 'I shared it with my sister, Greta.'

I nod. I'm not sure what to say.

'That one over there was my parents' room,' she says. Then she wanders back over to where I'm standing, still looking like she's in a trance or a dream, only not a very happy one.

'What happened?' I ask.

'What do you mean?'

'What happened to your house? What happened to your family?'

She swings my bag off her back, sits down on the ground and sighs. 'When Marsh Flu struck, it went through towns fast.'

'Everyone in your village died of Marsh Flu?'

She shakes her head. 'A lot. Maybe half the people.'

'Did your family die because of Marsh Flu?'

She doesn't look at me, just gawps at a spot on the ground, like she's thinking. 'My mum died of Marsh Flu when I was eight. That left me and my dad and Greta.'

'And they survived?'

She nods, but then she changes her mind and shakes her head. 'They survived Marsh Flu. But not New Dawn.'

'What did New Dawn do?'

'When the meteorite hit and people started to die of Marsh Flu, the whole of Bohemia – the whole of Europe – fell apart. The government collapsed. So men with guns took their place – New Dawn. They took control by force. And because they had the cure for Marsh Flu, people let them.'

'What does that mean?'

'It means that they made everyone do what they told them to do, or they killed them. It means they took everything – things that weren't theirs. They made the world all over again, with them in charge.'

I nod.

'And one by one they took over all the villages and the towns and they recruited the people who said they supported New Dawn and gave them the vaccine to stop Marsh Flu. They killed all the ones that didn't.'

And I can't help but picture the men in my mind, the ones in the black uniform. New Dawn. Commander Brune.

'One day they came here and they killed everyone, including my father and Greta.'

'But not you.'

She shakes her head, squizzes right at me. 'No.'

'Why not you?'

She gawps back at the floor and for a while she doesn't say anything. 'At first I hid. Under a table. Over there.' She points across at another part of the building, at a spot where there isn't a table any more. 'And when I had a chance, I ran and I didn't look back.'

For a few moments I gawp at her, trying to imagine it all, trying to imagine how scared she must have been.

'Did you go and live in St Jerome's after that?'

She shakes her head. 'Not right away. I lived in the forest,' she says. 'I stole from abandoned houses. I learned to hunt and I hid from people. I was in the forest for more than a year, just me on my own. But I was hungry. New Dawn caught me stealing food from an abandoned house. They took me to the home.'

Carina shivers. She looks up at where the roof should be, at the empty space where we can see the sky. 'It's starting to get dark,' she says. 'It'll be cold soon. We should light a fire.'

We start looking around for wood.

Blake

We sit in darkness in the car.

'This is where New Dawn found her,' Father Frei says, from the back. 'Not more than a mile from where she lived with her family. It's worth a look.'

'OK,' Huber says. 'That sounds like a possibility.'

This is my fault – the place is on the route I told Jesper to follow. I didn't know the girl's village was on the way. I feel the scroll sitting in my pocket. I need to warn them.

'It sounds like a long shot to me,' I say. 'They won't be sightseeing – they'll be trying to get as far away as they can, surely.'

Huber sighs. 'We're here now, Blake. We should check it out. It won't take long. Father Frei could be right. He knows the girl best.'

I nod. And then I check no one's watching me, before slipping the scroll from my pocket.

Carina

The fire spits and crackles. Jesper and I stare into it. From time to time there are sounds from the forest which make us swivel and look out into the darkness, scared, wondering whether we've been found.

All of a sudden, Jesper sits upright and quickly takes the black machine from his pocket.

'What is it?'

The glare from the screen bathes his face in light as he stares at it. 'It's a message.'

I get up and walk around the fire, sit beside him and look at the screen.

We're nearing Carina's old village. Get away now.

Jesper and I exchange a glance. Then he stares out into the forest, through the holes in the walls of our old house. And in his eyes I see the flickering fire reflected. I see fear too.

'We should get our things together,' he says.

'OK. I know where we can hide.'

But before we're even on our feet, there's a sound coming through the trees. The engine of a car.

Jesper

The noise gets closer. We grab all our stuff and leap away from the glow of the fire, into the forest. Bright beams of light blast through the gaps between the trees, so bright it lights our way. Behind us, the engine gets louder. And I'm thinking that if we can see their lights, they must be able to see us too. But I don't look round to find out; I run as fast as I can into the forest, trying to pick a route that the car won't be able to follow.

I hear a change in the tone of the engine and I know it means the car's slowing down. Seconds later I hear the sound of doors opening.

And then …

BANG.

The gunshot sounds like it's breaking the night apart. I duck instinctively. My eyes scan the area ahead of us for somewhere to hide.

'That way,' Carina says, pointing.

Up ahead is a building. I glance across at Carina. She nods and we race for it.

Another *BANG* splits the air.

And this time Carina drops to the ground.

Cos she's been hit, hasn't she?

I bend low to scoop her up in my arms and head for the shelter of the building.

Inside I lay Carina down and I hear the gunshots continuing to explode outside.

'Are you all right?'

Carina nods. She holds her arm up, turns it so she can look at it. And I can just about see in the dim light that she's been hit on the arm. The bullet has torn her shirt. There's blood leaking into the material. But as she pulls the material away, I see all it's done is graze her skin.

'I'm OK.' She winces through the pain. 'We have to keep moving. I know a place they'll never find us.'

I nod. I peek through a hole in the wall and see five figures coming our way. The tall man from the Huber Corporation out in front, shooting his gun like he did back in the town. The man with the scar on his face beside him. The Voice follows, keeping his gun pointed down at the ground most of the time, only lifting it when the others are watching him. And behind them Father Frei, who doesn't look like he has a gun, cos he certainly isn't pointing any weapon. And with him, looking this way and that, searching for us and holding a handgun, is Markus.

And they're all heading this way.

Carina

I get to my feet, pushing the pain from my mind. 'Follow me,' I say.

Jesper nods and we're off, flinching as the gunshots get closer to the old bakery where we're hiding. We dodge through the rooms and then out of the back doorway on to some scrubby grassland.

We cross the grass and head for the doorway of what used to be my friend Maria's house. We slip inside unnoticed.

It's dark, mainly because the roof's still in place and so are the walls. We head through to the back room – what used to be the kitchen – and then towards the small square of roughly cut floorboards that I know is a trapdoor leading down to the basement. I lift it up and peer into the darkness where the steps descend.

'I have a torch,' Jesper says. And right away he searches through his bag until he finds it. He goes first, lighting the way, stepping cautiously, and as he gets into the basement, he shines the torch around the whole room.

I shut the trapdoor behind us, sealing us into the cellar.

Jesper

I flash the beam of my torch around the room and what I see makes me jump. Because over in the corner of the room there are bones. Right away I want to get out, to push the trapdoor open and run into the forest, even if it means being shot at again.

Only I don't; I pry as Carina walks right over to the bones. At first she just gawps at them like I am, and we both see that these bones aren't human ones, cos they're the wrong shapes. They're from an animal of some kind. Then Carina kneels down, reaches out and touches one of them. I stay where I am, shining the beam of the torch towards the bones, squizzing nervously, wondering what the hell she's doing. Carina picks up the skull and brings it close to her face. Her lips move as though she's saying something, but she must whisper it, cos I don't hear a word. She gently places it back on the pile.

'It's Michel,' she whispers, walking back over to me. 'My friend Maria lived in this house, until New Dawn shot her and her parents. Michel was her dog. He must have hidden here when New Dawn came. Looks like he starved to death.' As she stands next to me, I see her wince in pain again.

'Is your arm OK?'

She holds it in front of her so she can look at where the bullet hit. I aim the torch beam and see a dark brown stain on her shirt where blood has soaked through. The graze is pink and raw and sore-looking. It hasn't started to heal. It should have done by now, shouldn't it? The wound should have sealed over, the blood should have seeped back in, the skin should have mended. And I wonder if there's something wrong, whether the bullet had something on it to stop her from healing.

'You're not healing.'

Carina gives me a look like I'm saying something stupid. 'Of course I'm not. I've only just been shot.'

A distant noise makes us both jump. A gunshot. Neither of us says a word. And for a second neither of us moves. Only then I'm thinking that we should hide ourselves, in case someone finds the trapdoor and comes down here. And the only place that looks like we could hide down here is under the steps. I put my hand on Carina's arm and point towards the space beneath the stairs. She nods and we move silently over there. And then she grabs the torch from me and switches it off.

And everything's black.

I take the knife from my pocket and hold it, sharpest blade out. In case.

Up above there's another gunshot, then another. I fight the urge to switch the torch back on so I can see.

The next gunshot sounds louder and closer. I wonder what they're shooting at, whether they're just trying to scare us into coming out. And all we can do is wait in the dark, listening and hoping they don't come this way. Every passing second feels like an hour.

Quietness descends again and I'm thinking maybe they've decided they've lost us and they've gone. But more and more silent seconds pass, and still I daren't move. I hardly dare breathe.

Then I hear a thumping noise which sounds as if it's coming from somewhere in this house. And then footsteps.

The footsteps sound like they're going upstairs, searching for us. After a minute they come back down again. And now there are voices and I'm sure one of them's The Voice.

Suddenly, through the cracks in the ceiling, I see a beam of light searching around up there. Cos they're right above us, aren't they? I listen carefully, trying to understand what they're saying.

'*Was ist das?*' one voice says, and it's Father Frei.

'*Eine Tür,*' comes the reply. Markus.

Then silence. And I'm trying to work out what those words meant, what he was saying. Beside me, Carina shuffles nervously.

'*Wir sollten sie öffnen,*' Markus says.

'OK,' says The Voice.

Carina lets out a little gasp, before composing herself again.

Light starts to leak into the cellar as the trapdoor opens.

Carina

The staircase creaks as footsteps descend into the cellar. We're trapped.

A torch beam flashes around the room, lighting up one corner after another. I take the gun from my pocket, hold it in front of me, finger squeezed tight against the trigger. I might not be able to shoot them, but maybe I can make them believe I will. I watch the beam of light dance around the room. It comes to rest on Michel's bones. The beam rests there for some seconds before all of a sudden it turns and leaves the cellar. The footsteps creak hurriedly back up the stairs.

'Nothing in there,' comes Markus's voice from above. 'Only dust and bones.'

'You haven't looked properly,' Father Frei says. 'You didn't even go in there.'

'Give me that,' says another voice.

A feeling of terror grips me as heavier-sounding foot-steps start down the stairs, clacking with each step. I grip the gun with one hand and Jesper's arm with the other.

The footsteps reach the bottom of the stairs and stop and, as before, the beam of light searches the room. This time though, the search is more thorough, more methodical, lighting each part of the cellar in turn, and I know right away we won't escape unseen. The light continues to travel slowly around the room, inching closer and closer to where Jesper and I are huddled. A metre away. Seventy-five centimetres. Fifty. Twenty-five. Ten.

And then it's on us. The beam of light wavers briefly as the man jumps when he spots us. It's the one Jesper said is The Voice. He keeps the light shining on us, and for what feels like forever he stares right at Jesper. We stare back, cornered. I think of the gun in my pocket, unloaded and useless.

As I watch his face, I see a smile flicker there in the dim light. He brings his free hand to his lips, puts a finger there, as though he's shushing us. Then he turns and the beam of light moves away with him. His footsteps clack towards the stairs and then out of the cellar.

'The boy's right,' he says, when he's back in the room above us. 'No one down there.'

In another second the trapdoor crashes closed with a thud and we're plunged into darkness.

Jesper

The Voice saved us, didn't he?

He saw us but pretended we weren't there.

He looked after me, like he always has done. Like I knew he would.

We stand silent and motionless in the darkness after he's gone and I grip the knife tightly in my hand.

Cos although they're not in the cellar, they're still directly above us, walking about. They all speak over the top of each other's words. But I can hear The Voice saying they should move on, that they're wasting time.

And the door above the cellar stays closed. After a minute the voices and the footsteps fade away until we're left in silence.

A silence that goes on and on and on.

Cos Carina and I are both too scared to break it.

I don't know how much time passes like that, but it feels like hours. Eventually though, I figure we have to do something, cos we haven't heard anyone for ages, so I whisper to Carina, 'Do you think they've gone?'

She takes a while before she whispers back, 'I think so.'

And then I relax. Just a little though.

I close the blade of the knife, take the torch and wind the handle as quietly as I can and switch it on. When I squizz over at Carina, she still has a look of fear, big dark circles under her eyes. I squizz at her arm as well, at the stain on her shirt where the bullet hit her, still not healing.

'What should we do?'

She thinks for a moment. 'Stay here till morning.'

I nod. 'You look like you need some sleep.' I open the toggle of the bag and search through, take out the blanket and hand it to her. 'I'll keep watch in case they come back.'

She nods, then bends down and brushes the dust aside on the floor with her hand before lying down and covering herself with the blanket. Within seconds I hear her breathing change and I know she's asleep.

I take the scroll from my pocket and drag my finger across the screen, waking it. To my surprise, there's a message waiting; I didn't feel it vibrate this time.

You're safe for now. I'll lead them away.

And then, as Carina starts to whimper in her dreams, I squizz through the scroll to see whether I can learn anything that might help us.

Carina

'Carina, wake up,' Greta says, panic in her voice.

My eyes open right away. It's still night-time. The room is dark, lit only by the flickering candle Greta holds.

269

She leans over me, her face etched with fear.

'What is it?' I ask.

'New Dawn – they're coming. You have to get up now.'

A moment passes, frozen in fear, before I throw back my covers and jump out of bed. I scrabble around, pulling on shoes and a coat over my nightdress. Greta puts her arm round my shoulders and hurries me out of my room, grabs the bag that's been packed for days, guides me towards the front room, where Dad stands to one side of the front window, holding his gun to his chest, peering anxiously at what's happening outside. As we enter the room, he indicates with his hands that we should stay down, out of the way of the window. We do as we're told. As we get to him, he brings us close, wraps us in his arms.

'We need to leave,' he says. 'There are too many of them. They'll take the village tonight.'

From outside I hear screams and thuds and bangs and horses whinnying. The sky has an orange glow to it. The air smells of burning.

'We'll leave through the back,' Dad says. 'Head straight for the wagon.'

As we reach the kitchen, something crashes against the back door. We stop in our tracks. Before we have time to think, there's another crash and the door shakes. Dad looks around. He grabs me by the shoulders and pushes me to the floor, shoves me under the table. I'm too shocked and scared to struggle.

'Stay there. Don't speak,' he mouths to me.

I do as he says, peeking out as he pushes Greta behind the kitchen door, hiding her, before turning to the back door. He holds his gun up and takes aim.

Cowering under the table, all I can think is that I want Dad to hide too. But he doesn't.

For a second, everything's quiet and still.

Then suddenly the peace is shattered as something slams against the door again and this time the frame comes away from the wall. A second later the back door crashes to the floor in a cloud of dust. From my hiding place, I see black boots stomp into the kitchen.

Then I hear a BANG.

I want to scream in terror, but I hold it inside. I watch as one of the New Dawn militiamen in black boots falls to the floor. A puddle of blood pools out from him.

BANG.

My heart jumps.

There's a thump as another body falls. I almost don't want to look. But I force myself, and what I see is another New Dawn soldier slumped on the ground, his eyes lifeless.

Hope raises in my chest. Maybe Dad can shoot them all. Maybe he'll save us.

But there isn't time to think, because there are more black boots at the back door and right away there's another BANG.

Another body falls. Once again I force myself to look, hoping that it's another militiaman.

But what I see is Dad lying still and silent. Blood leaks from him, making a pool of its own, joining with the ones around the militiamen. I can't believe what I'm seeing. This can't be real. I must still be dreaming.

'No. Dad!' Greta shouts.

I want to scream too. I want to cry. I want to go and hold Dad, to hug him and make him better.

But I don't. I stay where I am, silent, watching the boots trample over the bodies and towards Greta's hiding place. I turn silently on the kitchen floor so I can see. I watch as they pull the door and grab Greta. She screams and I want to scream too.

I watch as one of the men – a man I now know is Commander Brune – points his gun at her, and I say a prayer in my head, praying this is a dream, that this will be over soon.

'No!' says a voice. 'Don't do that.'

Commander Brune lowers his gun as another man steps forward – a short round man, with a bald patch on the back of his head.

'She's young,' says the man with the bald patch. Father Frei. Although he isn't Father Frei – he's Officer Frei. 'Isn't there another way?'

Brune thinks for a second. He nods. 'Hold this,' he says, and he hands Officer Frei his gun. I say a silent, desperate prayer. Then he grabs Greta, and she screams again. He pulls at her night-dress, almost rips it from her body, and then he throws her to the ground. And from my hiding place under the table, I watch Greta sob as the man undoes his belt and then drops to the floor.

Jesper

I wind the torch twenty turns before switching it on and shining it at her. What I see is what she's been doing for the last couple of hours – twitching, flinching, writhing, squirming. I can't watch her suffer any longer.

'Wake up, Carina,' I say.

Except she doesn't wake up, does she? She carries on sobbing and moaning. And I don't know what to do. I don't know if she's all right or if it's something to do with the bullet wound that won't heal. 'Wake up.'

With a gasp, she opens her eyes and gawps right at me, her face filled with fear and confusion. 'Greta,' she says.

Only I don't understand what she means, do I?

'Are you OK?'

Carina says nothing. She continues gawping at me and then around at the darkness of the cellar, looking like she doesn't understand what's happening. She breathes deeply, rubbing her eyes. 'I was dreaming,' she says. 'A nightmare I have sometimes.'

'I get those. What was it about?'

'Something that happened a long time ago.' She squizzes into the darkness. 'The day New Dawn came to the village.'

'Did you see your family?'

She sighs. 'Sort of.'

Neither of us says anything more for a while. Carina touches the place where the bullet grazed her arm. She winces. 'How long was I asleep for?' she says eventually, yawning.

I take the scroll from my pocket and slide my finger across the screen to check the time. 'Three hours.'

'What time is it?'

'Four in the morning.'

'Did you hear anything in the night?'

I shake my head.

'You think they've gone?'

I nod. 'The Voice led them away from us.' I wind the torch again.

Carina nods. She thinks for a second. 'You ought to get some rest too, Jesper.'

I shake my head. 'I'm OK. We should get going before it gets light. I'll find somewhere to rest later.'

She doesn't argue. We grab everything and pack it all back in my bag. We climb the cellar stairs, trying to creep up without making a noise. And when we get towards the top, I gently push the trapdoor open. A little light leaks into the cellar. We wait for a second, half expecting someone to jump out, to aim a gun at us. But nothing happens, does it? So I push the door right open and we climb out of the cellar and into the house.

And a minute later we're in the forest, all alone, heading north-west.

We've walked non-stop for hours through the forest without seeing another person or a building. Tiredness and hunger are starting to overwhelm us, when we stumble across a road and a scattering of tumbledown buildings and we stop.

'Let's go and have a look,' Carina says. The first words she's said for ages. 'We might be able to rest there for a while. You could get some sleep.'

And I'm so tired that I don't disagree.

We creep cautiously up the road towards the buildings. And as we get closer, it's obvious it's another village – just as abandoned and wrecked as the last one. The same sign stands in front of the village.

'What does this mean?' I ask Carina.

'Do not enter. Contaminated area.'

'What does that mean?'

'Marsh Flu,' she says. 'When the disease hit and they cleared the towns and villages, New Dawn put these signs up. It was to stop Marsh Flu spreading. That's what they said anyway.'

I think of all the buildings I've been in and I feel uneasy. 'Doesn't that mean we could catch Marsh Flu if we go in there?'

Carina shakes her head. 'People carry the virus, not houses. Besides, you must have been given the vaccine when you arrived at St Jerome's – everyone is.'

We get to the doorway of a house and both squizz nervously around us. All we see are squawks in the trees and bushes. And in the building there's just dirt and leaves and nothing much.

So we walk inside, going from room to room. A kitchen and a bathroom and two bedrooms and a front room. No stairs. Some broken furniture. No Huber Corporation. No pile of bones. No mad old man with a gun.

But in the front room there's a sofa that's damp and covered in dirt and leaves, which I brush off and sit down on, and a chair, where Carina sits. It seems like a good place to rest – easy to keep watch through the front windows to see if anyone's coming.

'Get some sleep,' Carina says.

'Just a few hours,' I say, taking the scroll out of my pocket to check the time and the arrow on the map. 'Then we should get moving again.'

She nods.

I take the bag off my back, pull out the blanket and then the knife. I hold it out for Carina. 'Just in case,' I say.

She takes it and smiles. 'Of course.'

Carina

I have so many questions about him and no real answers. So while Jesper sleeps, I play detective and look through his bag, hoping it contains answers.

What I find doesn't exactly help to clear things up though.

Like the official papers he carries – a *Personalausweis* and health card, all stamped in Baden. The name on both of them isn't his, but says 'Kasper Hauser'; no mention of Jesper Hausmann anywhere. In the spaces for 'Father's name' and 'Mother's name' is the word 'unknown'.

No answers. Just more questions.

I wonder about the documents I was promised, the new life. When will I get them?

And then I think of the little black machine The Voice gave him. Maybe that holds the answers. Awkwardly I take the machine from his pocket, hoping he doesn't wake while I'm doing it.

The black machine feels sleek and light in my hands. It looks alien. The screen remains dark as I handle the machine and a thought crosses my mind that maybe it only obeys his touch. But then I think of the way he handles it, the things he does to make it light up and show different information. I swipe my finger across it, and sure enough the screen glows and fills with little pictures, each with English words under them: messages, map, settings, phone, contacts. In the background is the time – 2.13 p.m. I place my finger on the little picture of an envelope above the word 'messages'. Instantly the screen changes and the messages appear.

I read every last word, searching to find whatever he's keeping from me. But I find nothing. Either he's not hiding anything, or he can hide things much better than I can find them.

So I put his machine back. And then I sit on the sofa and keep guard, taking the gun from my pocket and checking the chamber even though I know it's empty.

Jesper

I wake to the smell of smoke. And when I open my eyes and sit up on the sofa something's missing, isn't it?

Carina.

A thought flashes through my mind: maybe they came while I slept and took her.

Except straight away I realise that wouldn't make sense. *I'm* the one they want, aren't I? Why leave me?

I get up to investigate. I decide to follow the smoke, creep over to the window and peek outside. And what I see is Carina, crouched in front of a fire, gawping into it. I join her.

'What are you doing?' I ask.

'I was bored and hungry. I caught us some food. You hungry?'

I nod and sit down beside her and soon enough I'm gawping at the fire too. I see that she's placed a big stone in it. She slaps some pieces of meat on the stone. The meat hisses as it cooks.

'Where did you get that?' I ask, as the air fills with delicious smells.

'I caught it.'

'What is it?'

'Rabbit.' She carefully turns one of the pieces of meat with the knife.

'A hopper?'

Carina raises an eyebrow before nodding. She turns over the other piece of meat.

'How did you catch it?'

'A bit of luck,' she says, 'and a trap.'

'A trap?'

She nods. 'My dad taught me. You dig a hole in the ground in the middle of a rabbit trail, cover it with sticks and then with leaves, so the rabbit doesn't realise there's a hole there. Then you wait for a rabbit to run across and fall in. Doesn't always work, but this time I was lucky.'

She leans towards the fire, lifts one piece of meat off the stone and passes it over to me. It's hot, burning my hands, so I rest it in my lap, waiting for it to cool a little before I pick it up again and bite into it. The taste is amazing – hot and smoky and juicy.

'There are easier ways to catch a rabbit,' she says, taking the other piece of meat from the stone, 'but I didn't have all the equipment to do them. I used to catch them this way when I lived alone in the forest. Sometimes I'd be lucky – like today – and other times I'd go for days without catching a thing.'

I nod. For a while we eat, both silent. 'How's your arm?' I ask her.

Carina stops eating to look at her arm for a second. And I see that it still hasn't healed. 'OK,' she says. 'It stings a bit, but it's nothing serious.'

I nod and then scoff the rest of my meat hungrily.

Carina

As soon as we're finished eating we put out the fire and gather our things. Jesper checks his little machine and we're off again, following the direction of the arrow on the map, heading for the Low Countries.

It isn't long before the sun's going down and the sky darkens, but we keep going. And although we talk a little and Jesper asks more questions about my family and what happened when the militia came, we walk most of the time in silence.

The full moon climbs in the night sky and then turns red. The forest starts to fill with the sounds of night-time – hooting and howling and the beating of bats' wings – and I'm thinking again about somewhere to rest.

After a while I spot light up through the trees.

'Jesper, look,' I hiss.

We stop, bend down low and we look ahead.

'A house,' Jesper says.

He's right. There's a house with lights blazing inside it. And beside that is a collection of buildings that look like barns and stores and farm buildings.

I'm just thinking about what we should do – whether we should take another path to stay away from the house or whether we should sneak over there and see if there's anything we could take – when Jesper stands up and beckons for me to follow him as he walks towards the building.

We step warily, eyes fixed ahead. Neither of us makes a sound.

We pass the barns and the fields, which seem to be empty except for a horse and a wagon. As we approach the house, Jesper turns to me and points at something beyond it. It's an empty blue car.

'We could take it,' I whisper.

Jesper nods and nervously approaches the building and I follow him, ducking down low, passing beneath the window. As I pass the window, I hear muffled voices from within. I try to work out what the voices are saying, but I can't.

Jesper reaches the car first and grabs one of the door handles at the front to open it. 'It's locked,' he says.

'Leave it to me,' I say. I take a hairgrip and put it in the lock. A few moments later, the lock clicks open and we're in.

'Do you know how to drive?' I ask Jesper.

He shakes his head.

'Me neither. It can't be that hard. We'll just have to figure it out.'

Jesper climbs in the side where the steering wheel is. And then he sits there, looking at the controls, looking confused. 'We need the keys to start it,' he says.

Jesper

The engine splutters into life as she turns whatever it is she put into the keyhole.

The thrums and vibrations of the engine disturb the sleepy stillness of the forest.

And the next thing that should happen is that the car's engine should roar even more as I turn the steering-wheel thing and we start driving, tearing along the road. But it doesn't. The engine runs, disturbing the forest, but the car stays where it is and I gawp helplessly at the controls.

'I don't know what to do,' I say.

'Well, try something,' Carina says, 'otherwise whoever's inside that house is going to come out.' And she turns her head to look at the house.

So I start trying things – buttons and levers and pedals and the steering wheel.

But still we don't move.

'Hurry up, Jesper.'

'You can try if you want,' I say.

'There's someone coming, Jesper. Hurry up.'

I turn to see someone leaning out of the window of the house, shouting something that I can't hear. He leans back inside, disappearing from view.

I have to make this thing work this instant.

And then I notice the lever down by my right hand. I try moving it forward.

The man comes running from the house and in his hand he's holding a gun. He points it and shoots. One of the back windows of the car explodes, showering us in broken glass.

'Let's go!' Carina shouts.

I push the pedal to the floor and all of a sudden the engine roars and the car lurches forward and we're skidding away from the house and along the road. I turn the steering wheel this way and that, avoiding the trees, trying to keep the car under control. But even though it's my actions that are making the car go, it feels like the car's pulling me along and I'm just about managing to cling on.

'He's not following us,' Carina says, turning round and gawping out of the broken back window. 'We're safe.'

We speed along, passing great open spaces on both sides of the road, away from the forest now. And as the engine roars, I think about the map. I take one hand off the wheel and get the scroll from my pocket.

'Have a look at the map,' I say, handing it to Carina. 'Check we're going in the right direction.'

The screen on the scroll lights up as Carina touches it. 'OK. Yeah. Keep going this way,' she says.

We drive in silence for ages and I start to feel more like I'm in control. The sun rises and the moon fades and then disappears as the sky brightens. Carina checks the scroll from time to time, making sure we're still travelling in the right direction.

After a while she offers to drive and I'm too tired to argue. At first when she takes over the engine shudders and rattles and the car lurches and leaps along. But soon enough she gets the hang of it and we're moving smoothly along the road again.

And when the scroll vibrates in my pocket, I wake the screen and see there's a message.

I've been tracking your progress – another day or two and I'll see you again. How are you making such fast progress?

I read the message twice before answering.

We have a car.

Almost immediately a message comes back:

Good. Watch out for New Dawn patrols – they'll be looking for you. Stay safe.

I read the message through a few times before flicking back to the map. The pin showing our position moves quickly as Carina speeds along the road. Heading north-west as always.

Blake

'We won't find him on our own,' Huber says. 'He could be anywhere by now.'

Henwood nods. 'We need to get the message out there, to get the general public looking for him.'

Huber shakes his head. 'We can't do that, Henwood. If we let the world know that Jesper is loose, Commander Brune will also know he's been lost.'

Father Frei clears his throat. 'You're right. That would serve neither your purpose nor mine.'

'There's another way of course,' Huber says.

'What's that?' I say.

'I'll speak with a friend of mine at the newspaper,' Huber says. 'We'll get the whole country looking for them as soon as they open their morning newspapers, without knowing what they're really looking for ...'

Jesper

It feels like we've been driving forever, past fields and forests and hills and mountains and rivers. We've driven right through the day and now it's night again.

And now, as the sky darkens once more, I really need to pee cos I've been holding it in for hours and I feel like I'm gonna burst any second.

'Can you stop the car?' I say to Carina.

So she does, by the side of the road. I fling the car door open, ignoring her question of 'What are you doing?' as I run over to a couple of trees and go behind them, facing away from the road. I start peeing and it's such a relief. While I'm doing that, I squizz around at the trees and the shadows and the bushes and everything. And that's when something catches my eye, a couple of steps away from me.

Carina

Jesper runs towards the car carrying something in his hands and looking like he's seen a ghost, and I figure that there's a problem. He jumps back into the car. 'Look,' he says, thrusting a piece of newspaper in my face.

It's a copy of the *West Bohemian*. On the front page is a picture of my face and above the picture is the headline: TEENAGE MURDERERS ON THE RUN.

I grab it from him. 'Oh no. This can't be. That isn't true.'

'What?' Jesper says, leaning over to look at the newspaper.

286

'The headline says I killed someone and now I'm on the run.'

'But ...'

I carry on reading. 'It says I ran away from St Jerome's, killed a rich businessman and stole his car. It doesn't say anything about you, just that I ran away with a male resident of the home.'

Jesper stares straight ahead, shaking his head. 'But why does it say that?'

I don't answer, because I'm reading on to see what else they're saying about me. 'It says I'm dangerous, that anyone who sees us should get in touch with New Dawn immediately. It even describes the car we're in – registration plate and everything.'

Jesper sighs and stares out of the window. 'Who's going to see this?'

'Everyone. It's the newspaper. There's a number for people to call if they have information.'

He doesn't say anything, but I can tell he's thinking things through, trying to make sense of it. I read the rest in my head.

Allegations have resurfaced that Carina Meyer, daughter of deceased Spirit of Resistance member Peter Meyer, also committed murder and burglary in and around her home village after being made an orphan ten years ago.

As I read, a shiver runs down my spine.

'So everyone's going to be searching for us?' Jesper says.

'For me, yeah.'

I fold the newspaper and stow it away in the storage pod in the car door and then start the engine again. We haven't travelled more than a couple of kilometres when we see a town up ahead. I slow the car. 'Shall we risk going through the town, which will be quicker? Or we could take a detour.'

Jesper takes his scroll machine out of his pocket and looks at the map, then looks up at the town ahead. 'It'll be a long way round if we go back. What do you think?'

He shows me the road we'd need to take, but my head's reeling from the newspaper story too much to even think straight.

'We'll be through the town in a couple of minutes,' I say. 'It's night-time – no one's going to see us.'

He nods. 'Let's do it.'

Jesper

I stay low in my seat (so no one can see me) but as we speed through the town streets, it's clear no one else is around. All the houses are shut up for the night with the shutters drawn across the windows. We're out the other side of town in two minutes, according to the time on the scroll.

I rub my hands over my face. Neither of us has slept properly for days, just the odd hour here and there – and all the time dreaming that while I slept someone would come and find us – and sometimes a few minutes in the car when Carina was driving and my eyes closed and I was asleep before I knew it, only to be jolted awake again by a bump in the road.

'We should find somewhere to stop soon,' I say. 'We're both tired. We need to sleep.'

Carina shakes her head, eyes fixed on the road ahead. 'We're too close to the town. It's not safe. We should keep going. Another hour. It'll be safer to rest then.'

And I don't say anything, cos maybe she's right. Instead I look out of the car window, a heavy feeling in my eyelids, trying to stop them from closing.

I wake up when I feel an elbow in my ribs, and right away I squizz around to see what's going on. I'm in the car, Carina beside me. The sky's still dark. And the car's slowing down and then stopping. The reason is up ahead: cos a car's parked right across the road, completely blocking our way. Beside it stand two men in black uniforms. New Dawn. They're aiming their guns straight at us.

This isn't good news, is it?

'What do we do now?'

'I don't know,' Carina replies. 'Do nothing. Stay calm. Let them make the first move.'

So I do exactly as she says, breathing deeply as I gawp at the men yomping towards us with their guns pointed our way the whole time. One of them aims his gun downwards a little, like he's pointing it at the ground in front of him. There's a CRACK and a puff of smoke and Carina's side of the car collapses. He points the gun again, there's another CRACK and another puff of smoke, and my side collapses too. And I figure he must have shot out the tyres so we can't drive off.

The men each come round one side of the car, to the doors – one to my door and one to Carina's. All the while their guns are fixed on us. The man at my door shouts something in German. Only I don't understand what it means. I watch Carina, see her hide something in her boot. Then she opens her door and gets out, hands raised, and I figure I should do the same.

The men gawp at Carina for a while, before one of them says, 'Carina Meyer?'

She shakes her head.

The man shakes his head, spits on the ground. '*Lügnerin*,' he says. '*Das Foto ist in der Zeitung.*'

And then, as one of the men keeps his gun trained on us, the one closest to me searches us, patting us down, taking my knife and bag away. But he doesn't find my scroll, does he? Cos it's too close to my privates and he doesn't search there.

'*Geh zu unserem Auto*,' he says, poking his gun in my ribs. The other militiaman does the same to Carina, and I see her start walking to their car, so I do the same.

And as we wait in the back of the car, the man who isn't in the driving seat picks up a device from the dashboard and speaks into it. *'Wir haben Carina Meyer und den Jungen … Kaspar Hauser.'*

When their car's moving and we're getting rattled around in the back and neither of the men are prying at us, the first thing I do is I squizz at Carina.

She looks back at me and starts moving her eyes, nodding towards my hands, and then making a little movement with her own, trying to show me something. One hand flat, the other curled into a fist, except for the first finger, which she pretends to kind of slide across the flat hand. Once. Twice. Three times. Only I don't understand what she's trying to tell me. So I look straight at her and I silently make the word 'What?' with my mouth.

She quickly squizzes at the front of the car, checking they're not prying at her, and when she's happy they aren't, she mouths the words, 'Your machine.'

I nod. I should have known. The scroll.

Straight away I reach my hand in my pocket, grab the scroll and slowly, slowly, slowly take it from my pocket. Right away, Carina reaches over and grabs it and I watch as she holds it out of sight of the men and she starts to send a message:

We've been captured by New Dawn. They're taking us to the station. Please help.

Blake

Henwood drives us from village to village, from town to town, all of them deserted. Each time it's the same: we search the place, guns at the ready, but all we find are piles of bones, dust, crumbling buildings. Every move is informed by nothing more than a hunch – sometimes from Huber or Henwood and sometimes from the priest, Father Frei, who seems even more desperate than Huber to locate the boy. But the truth is, with each search we're getting further and further away from them. Or they're getting further and further away from us. We've lost them. We have no information about their whereabouts.

Or at least, Huber and Henwood and Frei have no information. I know precisely where they are at any given moment.

In their ignorance, and with my help, Henwood and Huber are taking us round in circles. So it is that we pull off the road near another deserted town (Gugendorf) where Jesper and Carina won't be found, and we're back to where we started, no more than a few kilometres from Schweilszeldorf, where I found Jesper's coat.

The town bears the same hallmarks as all the others we've searched – bombed and fire-damaged buildings being reclaimed by the forest, warning signs, cracked roads. No sign of any people.

But Huber and Henwood and the two goons from the orphanage don't know that. They creep about the place, nerves on edge, guns loaded, ready to blow anything that moves to pieces. I pretend to do the same. I creep around, checking gaps between buildings, gun held out in front of me.

The first chance I get, I slip inside a house, out of sight of the others. I go straight to the most out-of-the-way part of the house I can, which turns out to be the back room, and I take the scroll from my pocket.

It vibrated some time ago, as we drove through the forest, when I couldn't take it out to check. I run my finger across the screen and it lights up. Immediately a message icon pops up. A message from Jesper.

My heartbeat quickens.

They've been found. New Dawn have them and they're on their way to the station. I check the map and see they're heading for a town called Dunkelstadt.

I have to get away from Huber and Henwood now.

I check that I have enough bullets in the clip of my gun and snap it back into place. I edge my way out of the building with my gun held in front of me. And now my heart's racing, my palms are sweaty, my eyes dart around to check I'm not being watched. I'm ready to shoot anyone who gets in my way. I make it to the doorway of the building and look around the deserted streets, checking the coast is clear.

I hurry back through town towards the car and there's no sign of the others. They must be caught up in searching. I reach the car and open the driver's door, see that the keys are in the ignition. I turn the key and start the car. I throw it into reverse and put my foot down, skidding the car around.

When I look out of the front windscreen, I see Henwood in front of me, standing in the car's path.

'What are you doing?' he shouts.

I rev the engine in answer.

'Stop, or I'll shoot!' he shouts.

But I have no intention of stopping. I take my foot off the brake, accelerate and speed away.

Henwood aims his gun and shoots at the car. *BANG*. The side window shatters and falls on to the passenger seat.

I duck, steering the car towards the road, still accelerating. Then another shot: *BANG*.

This time the car jerks and collapses on the passenger side. He's hit the tyre.

I don't stop though. I keep my foot on the accelerator, keep low as the car bumps along, away from Gugendorf, leaving his gunshots in the distance.

Carina

They take us to Dunkelstadt, to the old town hall – New Dawn's headquarters in the town. Huge letters spell out the word '*RATHAUS*' in the stone above the doorway.

Jesper and I shuffle wordlessly through the entrance hall, beside the officers, whose footsteps click and clack and echo around under the high ceiling. At the end of the hallway we're taken to a desk, behind which sits a large red-faced man with small round glasses that have to stretch to fit his face. He wears a New Dawn uniform. He raises an eyebrow disdainfully as we approach.

'I called the number in the newspaper,' he says to the officers. 'They're on their way. It's the boy they're really after. The girl doesn't interest them. Take her to the cells. Do as you like with her.'

Immediately the officers march me away, through double doors and then a maze of unlit corridors. We stop outside a green door which the officer unlocks. He shoves me into a room, closing and locking the door before I've even recovered my balance.

The cell has a row of dirty, uncomfortable-looking beds, and bars across the single window at the end. I notice with a start, that I'm not alone in here. There's a woman sitting on one of the beds, rocking backwards and forwards, muttering something to herself under her breath, playing with something in her hands that I think must be rosary beads. As I watch her finger the beads, I see she has no fingernails, just sore red patches where they should be. How did that happen? Did she do that to herself, or did the militia do it to her?

Whatever the answer, I decide right away that I'm taking a bed as far away from her as I can.

I choose the one nearest the door – furthest from the mad lady – and sit, trying to ignore her. Fortunately she ignores me too. The words of the guard rattle around my brain: '*Do as you like with the girl …*' It doesn't need a genius to work out what that means. It means what Commander Brune and Officer Frei did to Greta before they shot her. It's what they'll do to me.

And there's nothing I can do to stop them, is there? I mean, I have a gun – they didn't search me thoroughly and didn't find it in my boot. But what use is a gun without any bullets?

I try thinking about Jesper instead, about what they're doing to him right now. Maybe they've already handed him over to the Huber Corporation. Maybe they already have their bounty. He could already be dead.

Maybe I'll never even find out what happens to him.

Unless I do something about this situation.

Blake

The faded sign for the village of Schweilszeldorf comes into view as I bump along the road. I steer the car on to the road-side and leave it hidden amongst the trees and bushes, taking everything that might be of use.

I run to the spot where I left the van a few days ago and get in. I start the engine, check my scroll for directions to Dunkelstadt and drive.

Jesper

They leave me alone in a small room with a locked door and a bed. And although it's night-time and I'm tired, I don't go to sleep, do I? There are too many things going through my mind. I'm scared. And I hear noises coming from somewhere. Shouting. Screaming. Crying.

I try as hard as I can to block the sounds out, to sit on the bed trying to deal with the millions of thoughts and questions flying through my mind. But it doesn't work, and every time someone shouts or screams I flinch.

And it's a while after the sun's come up when I hear a different sound that makes me think something's about to happen – movement outside the room – footsteps and keys.

The door opens and in walk two guards dressed in the black uniform of New Dawn.

They say something to me in German, and before I can even try to think what it means, they grab me by the arms and take me from the room, locking it behind us.

We travel along a corridor, past rows of identical doors. And from behind the doors I hear the screams and cries and shouts and I wonder what's going on in those rooms and whether that'll be me in a minute.

We stop by a door. One of the guards lets go of me to unlock it. And my guts knot themselves up.

The door swings open and I'm pushed inside …

… into a room where a man sits alone behind a table. It's the third man from Huber, isn't it?

The Voice.

'*Du hast fünf minuten,*' one of the guards says. And then he slams the door closed and locks it.

For a moment I gawp at the man in front of me and he gawps back. And even though I'm relieved, there's still a knot in my stomach.

'Jesper, it's so good to see you,' he says.

And it's his voice.

He *is* The Voice. There's no doubt in my mind. And he's here. He's an actual person. A real thing. Not just a voice. All that time I lived in My Place and he was just a voice, I never even imagined what he looked like.

My mind fills with all the thoughts and feelings and questions I've been carrying around since he left me in the forest, all the things I've been wanting to ask him.

Only when I go to open my mouth and speak, nothing comes out.

He smiles at me. 'How are you? You look well.'

I nod. I open my mouth to speak again, and this time I manage to croak out a question. 'What's happening? Why did you take me from My Place?'

And before he replies he takes a deep breath and then slowly blows it out. 'I had no choice, Jesper. You were in danger. They were going to kill you. I had to get you out of there for your own safety.'

'Who? Who was going to kill me?'

'The Huber Corporation. Let me explain. They run what you call My Place, Jesper. You'd reached the end of your usefulness to them, so they were going to end your life. They were going to kill you. I couldn't stand by and watch that happen, so I set you free.'

'But you left me in the woods. I could have died.'

He shakes his head. 'I didn't just leave you in the woods though. I'd been preparing you for months. I showed you clips on The Screen which I knew would help you survive in the forest.'

I nod. Cos that's true, isn't it?

'And I tracked your movement as you walked through the forest, until you lost your tracking chip.'

'But I still don't understand why they want to kill me.'

'It's too complicated to go into here and now, Jesper. We don't have time. But you're related to the original carriers of Marsh Flu. You were held in the Huber facility – My Place – for research purposes. Huber developed a vaccine against Marsh Flu. But recently a new form of the disease has been

299

spreading. Huber fear that it will be traced back to them, so they decided to destroy any evidence that could incriminate them. And that includes you.'

I say nothing. I let the information sink in, try to make sense of it. But I think of the boy in the bed beside mine at St Jerome's, how he died not long after I arrived there. 'Do I carry the disease?'

The Voice shakes his head. 'No.'

'Then why do they want to kill me?'

He sighs.

I hear keys rattle outside the room.

The Voice squizzes over at the door and then back at me. 'We don't have time to discuss this right now, Jesper. It's complicated.'

And before he says any more, the door opens and the guards step into the room.

Carina

A militiaman collects me from the room and I can't help but feel dread about what might happen next.

He walks me through the corridors – dark green paint peeling from the walls, pictures mouldering in their frames, the windows high up on one wall casting dim light and shadows

300

around. We pass armed officers at every door. They look me up and down as I shuffle past, making me nervous about who wants me and what their intentions are. I put my hand in my pocket and feel the gun, for reassurance.

Eventually we stop in front of a door – identical to all the others. My hands go clammy as the guard puts the key in the lock. When the door's open, he jabs me in the back with his gun to make me move.

What I'm expecting on the other side of the door isn't what I see at all. Because sitting around a big wooden table are Jesper, the red-faced militiaman from the front desk and the man Jesper calls The Voice.

'Sit,' the guard orders.

So I do.

Jesper looks across the table at me. He looks confused. I'm confused too, but I smile at him.

'You say you know this young man and this young lady,' the militiaman says in German to The Voice.

'Yes,' The Voice answers in German. 'Kasper Hauser is my son.'

The militiaman looks at the identity card, the one I found in Jesper's bag. He raises an eyebrow as he looks back at The Voice. 'This says "father unknown".'

The Voice nods. 'I realise that. There was a time of great turmoil when he was born and he was taken from me. He ended up in a home. We need to get his papers corrected. But as you know, that isn't easy …'

The militiaman looks anything but convinced. 'And the girl?'

'My niece. Stefanie Hauser.'

The militiaman takes another long deep breath. He knows this isn't true. He caresses his red flabby cheeks with his right hand as he thinks. 'Why doesn't she have any papers?'

'I have her papers here.' The Voice lifts a black leather briefcase on to the table and clicks it open. He reaches inside and brings out a pile of papers, which he places on the table.

The militiaman leafs through them, then pauses to give me a searching look. When he's done, he pushes the papers back into the centre of the table. He looks at The Voice with a raised eyebrow and the room is silent.

'I'd be grateful if I could take my relatives home now,' The Voice says.

The militiaman doesn't say anything in response. Instead he lays a newspaper down on the table. A different newspaper from the one Jesper and I found, but the same pictures stare out from its cover along with a similar made-up headline. 'Mr Blake, the young lady looks a lot like the girl in the newspaper, would you not agree?'

The Voice glances at the paper. He shakes his head. 'This is a different girl.'

The militiaman frowns. 'Really? The similarities are remarkable, don't you think? Her appearance. The fact that we stopped her in the same car reported here. The fact that she is with a male accomplice.'

I glance at Jesper. His eyes dart from person to person, confused and nervous.

'I've given you official documents proving these children are who I say they are,' The Voice says. 'I'm their father and uncle respectively. Let them come with me. They haven't committed any crime.'

'They were in a stolen car.'

'True. But I'm more than willing to pay any fines they might have incurred ...' The Voice says, reaching for his briefcase again.

'It isn't that simple. There's a bounty out for the return of these children. Twenty thousand crowns. I've already called the number to report them.'

The Voice stares back at him. 'Have you?'

The red-faced man nods.

'I can pay. How much is the reward?'

The militiaman takes his glasses off and rubs his eyes. 'Mr Blake, you must understand that this isn't possible. These young people are wanted in relation to very serious crimes. Murder. Theft. I can't simply hand them to you.'

The Voice – Mr Blake – squirms a little in his seat. 'You and I both know there's every likelihood the crimes these children are accused of are purely fictional.'

I try not to catch anyone's eye.

'There are people from the Huber Corporation on their way here at this very second –' the red-faced man says.

'They can't be handed over to those men. They'll be killed.'

The militiaman puts his glasses back on his face, shrugging. 'This changes nothing. As I have said, I can't simply hand them over to you.'

The Voice sighs. 'Maybe you can be persuaded.'

'Perhaps. You can try to convince me at least.'

'I can offer you twenty thousand.'

The militiaman sighs. 'Huber are offering me twenty thousand ... If I hand them to you, there'll be complications for me. I'll have to lie about what happened. Either I'll have to say you broke them out of here or that we were mistaken about their identity in the first place. I'll need compensating for the inconvenience and for the loss of my reputation.'

The Voice raises his eyebrows, thinking. Then, slowly, he nods. 'OK. I'm willing to pay twenty-five thousand.'

'Thirty and we're closer to a deal ...' says the militiaman, face set hard, unmoving.

The Voice thinks for a second. 'OK, thirty it is.'

The militiaman's face is split by a smile as he gets to his feet and leans across the table to shake hands. 'You shouldn't delay your departure,' he says. 'The Huber Corporation will be here soon.'

Jesper

One second they're all talking German and I don't know what's happening and the next they're getting out of their chairs and I still don't know what's going on.

As everyone heads towards the door, Carina comes over and stands by my side. 'We're free,' she whispers in English. 'He's paying them thirty thousand crowns to let us go.'

Before I get a chance to reply, we're moving out of the room, through the corridors, back to the desk where they took my bag last night. And The Voice stands there, smiles at me, before checking his watch. He takes some thick envelopes out of his bag and hands them to the red-faced officer.

The officer takes them, stuffs them in his pockets and nods. They speak to each other in German as the officer hands back my bag.

'We have to leave immediately,' The Voice says.

Right away we're rushing across the hallway, The Voice's feet clacking and mine and Carina's shuffling on the stone floor as we run for the doors.

Outside, the wind's cold and biting. The Voice leads us down the steps and then along the pavement, dodging in and out of people going about their business. And I notice that all the time he has a gun held in his right hand and I wonder whether I should get my knife out of the bag. We stop in front of a black van.

'Get in. It's best if you two ride in the back,' The Voice says. 'There's a sheet you can cover yourselves with so no one'll see you. Be careful of the freezer.'

As soon as we're in, the door slides closed behind us. The same sliding metal sound I heard when I was left in the forest.

A second later and the engine starts with a splutter, the van *RRRRRRRRRRR*s into action and we start moving.

Carina and I are thrown around as we zoom along. I hold on to a handle on the side of the van and look out of the back window, cos it turns out that when you're inside, you can see out through it even though it doesn't look like a window from the outside.

Carina nudges me. 'There's a car.'

And she's right. It's behind the van, following. We both know what this means. We travelled for days and didn't see another person or a car. Not until we were stopped. And this one that's behind us looks just like the one we saw before, when we first escaped from St Jerome's – same shape, same sign on the front, same blacked-out windows so we can't see who's inside.

'It's them, isn't it? Huber?'

I nod and then I bang on the metal where it separates the front of the van from the back. 'They're following us,' I shout to The Voice. 'Huber.'

He doesn't reply, but immediately the engine *RRRRRRRR-RRRR*s louder. The van picks up speed, turning this way and that, throwing Carina and me around.

I grip the handle tightly, crouching so I can squizz out of the back window. Buildings and trees flash past, faster and faster, until they're nothing but a blur. We take sharp turns – left and right and left and right – zooming along small side streets. And all the time the other car is right behind us – sometimes closer, sometimes further back, but always following.

We speed past the edge of the town and out into countryside. Trees and grass and fields flash past. And the black car stays directly behind us, watching us, just waiting for us to stop.

And then a hand holding a gun appears out of the car's side window.

BANG.

Carina and I duck down, exchanging a glance. And I know she's thinking the same thing as me: there's no way we're gonna get away from them.

Carina

Jesper and I are rolled around the back of the van as The Voice drives faster and faster, taking turns at the last minute, trying to throw the black car off the trail.

We're not the only things being thrown around, because on the floor of the van I spot something. Two small metallic cylinders. Bullets. I pick them up from the floor and put them in my pocket.

And when I look out of the back window again, I see the black car easily matches our every burst of speed and sharp turn. All the time they're shooting at us, hitting the road and the body of the van. As I'm thinking that I should load the bullets into the gun and shoot back, something happens that I'm not expecting. The van turns so suddenly and violently that Jesper and I are thrown against the metal sides. The ground beneath us suddenly feels bumpy instead of smooth. And out of the back window I see why: we've steered off the road, across grass and mud towards the forest. The van bumps along, throwing us up and down and from side to side.

Above the bumping and the engine noise, The Voice shouts in English from the front of the van, 'I'll stop in thirty seconds. As soon as I do, run for the cover of the trees and don't stop.'

I look out of the window, see that the black car's struggling to get across the mud and past the trees, and I start to think maybe we can do this. On roads the car might be better, but out here in the forest, it's slowing.

Jesper and I look at each other. He's gripping that knife for dear life.

'Are you ready?' he says.

I nod. 'Stick together.'

There's another shout from the front of the van – 'NOW!' – and then the van skids round and stops.

Jesper gets his hand on the door handle first, turns and pulls it to the side and the door slides open. In less than a second we're out and we're running.

Jesper

We don't take a moment even to look around. The three of us run as fast as we can.

As I head for the trees, I hear the door of the black car open and people running, shouting in German. A gunshot splits the air and a bullet whistles past, thudding into a tree, making all the squawks in the trees flap their wings as they take to the sky.

But we don't stop. We dodge around trees, using them as cover so we're not easy targets. And even though running comes easier to me than to The Voice or Carina, we're managing to get away from them.

Within a couple of minutes there's a gap between us and the men from the car. The Voice dodges behind a tree, taking shelter. Carina and I do the same. He squizzes back at the men running through the woods – the two men from Huber, Father Frei and Markus – and he takes aim and shoots.

CRACK.

The bullet whizzes through the air, missing everyone. And right away he shoots again.

CRACK.

This time the bullet hits a tree and bits of bark and wood fly off.

The men dodge for cover, hiding behind trees. And then they return fire.

BANG BANG BANG BANG …

The forest fills with the sound of gunshots flying back and forth, hitting no one but emptying the forest of squawks and hoppers and bushtails.

Until suddenly the gunshots stop and the forest is eerily quiet.

'They're reloading,' The Voice says. 'Quick, let's make a move.' He aims his gun one more time – *CRACK* – and then we're running again. As we run, I squizz over my shoulder and see the men are running again too, fiddling with their guns as they go. And as I watch, I see Markus stop, see him lift his hands, pointing his gun, aiming.

BANG.

It happens slowly and silently like in a clip on The Screen. The bullet fizzes through the air and thwacks high up into The Voice's leg. And I'm powerless to do anything, except gawp as his leg gives way and he collapses to the ground.

Carina

In no time at all there's blood everywhere, soaking into the leaves. Jesper leans over The Voice, looking like he's in shock.

Bullets continue to fly past us.

'Go. Save yourselves,' The Voice says. 'Don't wait for me.'

I turn to see the four men all holding guns in front of them as they run towards us, firing off shots. The Voice is right. The only way is for me and Jesper to run, to try to save ourselves.

'Come on, Jesper. We have to go.'

Jesper looks back at the men, then down at The Voice. He bends low, picks The Voice up and hoists him on to his shoulders. I stare, because it shouldn't be possible for Jesper to lift him at all, let alone make it seem that easy.

'Grab his bag,' Jesper says to me.

I do as he says and then we run. And somehow Jesper runs just as smoothly as before, as though he's carrying nothing heavier than a rucksack on his back. I have to sprint to keep up with him, and we run deeper and deeper into the forest.

Behind us, the men call out in English:

'Stop, Jesper, it's useless; there's no way you can outrun us.'

And: 'Stop. I'll shoot.'

Another flurry of bullets flies through the forest, missing us. But it can only be a matter of time until one hits me or Jesper. We have to get away from them.

So I just concentrate on running, ignoring the sick feeling that's building in my stomach.

Jesper

We run on and on, not stopping, not looking around. It isn't until the sound of gunshots has stopped that I chance a squizz over my shoulder and I see they're not even in sight.

We've lost them completely.

I can feel from the way The Voice is bleeding on me that he's not healing. His wound needs attention. So when Carina spots a cluster of buildings, we hurry to the closest and take him inside. I bend to my knees, carefully lowering him to the floor. He groans and grimaces as I lie him down.

All the time, I feel Carina's eyes on me. 'How did you do that?' she says, putting The Voice's bag down next to him. 'How did you run like that with a man on your back?'

Only right now there are more important things than how fast I can run, aren't there?

The Voice tries to sit up.

'What do we do? His leg's not mending itself.'

Carina kneels beside me, gawping at the wound. 'We have to stop the bleeding. We can use clothing to make a tourniquet.'

And I remember the way she tried to heal my wounds, ripping clothes into strips and tying them tight. I unbutton my shirt, which already has The Voice's blood soaked into it at the shoulders anyway, and hand it to her. She gets to work, wrapping strips of material around The Voice's thigh, above where the bullet hit him, where there's a big gaping fleshy hole and the blood's leaking out. And when she's wrapped it around, she pulls it so tight that it looks like it's gotta hurt. The Voice grits his teeth, breathing through the pain.

And then there's a moment of stillness in the room, even if there isn't one in my head. The Voice struggles to sit up, wincing in pain as he puts pressure on his leg. I search through my bag, find my bottle and offer him the last of my water. He nods as he takes the bottle and then he drinks deep.

'Thank you, Jesper,' he says. 'You saved me. They'd have killed me if it wasn't for you.'

I say nothing. But I'm thinking that maybe they've already done the killing, he just hasn't died yet.

'And I realise you're owed an explanation,' he says. 'You need to know who you are.'

I gawp at him. I know who I am. I'm Jesper. My guts twist themselves around in knots inside my stomach.

'We don't have time,' Carina says. 'They'll be coming after us ...'

'He deserves the truth,' The Voice says.

I nod. 'I want to hear this. They're miles behind us.'

And while Carina raises her eyebrows, The Voice takes a deep breath which sounds like an effort and then speaks. 'Until two weeks ago, you'd spent your whole life locked away in the Huber Corporation facility – a medical research base. Your official name was Boy 23. But the name by which I knew you and you knew yourself was Jesper Haus-mann.'

I feel Carina's impatient gawp, but I just concentrate on what The Voice is saying.

'As far as you knew, you didn't have parents,' he goes on.

I nod.

'Jesper, you need to know, you have a mother and a father.'

Something like a jolt of electricity zaps through my body. I don't know what to say. I don't believe it. Cos I *don't* have a mum or dad, do I? I gawp at The Voice, trying to understand what he just said.

'Your biological mother is called Hanne.'

Why is he saying this? It's impossible. 'I really have a mother?'

He nods slowly.

And The Voice doesn't tell lies, does he? He looks after me, helps me, guides me. Only now he's telling me that I have a mum and a dad. 'Where is she then? Show me her.'

And that's when his face changes, when he grimaces, and I'm not sure if it's because of the pain or something else. 'It isn't as straightforward as that,' he says, not meeting my eye. 'Your mother was in Huber, just like you. She was a research subject too.'

'Research subject?' Carina says.

The Voice sighs again, and this time I'm sure it isn't cos of the pain. At least not in his leg. He nods. 'There's no easy way to say this. Your mother isn't the same as everyone else.'

314

'What does that mean?' Carina asks.

'Twenty years ago something fell to Earth out in the forest, close to Fredelburg.'

Carina nods. 'Yeah, everyone knows that. The meteorite which wiped out whole villages and towns and brought Marsh Flu.'

'Yes and no, Carina,' The Voice says. 'What you say is what was reported, but the reality was somewhat different. There is a truth which has been kept secret.'

Carina raises a disbelieving eyebrow. 'What?'

'What landed in the forest was a craft. A star voyager from another planet. Carrying life forms. It caused the damage which you can still see in the forest, which was attributed to a meteorite.'

Carina shakes her head. 'I've heard that story before,' she says. 'But it's just a conspiracy theory.'

Blake shakes his head. 'No, Carina, it's true. Jesper's mother and others like her were aboard. We named them the Sumchen.'

Carina says nothing.

'Fourteen Sumchen survived the impact. Six male. Eight female,' The Voice goes on. 'Physically there was almost no difference between Sumchen and humans, certainly not at a glance.'

Carina's expression becomes a knot of lines as she screws her face up. 'Prove it.'

'You have the proof in front of you, Carina,' he says, pointing at me.

And Carina doesn't answer that, does she?

'The specimens were kept secret from the world. The story about the meteorite was put out to explain the crash.'

Carina makes another noise like she doesn't believe it.

'The specimens were taken away for examination. And we didn't realise it at the time, but one of the Sumchen women carried Marsh Flu – the original strain of it – to Earth. It didn't affect her or the other Sumchen because their bodies had developed resistance to it over millions of years. But to the people of Earth, who'd never come into contact with the disease, it was contagious and deadly. People began to die and Bohemia, and then all of Europe, became unstable. Governments toppled. Others seized power.'

'New Dawn,' Carina says.

Blake nods. 'Exactly. Neither New Dawn nor the Huber Corporation wished the world to know that they'd harboured the hosts of a deadly new disease. So the outbreak of Marsh Flu was put down to the meteorite people believed had landed in Fredelburg.'

And the look on Carina's face has changed. She listens, nods. She believes what The Voice is saying.

'New Dawn instructed Huber to work on a vaccine. And so we did, successfully. But when the vaccine was finished, New Dawn used it like a weapon – they spread panic amongst the population and then withheld the vaccine from their political opponents, strengthening their own position of power. It made New Dawn and Huber incredibly rich.'

The Voice pauses and closes his eyes for a second. He's in pain, isn't he? He's dying.

'The Huber Corporation were instructed by New Dawn to destroy all evidence of Sumchen and Marsh Flu once the vaccine was discovered. But that didn't happen. Huber had observed that the Sumchen enjoyed many physical advantages over humans – they healed almost instantaneously when injured, and they were faster and stronger. So a programme of experimentation and breeding was introduced.'

And this is too much to take in.

'The aim was to breed a being with the best traits of both species. A new hybrid. You were one of the first successes, Jesper.'

I get a tight feeling in my temples. My heart races.

'I have all the documents about Jesper and his family in my briefcase – look for yourself.'

Carina steps forward, scoops up The Voice's bag and opens it. She starts looking through the documents. As she reads, she shakes her head like she can't believe what she's seeing.

'See?' The Voice says. 'It's all there. Every shameful detail.'

And I can tell from the way Carina keeps studying the documents, from the way she doesn't argue back, that it's true.

But all I can think is that I have a mother and a father.

'Do you have a picture? Of my mother?'

The Voice turns back to me and nods. 'There are pictures of you and Hanne and your siblings too.'

'Siblings?'

'Two sisters and a brother.'

And again my insides are turning over and my temples are tightening, struggling to take all this in. Carina steps towards me, holds out a photograph. 'Is this her?'

But even before The Voice has said a word, I know it is. Cos with one look I can tell she's the woman who was sometimes in my dreams. No question.

'I don't understand,' I say. 'Why didn't I know any of this? Why didn't I meet my family?'

The Voice doesn't answer. He looks down at the ground and grimaces in pain.

'So if this is my mum, who is my dad?'

And at first he says nothing. But slowly he looks up at me, and before he's even opened his mouth I know the answer.

'I am. But I ... we didn't ... I was your donor, Jesper. I'm your dad.'

And the world seems to spin around me.

Carina

How can any of this be true? There's no such thing as alien life forms. But the evidence is in my hands in black and white. There are even pictures of Jesper and his mum and brothers and sisters. The only person that's missing is his dad. The Voice.

318

The Voice grimaces in pain as he shifts his weight. 'I can't justify it,' he says. 'All I can do is explain.'

But then he doesn't explain; he winces in pain again and adjusts the way he's sitting up.

'How could you let your son – Jesper – grow up in that place? Why didn't you tell him who you were? Why didn't you tell him who he was?'

He sighs. 'It wasn't as straightforward as that. I'm sorry.'

'So why let Jesper go now?' I say. 'Why not before?'

'It suddenly became obvious that the experiment involving Jesper had run its course. He was due to be decommissioned.'

'Decommissioned?'

'Destroyed. Killed. Shot.'

Jesper listens, silent.

'Why?' I ask.

'One of his generation developed flu-like symptoms. At first we thought it was simply Marsh Flu. But blood tests revealed it was an entirely new strain of the disease, which proved resistant to treatment.'

I watch the expression on Jesper's face change. He looks worried. I say nothing. I think of Sabine and what Father Liebling said to me after she died: that there might be a new strain of Marsh Flu.

'The girl died and Huber realised they had a new disease on their hands. Their reaction was to do four things. One, develop a new vaccine. Two, spread the new disease out in the world, in the hope of creating a new pandemic and a clamour for a cure. Three, destroy any evidence that could trace the outbreak and spread of the new strain to Huber. Four, supply their new vaccine to the world and become even richer and more powerful. We're currently at the second stage.'

The Voice grimaces as he adjusts his bandage. He needs a medic. He won't survive without help.

'So what are we going to do? How do we save ourselves?' Jesper asks.

'You have to get away from here,' The Voice says. 'I saved you, Jesper, and now you can save the world from the new strain before we have a pandemic. You must find the Spirit of Resistance in the Low Countries and hand the research I took from Huber to their scientists. In the back of the van there's a freezer with a vaccine inside it. They'll develop it and distribute the cure to everyone.'

'How are we going to do that though?' Jesper says. 'New Dawn are looking for us. Carina's picture was in the newspapers.'

The Voice breathes heavily for a second, and I think he must be letting a wave of pain wash over him. 'There are new papers – identity cards, birth certificates. New passports. New names. Everything you could possibly need is in my brief-case.'

'That won't fool anyone though,' I say. 'They have my picture. Our faces are easily recognisable. Our papers won't fool them if they can see who we are.'

The Voice adjusts how he's sitting again. He closes his eyes for a second or two. 'You need to change your appearances,' he says. 'In the van there are scissors. Cut your hair. There's hair dye as well. There are lenses to change your eye colour. A change of clothes. Documents. Everything ...'

But before he finishes his sentence, there's a sound outside the building.

Jesper

There are voices and heavy footsteps. They've found us.

The three of us fall silent. I turn towards The Voice, hoping he'll tell us what to do. Sure enough, he pushes himself up on his hands so he's sitting up straighter. 'You have to go,' he says. 'Take my case. All the papers and details of where to head when you reach the border are in there. Everything you need. Leave now. Take the van and get to safety.'

The voices outside grow louder, even though I can tell they're trying to keep them hushed. But I'm frozen to the spot. Cos we can't leave him, can we? He's The Voice. He's my dad. They'll kill him for sure.

'Take the case,' he says. 'Be quick. There isn't time to delay.'

Carina and I look at each other.

'But what about you?' I say. 'You're coming too, aren't you?'

He shakes his head. 'Look at the state I'm in, Jesper. I'm dying. I'd slow you down.'

'But if you stay they'll kill you.'

He shakes his head once more and picks his gun up from the floor. 'I have this. The best chance we all have is if you leave me here. Now get going.'

And still I'm in two minds. I stay frozen to the spot.

'Go,' he urges. 'Leave me here, Jesper. You have a job to do.'

'He's right, Jesper,' Carina says. 'It's the only way. Come on.'

The footsteps get closer. I sense them at the front of the building. Carina gawps at me, and without saying a word we both know what we're gonna do. We scoop up the case and the papers and my bag.

'Good luck,' The Voice says.

And then we race through the building to the back room, climb through an empty window and jump down, keeping low. We creep through bushes, in and out of the trees, getting away from the building, but turning and watching it with every step.

And all the time I'm thinking that we shouldn't have just left The Voice there like that. I could have carried him on my shoulders, couldn't I? We could've all been safe. I could've had a family.

But we can't go back now. We creep through the forest, getting further away, escaping. And even when I feel the scroll vibrate in my pocket, I don't stop, do I?

I hear shouting in the distance, coming from the building, and I know that they've found him.

Gunshots fill the air.

Carina

CRACK. CRACK. CRACK. CRACK.

Four gunshots pierce the silence of the forest. We stop running, drop to our knees and scrabble around to face the building. I put my hand in my pocket. Two bullets. Not enough. My heart races.

'I counted four gunshots,' Jesper says. 'There were four men. The Voice shot them.'

I say nothing. Those shots could have been fired by anyone. And I can see on Jesper's face that he knows it too.

'We should go back and get him out of there,' Jesper says. 'If he shot them all, we can take him with us. It doesn't matter how slow we go if he's shot them. There'll be no one after us.' He gets up as though he's gonna run back there.

I grab his arm to stop him.

'We don't know what happened in there. It'd be suicide to go back right now. Wait here. If no one's come out in a minute's time, we'll go back in and get him.'

Jesper shakes my hand away from his arm. He stares at me angrily. He has The Voice's dried blood on his neck. I try to hold his stare. I reach my hand out and put it on his bare shoulder, trying to reassure him. Eventually he looks away from me and crouches back down, watching the building, still angry and twitchy.

For ages nothing happens except some crows return to the trees, wings beating, cawing loudly. I start thinking perhaps Jesper's right: Blake has shot them all. Four shots, four men. *Bang, bang, bang, bang.*

Then something moves and at first I can't tell what. We both crane our necks to see. Markus emerges from the building. Behind him are the two men from Huber and Frei, all holding their guns out in front of them, searching for us. The only one who doesn't come out is Blake.

I sense Jesper getting more and more tense and angry. And I think of the weapon in my pocket.

I position myself so I can't be seen and I keep watching as they skirt round the other buildings, guns raised, ready to shoot. All the time I think about Blake. It's obvious what's happened to him. And I wonder what Jesper's thinking right now.

As the four of them disappear into another of the houses in search of us, I'm thinking about what we should do and there's only one sensible solution. 'We should leave now, while they're searching,' I say. 'We can get away. We can get to the border and find the Spirit of Resistance.'

But as I'm talking, Jesper's already on his feet. He looks at me, shaking his head. Without a word, he takes his knife out and walks back towards the buildings.

'That's my dad in there,' he says.

Jesper

'Jesper,' I hear her saying from behind me. 'What are you doing? You can't …'

But even though I hear her, I'm not listening. I'm yomping back through bushes and trees towards the buildings, keeping low and prying on the house they just entered. I'm not leaving him there to die alone. We should have taken him with us. We let him down. I left The Voice to die. He brought me into the world. He spent his life helping me. He saved me and I let them kill him.

I hear footsteps behind me, trampling the leaves and the twigs and I know Carina's following. I turn round and give her a look, tell her she should stay where she is.

And then I'm yomping through the undergrowth again, gathering speed, feeling the anger build inside me.

I spot them coming back out of the building, guns still pointing, squizzing around for us. I drop to the floor and hear Carina do the same behind me. The men haven't seen us though. I pry on them as they move towards another house and go inside it. I turn and see Carina's squizzing at me.

'Stay there,' I hiss. 'I'll be back.'

And in a second I'm on my feet again and I'm moving through the bush, back towards the house, getting closer and closer. And before the men have come out of the other house, I reach the building where we left The Voice. It's silent. I rush in through the space where the front door's meant to be, straight to the front room, where I find him.

His eyes are closed. There are two bullet holes in his head and two in his chest to go with the one in his leg. He lies in a pool of his own blood that's getting bigger each passing second. He isn't healing. He's dead. And all I can do is stand there and gawp like some kind of fool, useless and helpless and not believing what's in front of me and not knowing what to do about it either. And feeling guilty, like this is my fault, even though I didn't pull the trigger.

His right hand still holds his gun. And for a moment I gawp at it and I think. Cos I can't make this right again, not now; I can't bring him back to life.

But I can do something for him. And for me. I can make sure we get away, that we take the information to the Spirit of Resistance.

I prise the gun from his cold hand and leave the building.

Outside I crouch low, creep along by the walls, using them to cover me, prying on the building I saw the men go into last. My insides feel strange – stomach tying itself in knots, heart thudding. And as for my brain, it's racing with information, with thoughts, imagining what's gonna happen, raking back through what's already happened and what it means and who I am.

I say a silent prayer to God, asking Him to guide me to do the right thing, to protect me.

And then I see them. The two men from the Huber Corporation and Father Frei. I freeze where I am as they come back outside. They squizz around, guns held in front of them, but they don't see me and move off towards the next building.

I stand where I am, cos all of a sudden I've lost the ability to do anything – think, move, make decisions. I look down at my right hand, at The Voice's gun. And all of a sudden I'm aware of how heavy it is, how unnatural it feels in my hand, how I've never even held one in my life before, let alone used one. And I start to ask myself the same question over and over again: *What are you doing, Jesper?*

Except my brain comes up with an answer, doesn't it? Cos a picture of The Voice lying slumped in the other building pops into my head and won't go away. They killed The Voice. My dad.

And I'm gonna kill them.

And that's when Markus comes out of the building in front of me. He comes out with his gun held in front of him, squizzing this way and that, just like the others. He doesn't see me though, does he? And this time my brain fights against my body, makes sure I'm not frozen to the spot. And as Markus moves towards the next building, I follow at a distance, gun pointed at him. Just before he's about to go into the building and my chance disappears, I open my mouth and I call: 'Markus!'

He turns in my direction.

He sees the gun, but it's too late for him to do anything about it, cos I force myself to squeeze the trigger.

BANG.

Immediately he collapses to the floor, screaming out in pain. I can see from here – ten metres away – that I haven't killed him. The bullet hit his arm and he dropped his own gun and fell to the floor and now he's writhing around in the dirt. At first I think it's just the pain making him writhe around, but then I realise he's trying to get to his gun. I've got to do something before he picks it up and kills me. He won't think twice, will he? So I raise my gun again and I squeeze the trigger. Only this time it kind of clicks and there's no bang and no bullet. So I squeeze again and still nothing happens except a click. And again and again.

Cos I've run out of bullets, haven't I?

So I drop the gun and run towards him, just as his fingers are edging towards his gun. I stand on his hand to stop him and he yells in pain again.

'Scheiße!'

I bend down and pick up his gun.

328

My mind races with thoughts of what I should do now, but a noise interrupts them, makes me look towards the door of the building in front of me.

The men from the Huber Corporation are staring at me, guns pointed at my head. With them is Father Frei, his gun held down by his side.

And all I do is stand there, useless. Cos if I lift my hands to point Markus's gun at them, they'll shoot me before I'm even done, won't they?

It's useless. There's nothing I can do. I'm going to die.

Except then I think of something. I point the gun at Markus's head. 'Put your guns down or I kill him,' I say.

But instead of putting their guns down and looking scared, they laugh. The taller of the two men aims his gun at Markus and he pulls the trigger. There's a CRACK that splits the air, makes Markus's body jump and then slump to the ground. And as I gawp at him, I watch the life go from his eyes.

'Drop your gun, Jesper,' the taller man says, 'before you get hurt as well.'

So I do what he says. The gun thuds to the ground.

'Nobody else needs to get hurt, as long as you do as I say.'

But I know that's a lie. They'll kill me whatever I do.

And the way I see it, I have three options.

One, stay here and do as they say and they kill me anyway.

Two, run away as fast as I can and they shoot at me and I die.

Three, I shoot them, except by the time I've aimed at them, they'll have shot me.

There's no option that keeps me alive, is there?

And so I stay where I am while they point their guns at me and step slowly towards me.

'I don't want to harm you, Jesper,' the taller one goes on. 'I want to take you back to your home. My Place. Will you cooperate?'

I stand where I am. I know he's lying. He takes another step towards me.

Only then there's a noise that no one's expecting. It comes from somewhere in the forest.

CRACK.

The bullet hits Father Frei in the shoulder and he falls to the ground, dropping his gun.

Before I have time to think about what just happened, there's another *CRACK* and the taller Huber man falls. Dead before he hits the ground. Eyes glazed.

And for a split second the man from Huber who has a scar that runs down his face just gawps, frozen to the spot.

I take my chance, pick up Markus's gun and I point it at the man with the scar. And as soon as he realises there's more than one gun pointed at him, he puts his hands up, starts backing slowly away. And then he makes a run for it, into the woods.

I stand frozen to the spot, gawping at the dead bodies and the injured Father Frei, wondering who shot them. Cos it wasn't me and it wasn't The Voice.

Carina

The short man runs off, and though I point my gun in his direction, I know there are no more bullets left in the chamber and so he escapes.

I walk out of the undergrowth towards Jesper, who's open-mouthed, not comprehending what's just happened. He stares at Father Frei and then at the man from Huber, frozen in his thoughts.

'You shot them,' he says.

I nod. 'I had to. They were going to kill you.'

And from the ground I hear Father Frei: 'Help me. Jesper, Carina. Please.'

He's bleeding. He needs my attention. I don't tend to his wounds though. I hold my gun and I stare at him. A memory fills my mind: Father Frei, back when he was Officer Frei of New Dawn, when he watched as Commander Brune used Greta and then put a bullet in her head. All the anger I've held inside for ten years surfaces. How is it right that he gets to still be alive when Greta's dead? How can he even think to ask for my help?

My index finger closes around the trigger of the handgun. I raise it and aim at Father Frei's head.

'Please, Carina, have mercy. I haven't done you any harm.' He makes the sign of the cross.

But he's lying. 'You let Commander Brune rape my sister. You watched. You stood there as they put a bullet in her head.'

331

The look upon his face changes instantly – realisation replacing pain. He opens his mouth but no words come out.

My finger squeezes the trigger.

'Don't do it,' Jesper says. 'We need to go.'

'Help me,' Father Frei says.

But all I see is Greta's face, her tears. All I hear is her screams for them to stop. Their gunshot. And silence.

And the anger inside me bubbles over. I pull the trigger.

Father Frei's eyes bulge as he panics.

But the gun just clicks.

The chamber's empty.

Jesper grabs my arm and starts pulling me along, away from the buildings, back into the woods.

We run back through the forest. We hear no gunshots, and I assume that means we're not being followed, but that doesn't stop us from running on and on and on.

It's only when the two vehicles come into view – The Voice's van and the black car – that we slow. The engine of Blake's van is still running where he left it, but it's filled with bullet holes and the tyres have been shot out.

'We'll have to take their car,' Jesper says. 'It'll be faster than the van anyway.'

We grab everything from the van – including the portable freezer from the back – and stuff it into the black car and Jesper offers to drive. The car starts with a quiet but powerful roar. Jesper looks at the buttons and dials, figuring out how to make it work. He pushes a switch and the lights at the front of the car come on, lighting up the darkening forest.

'You were going to kill Father Frei,' he says.

I shake my head. 'I knew there were no bullets left.'

'So why pretend?'

I say nothing. The mental image of Greta and Father Frei returns. And I begin to wish I'd had another bullet. Maybe shooting him dead – doing something for Greta – would have finally got rid of the memories. 'I wanted to watch him suffer,' I say.

Jesper's quiet for a while, staring out through the windscreen, thinking. 'They killed The Voice,' he says eventually. 'They shot him in the head twice. I saw him lying there.'

I say nothing.

'It was my fault. I shouldn't have left him.'

Suddenly, as though he's just thought of it, he puts his hand in his pocket and brings out his machine. The scroll. He switches it on. He stares at it, the glow of the screen reflecting on his face.

'He sent me a message,' he says. 'He must have done it just before they found him.'

He holds the machine out so I can see the message.

These are the files. Take them to the Spirit of Resistance. Good luck.

'That's what we do now,' I say, pulling the leaflet from my pocket.

He takes the leaflet from me and looks at it. It's in German though, so after turning it over in his hands he passes it back. 'We have to do this. For him.'

I nod. 'We need to stop somewhere first though. We should change our appearances, like he said.'

Jesper puts the car in gear, presses the pedal and the car lurches jerkily forward.

By the time we reach the border, we've abandoned the car and it's late at night, nearly morning. Jesper and I look completely different. His hair is cropped short all over and dyed blond rather than his usual brown. Contact lenses have turned his brown eyes blue. He wears round glasses too. My long hair is gone and it looks almost boyish now. My green eyes are now also blue. I'm unrecognisable from the picture in the newspapers. And as we step towards the two armed officers guarding the border, bags on our backs, we hold our new papers.

Maria Schultenberg and her brother Magnus.

An officer points his gun at us as we near him. 'Halt,' he shouts. 'Hand over your papers.'

We hold them out and the other officer grabs them. He takes a torch from his belt and aims it at the papers, examines them, looking us up and down, while the other one points his gun at us.

'What's your business in the Low Countries?' he asks Jesper.

Jesper stares blankly at him, not understanding.

'He's deaf,' I say. 'We're going to stay with our uncle. In Aachen.'

'How long for?' the officer says, this time talking just to me.

'For good.'

'What's in the boy's hands?' he asks, pointing at the freezer with the vaccine inside it.

I shrug. 'It has his medication in it,' I say. 'He's diabetic.'

The officer grabs the handheld freezer from Jesper and looks inside.

My heart stops beating. I watch his face as he examines the test tube. But then he shrugs, puts the vaccine back and hands the freezer back.

He hands us our papers and the other officer lowers his gun. Then with a nod of his head he lets us across the border.

We walk on for a while, until the border is well out of sight. And then we find a place by the side of the road to sit and rest.

Right away Jesper takes the scroll from his pocket and wakes the screen up. He looks at the map first of all, and then starts searching through the messages, looking at the last messages he received from The Voice.

I take the files from The Voice's case and flick through them. Because what he said was a lot to take in, and some of it was difficult to believe. I want to check the details in the file. Some of what he said – the star voyager and Marsh Flu, and how New Dawn spread the virus before they released the vaccine – is stuff that I've heard before. None of it's new. But I've never believed it. It always seemed like conspiracy theories to me.

But as I flick through the sheaf of documents, it becomes clear to me that The Voice was telling the truth.

It's all here – pictures and data and reports. There's no doubting it. I skim through until I come to the files about Jesper's family. I look at the picture of his mother, Hanne, see how her face looks a lot like Jesper's. Her cheekbones are high and pronounced, just like his. Her eyes are deep, deep brown like his. There's no doubting the similarities.

'Can I have another look at that?' Jesper asks, putting his scroll back in his pocket.

I hand the picture to him and look at the next page – a sheet with all his details on it: name, birthdate, birthplace, mother, siblings. And in the box marked 'Donor' is The Voice's real name – Mr Mark Blake. He was telling the truth.

'Jesper, you should look at this.'

He glances over, puts down the picture. 'What?'

I pass the sheet of paper to him. 'Look at what it says …' And I point at the box marked 'Donor'.

He stares at it for a while and then he lets the paper drop to the ground, covers his face with his hands.

Jesper

After a while, I feel a hand on my shoulder. I flinch. But it's only Carina, isn't it? She smiles at me. 'Are you OK?' she asks.

I nod, even though it's a lie.

'We should get going,' she says.

Carina's right. I can't sit here forever.

Carina takes a piece of paper from her pocket and holds it for me to see. 'We have to find these people: the Spirit of Resistance. We take them the files The Voice sent you. What's on your device could stop another pandemic,' she says. 'This is important. That information could save millions of lives.'

I get up off the ground and we start yomping again. Cos we have to save the world.

Acknowledgements

There are a few people I should thank for helping with the writing of this story. But I should start with the people whose real-life tales inspired this one. I'm always fascinated by the stories of people who live apart from society, and one day in September 2011, I read about a boy called Robin Van Helsum, who walked out of the forest and into a German town. When the police spoke to him, he claimed he'd lost his memory. He did, though, tell them that he'd been living in the forest with his father since the death of his mother in a car accident, and when his father had died and he was left alone he decided to walk to a town.

His story turned out to be a hoax, but it inspired me to look into the lives of other 'wild' children. One such famous case was that of Kaspar Hauser, a teenage boy who turned up in the town of Nuremburg in Germany in 1828. He said he'd been brought up in a dark cell, completely alone. One day a mysterious man, whose face Kaspar never saw, arrived and taught Kaspar to stand and walk. Then the man took Kaspar from his cell and left him in the forest with a note.

I discovered many similar stories of children who have grown up away from other people. A great place to read about them is Michael Newton's book, *Savage Girls and Wild Boys: A History of Feral Children*, which helped me lots while I was researching.

Boy 23 grew from the seeds which those stories planted in my mind. But without the help of others, it certainly wouldn't have become the book it has. I'd like to thank Emma Matthewson, Caroline Sheldon, Rebecca McNally, Ellen Holgate, Polly Whybrow and Helen Vick for their time, patience, encouragement, advice and expert editing skills.

I'd also like to thank my family and friends for their patience whilst I've been researching and writing *Boy 23*, especially Lloyd for sharing his experiences of Romanian orphanages with me, and Sonja, Daisy, Flora and Billy for always listening and encouraging me.

About the author

Jim Carrington is the author of four books for young adults. His first novel, *Inside My Head*, was nominated for the Carnegie Medal, and the Branford Boase and UKLA awards. His third novel, *Drive By*, won the James Reckitt KS3 Book of the Year prize. He has also written two books for younger readers. He lives in London with his family and teaches in a primary school in his spare time.